THE HIGHER EDUCATION OF NOAH RILEY

(Crimson Crew Book 1)

A. Whitcoma

ISBN-13: 979-8504932248
eBook ASIN: B09523VQVY

Cover design by: Rowan Arts Graphic Design
Library of Congress Control Number: 2018675309
Printed in the United States of America

For Charlene

WARNING: Sensitive content which may be triggering. For mature readers only.

TABLE OF CONTENTS

Books By This Author

PROLOGUE

The little body trembled as it fought for air in the dark closet. They prayed for light, for rescue, for love and gentle hands. But it never came.

Sometimes Mother would throw open the door and pull them out of the dark abyss. Sometimes she wrapped her arms around them, chasing the shame and fear away, even if it was just for a few fleeting moments gone all too soon. Sometimes Mother smiled down on them and saved them from themselves and the monsters all around.

But those reprieves were fewer and farther between now. As the slow, agonizing minutes ticked by and the walls began to close in on all sides, that small hope was extinguished alongside the light.

There was a whimper then, but it was low and soft. They'd learned long ago that crying out loud only made it worse. It made the other hands that much angrier when they were eventually pulled out, so they stayed quiet even as they gulped for air and squeezed their eyes shut, trying desperately to keep the overwhelming blackness from assaulting and obliterating their senses.

But the dark was an all-consuming, relentless force pushing at them from every side and all but collapsing them in unto themselves. Soon the darkness was a tangible weight that sat so heavy upon their heart, their small chest, pushing and squeezing, making it harder and harder to breathe. It made the gasping and whimpering more erratic even as they fought with themselves to stay hushed. They had *to be silent. They* had *to disappear into the nothingness. They tried not to exist whatsoever.*

They curled into a tight little ball on their side, shrinking as far into the corner and into themselves as their traitorous body would allow, wishing they could evaporate entirely into thin air. If they could become the air itself, they wouldn't suffocate... they wouldn't be shoved into the dark void of cages and closets. They'd no longer be imprisoned by four tight walls or their small, shrinking chest cavity. They'd finally be light and free...

As the long minutes dragged on endlessly, they began to shiver in distress as they fought another battle, this time with their bladder. A slow, agonizing hour past and they could no longer hold it. As they peed themselves and the warm, odorous liquid slid down their backside and legs, into the carpet, they began to softly cry. They knew then with absolute certainty that it was all true. They were *bad and hard to love, and they would be punished for it.*

CHAPTER 1

Lainee Reed pushed herself as she always did the last few minutes of her daily workout inside the Malkin Athletic Center, or the MAC as the students here at Harvard referred to it. She ratcheted up the resistance on the elliptical, all but wrestling with the mechanical contraption as if resolutely scaling, clawing her way to the top of some beast of a mountain with an imaginary plateau only she could see. Even though it didn't exist, she would never stop trying to reach it.

Lainee made it a habit to push herself hard in all things under her control, and most things were now and these days, thank her mother's God, since leaving home for college. Finally, here, at one of the most impressive, historic collegiate institutions in the country, she was in her element. She was in control. She was focused and disciplined. She was in the top ten of her junior class to prove it. That was no easy feat at this particular prestigious private university, whose acceptance rate was a mere 5% to begin with.

Finally finished with her cardio, Lainee gracefully stepped off the machine, sweat rolling down her neck as her long, chestnut-brown hair hung heavily down her back. It was much hotter, leaving her hair down versus pulling it back into a ponytail, as was the long sleeve, slate gray Under Armour shirt and matching running tights that were her usual uniform. She strategically preferred it that way, protecting and hiding as much of herself as she possibly could. She had enough prying eyes on her as it was.

Lainee sipped some water from her thermos, almost oblivious to the stares as she moved to the other side of the expansive gym to where the machines and free weights sat. Strength training was an important part of her daily workout routine, too. She had sculpted muscles already but she strove for more than just sustained total body conditioning.

She needed to be stronger, smarter, better. She needed to be in control at all times and in every situation. It wasn't optional.

Putting her disciplined practice to good use, she carefully ignored all the stares around her as she moved to the first weight machine in her circuit, never making eye contact with those around her or removing her ear buds. She never wanted to encourage social interaction and conversation, after all.

She was in her own, small little world just as she preferred it. She was alone, she reassured herself. She was strong and resilient. She was an army of one.

Noah Riley worked the rowing machine as if his life depended on it, as if he was being chased down by the grim reaper himself here in the prime of his life. He had been honing the muscles on his lean, 6'2" frame since high school. Now in his third year at Harvard, Noah was a fine-tuned specimen with exceptional good looks and an outstanding talent both on the lacrosse field and theater stage alike. When he took stock of these things, it was with clinical assessment, a bit of pride and absolutely no arrogance... well, very little arrogance anyway.

As lead in a majority of the prestigious school's plays, as well as a bit of a Broadway and Hollywood player on the side, he was used to all eyes on him. If he was honest with himself, he liked the attention more than most because he needed the validation like lungs needed air, but it really had absolutely nothing to do with vanity and arrogance. If only it was that simple.

Periodically during his workout today and every day, people would approach Noah, usually very pretty and confident girls, and they'd strike up a conversation about the latest game or play, or really any hot topic on campus they could use as an excuse to engage. He was used to this and didn't mind it one bit, even here in the gym. In fact, he craved the attention here and, hell, everywhere. He wasn't sure what that said about him exactly but, as always, he dismissed the self-analysis quickly and uncomfortably.

As another hot girl in tight workout clothes sidled up to him and started a conversation, he smiled up at her, his amber eyes flashing with charm and flirtation, making her knees go weak and her cheeks flush. Noah was grateful for both the attention and the distraction from the troublesome territory of self-analysis he'd been tip-toeing dangerously near, but he kept rowing as they conversed, otherwise he'd never be in shape considering how many times these interruptions occurred.

Unable to help himself, as if they had a mind all their own and were pulled by an invisible, nefarious force, Noah's eyes kept sliding around the chatting, flirting girl right in front of his face and across the room to someone else. Despite his best intentions, his gaze was once again drawn to the one and only female in the gym, maybe the whole school, that hadn't shown him any interest at all, hadn't even glanced his way once. Ever.

Who the hell is this girl? Noah watched her adjust the weight on the chest press, her long brown hair falling around her face like a curtain as he all but willed her from across the room to turn her eyes his way. She didn't. She never did, but for some reason he knew her eyes were large, almond shaped and piercing blue anyway.

They'd been working out at the same time every day here at the MAC since the start of the school year a few months back. He had her routine down to a science now, knew which machine would be next and how many reps would be completed at each installation, knew she would never acknowledge him in any way throughout all of it. She never deviated from her routine in the slightest.

To say he was fascinated by her was an understatement. Perhaps it was because she continued to completely ignore him here at the gym, day after day, as well as when they happened to cross paths on campus. Perhaps it was because that peculiar behavior of ignoring him was quite singular to her, but it goaded him at the exact same time that it intrigued the hell out of him.

Inexplicably, he couldn't seem to take his eyes off of her. That, too, was singular to her. Noah never got hung up on any one girl. Why would he when he could pretty much have 'em all? Case in point, Miss Chatty-Cathy-in-Tight-Latex carrying on a one-sided conversation right in front of him at that very moment.

If he was more obnoxious, or confident a small voice chided in the back of his brain, he would have walked right up to the mysterious girl and forced her gaze and an introduction. But Noah didn't, maybe couldn't, for some odd reason.

What is her story? It wasn't the first time he'd asked that question to himself in his head, and he knew it was far from the last. He really couldn't figure it out, couldn't figure *her* out or the powerful pull she had over him. She was a complete enigma and oddity in his otherwise flawless collegiate existence.

He couldn't believe he'd never noticed her until this year, though all signs pointed to her being an upperclassman, too. Probably because she wasn't a theater major like he was, so their paths hadn't crossed until now.

Probably because she's ridiculously intelligent, studying for a legitimate career and actually belongs at an institution like Harvard...unlike me, Noah conceded with more than a little self-deprecation. He had no doubt she'd gotten in with her killer grades like most of the students here, where as he'd gotten in with his father's money and a little bit of talent on the stage and lacrosse field.

Now the two of them seemed to be on the same workout schedule at the same gym every day. He made sure of it. Noah was pulled to her that way, more and more. He never bothered with the other gyms on campus now. He'd certainly never been more dedicated to his workout regime, even during lacrosse season.

He seriously couldn't keep away. She was such a mystery, so utterly baffling and... different. Not only because she never gave him the time of day but because she never gave it to anyone. She never smiled, never spoke, just gracefully and habitually showed up here every day at noon, attacked the machines and weights with singular focus, covered almost completely from head to toe with as little skin showing as possible.

She was freaking fascinating, in great shape and, yes, strangely beautiful. Despite the long, haggard scar along one side of her face. Hell, maybe more so because of it.

Noah knew his interest and curiosity in the girl was unnatural. He thought of that face, that scar, more often than he'd like to admit. It had quickly become an uncomfortable obsession.

As the chattering girl beside him finally got the hint and walked on, Noah continued to stare... stare and row... row and stare.

As usual, his mystery girl never took her ear buds out, never talked to a soul, never turned her lips upwards in a smile. More importantly, she never looked his way, which was still oddly annoying even after all of these weeks. He was just so used to being noticed and... wanted. Perhaps he needed the attention too much. He absolutely needed the validation. But this girl, so different from all the others, just religiously worked her fine ass off day after day and pretended the rest of humanity didn't exist, even him... especially him. It rubbed in strange ways. All of it. All of *her.*

The few times Noah had been lucky enough to see her outside of the gym, his eyes had zeroed in as if unnaturally pulled even from a distance. She was always alone then, too, usually striding purposefully across the expansive Harvard Yard to the library or class. He, on the other hand, was mostly leisurely meandering with a lazy smile, surrounded by friends, teammates and admirers alike. Unlike this girl, Noah was never alone. He made sure of that, too.

The juxtaposition of their outward appearances made for a startling, stark contrast. Night and day, really. The outside world no doubt looked on at the two of them and saw polar opposites. But Noah knew better.

Unbidden, he recalled a line from a Greek play he'd starred in a few years back in high school. *"The first appearance deceives many... the intelligence of a few perceives what has been carefully hidden."*

Noah continued to row and stare, reluctantly acknowledging that he could apply this Greek proverb and its accompanying insight to the both of them equally. But he was undoubtedly the only coward between the two of them. And in that moment of brutal honesty, he admitted to himself for the very first time that he was probably primarily pulled to his mystery girl because she was scarred and damaged.

Just like him.

CHAPTER 2

Lainee efficiently tapped her phone to start a new classical playlist, adjusting the weights on the seated leg press. Then she sat down and got back to work, running through her quantum physics study guide in her head all the while. She had a quiz later that afternoon and had been studying every free hour over the past week. She already had her self-made study guide of Q&A's memorized but she ran through it again and again as she pumped her legs until they were fatigued and shaking.

She had to be stronger, smarter, better, she reminded herself, pushing herself to do 10 more reps and one more mental run through of her study guide. She had to be in control at all times and in every situation. It wasn't optional.

◆◆◆

It's like looking in a mirror... that ghost of a thought flitted carelessly unbidden through Noah's mind like an eerie caress. That startling, brutal truth finally had him ripping his eyes away from his mystery girl. He frantically squelched that line of thinking, rowing harder and faster, grasping around for a safer train of thought.

Hamlet, Noah thought rather desperately as he did his damndest to ignore and override. He needed to start reviewing his lines and prepping for the play, he briskly reminded himself, refocusing and redirecting his traitorous mind. Thankfully, rehearsal would begin soon for the year's first production, giving him the ultimate distraction.

Noah was looking forward to playing the titular and tragic Prince turned King of Denmark. This was his ultimate passion, his easiest escape in which he excelled, so he felt little to no pressure here, only eager anticipation. And immense relief.

The school's theater company always put on a couple of Shakespeare productions throughout the season, as well as a few contemporary ones, ensuring Noah was lead in most due to his talent, popularity and appeal. They were also good about shifting him to more secondary and supporting roles during the February-May time frame when he competed in lacrosse.

Truthfully, he was a much better actor than lacrosse player, but Noah held his own on the field and enjoyed the team camaraderie and physical outlet. Too, all the girls seemed to love that about him, getting all hot and bothered whenever he slid on his maroon and white jersey with the lucky number 33 emblazoned on the front... *well, most girls anyway.*

Noah distractedly glanced at the blue face of his Harvard-edition TAG Heuer Aquaracer sports watch. Still ten more minutes on the rower to actively *not* think of the one exception to every rule. Suddenly he wished the babbling hottie would come back for an easy distraction and ego boost.

And, just like that, he was thinking about *her* again and his eyes were wandering against his will... back across the room, back to the enigma that had seemed to burrow into his brain matter.

Jesus, get a grip, Riley, you fucking stalker. What is wrong with you, he berated himself even as he wondered what music she was listening to and if her self-imposed isolation had more to do with being an extreme introvert by nature or, more likely, that permanent slash across her cheek?

He was really quite desperate to know the story behind it. A knife? A childhood accident? Whatever had happened, it couldn't have been pleasant or easy. That scar was clearly the life-changing souvenir of the most influential and traumatic moment of her life, on display for the whole world to see.

Noah physically shuddered then at the mere thought of that kind of stark exposure to the rest of the world, and his gut twisted in empathy. Frankly, he was awed by her strength and resilience no matter what the back story. He wanted to somehow communicate that to her, and also tell her she needn't hide away, especially from him. Hell, she should be damn proud. That scar was badass and strangely beautiful. It also bespoke of an immense inner-strength and willpower to overcome which few possessed, especially him.

The scarred stranger pulled at Noah for this and a million other reasons.

He turned this all over in his head as he clocked the speed of his rower and started to ease up. He realized with some self-serving relief that it wasn't so much morbid curiosity like it might be for some of the others, because they were certainly staring, too. No, for him the scar inspired something like awe, compassion and... *understanding.*

Noah shook his head now, trying to dislodge the unwanted thoughts that were coming more and more frequently. It was strange, unnerving and, frankly, terrifying territory he was inching towards as he watched and analyzed this girl. He usually made it a habit to stay the fuck away from that dangerous minefield of self-examination, so he assured himself now that the two of them were actually nothing alike, and he backed away from it, nice and slowly.

He was just fine, thriving even, Noah selfishly told himself as he eased off his machine completely. He was nothing short of successful and popular, he catalogued clinically. Didn't he have the scores and the fans alike to prove it? So clearly, he quickly concluded, he was nothing like the reclusive, damaged stranger. He was normal, healthy... flawless.

Noah winced at his own shallow, narcissistic need to prove himself different and better than she when he wholeheartedly already knew it was not the case. There really was no question about it. His mystery girl was the epitome of dignity and grace. She was stronger than he ever could be in all the ways that mattered. She was the ultimate survivor, day in and day out. It was literally written all over her face.

Noah shuddered again at the mere thought of his sleek, good looking facade slipping even a little bit under the weight of a visible facial scar. It wasn't entirely vanity. It was also self-preservation.

As he pushed up to his feet beside the rowing machine, drinking from his water bottle for some hydration, Noah felt quite guilty about his immense relief that this was her cross to openly bear and not his. He wasn't nearly as strong as she was, after all. Noah knew this with absolute certainty. She was everything he wanted to be, needed to be, but only pretended to be.

He drank for long minutes more, ignoring his sweat-slicked, straining muscles and every other person buzzing around the room, his amber eyes as always locked on the girl, the stranger, the enigma that pulled at him in more and more uncomfortable ways. He was bewitched, spooked, haunted to his core.

All the other workout inhabitants coming and going shot curious glances her way, too, and often. They were quicker to look away than Noah, though, seemingly uncomfortable by either the scar or the sorcerer herself. His enchanted eyes always lingered, as did his thoughts. It wasn't really a choice.

All the while, the girl carefully kept her eyes averted, head bowed low so that her hair served as a curtain across her slashed cheek as she worked the repetitions of her current weight machine, methodically, carefully, rep after rep, day after day. She tried her damndest to hide away from the rest of the world, but Noah saw her nonetheless.

He was just a weak, mere mortal under her otherworldly spell, and she the ultimate survivor of what came before, and the victor of what came next. She all but demanded his devotion on this haunted battlefield without so much as a word to him.

I see you, my little warrior, Noah thought with a mounting emotion that was equal parts affection and unease as he walked toward the exit, still tracking her with his gaze. *You can't hide from me.*

Noah walked out the door with the uncomfortable understanding that he probably couldn't hide from her either.

CHAPTER 3

In classic avoidance behavior that had taken him years to perfect, Noah took it upon himself to party each and every night of the week thereafter, skipping the gym all together in favor of a run or two across campus punctuated with some admirable bedroom Olympics.

He went through a lot of condoms that week.

He also artfully dodged his father's pestering phone calls about slipping grades and some subsequent tutor while simultaneously steering clear of a stack of growing assignments in biochemistry and applied mathematics, thus cementing his very near future married to aforementioned tutor.

When the school's Student Support Services also began calling him, Noah knew the jig was up. Even he, theater prodigy and fan favorite lacrosse player, could not get around grades for too long at an establishment such as Harvard. It had an academic reputation to uphold even if he did not.

Noah resigned himself to his fate after one last weekend of hard partying and pliant girls.

◆◆◆

Lainee had practically permanently reserved the table in the southeast corner of the Loker Reading Room in the Widener Library years ago as a freshman, so frequently she was there. Widener was the main library on campus and, in her eyes, the most impressive and inspiring of them all. Harvard held the world's largest private library with almost 19 million books across 70 libraries and Widener was its centerpiece. Lainee adored it like a dear friend.

The plethora of white marble pillars raising high the ornate and pristine ceilings, embellished with royal sky lights and chandeliers throughout, comprised the perfect crown jewel for the world's grandest bibliotheca. For a scholar like Lainee, this was her church in which she frequently worshiped. She revered the awesome, expansive collection of tomes and the historical architecture embracing it, yes, but it was also the lighting, the ambiance, the very *smell* of it that had her coming back time and time again. It was a soothing, silent place in which to study and focus. It was the equivalent of a constant companion when she had no others.

It was here that Lainee also met the students she tutored, and it was now when she would face off with her newest one, who also happened to be her worst nightmare come to life. Resolutely, Lainee stiffened her spine and pulled out her books and laptop. *Stronger, smarter, better*, she chanted as she mentally prepared for this difficult exercise.

She was an army of one she reminded herself. She was intelligent and capable. She was also prepared and had the tactical advantage on her home turf. She could do this, she assured herself, because she could do hard things. Still, she waited with shallow breaths and butterflies she couldn't quite rationalize away with her big brain.

Noah popped in a fresh piece of cinnamon gum and groaned internally as he walked into the pompous, intimidating building that was the Widener Library, a place he'd been actively avoiding most of his academic career up until now. He slowly trudged in past the dozens of overdone pillars and out of place, high-tech security system. As always he avoided the elevator in favor of the stairs and climbed up to the Loker Reading Room with heavy footfalls.

Upon arrival, he looked down the expanse of the long, rectangular room void of all color. It seemed to stretch on endlessly, all white from floor to ceiling... *like a freaking mental institution.* God, it smelled old, too, he thought, crinkling his nose in distaste. Noah decided he loathed the place then and there while searching out his new "tutor," also known as the paid parental spy his father had insisted on. Fuck his life. Even an hour away and a grown adult, his dear old dad still managed to exert his overbearing control over him. It was humiliating.

With a disgusted sigh, Noah remembered the text instructions implicitly specified they'd meet in the southeast corner of the ridiculously long and narrow room. Sure enough, he saw a lone figure tucked away neatly in that very corner amongst all the stacks, exactly where his new tutor said she'd be. At a distance he saw she was already raring to go with her laptop out and fired up, head bowed with a curtain of dark hair hiding her profile as she typed furiously away.

Noah groaned-whined right out loud then like a petulant child might and slowly, begrudgingly made his way over, for once ignoring all the stares by appreciative eyes that followed his every step. For the first time in a long time he was too consumed in his own miserable thoughts to even notice the attention.

Truthfully, he was relieved to have the academic help, but it was a bitter pill to swallow that it was a tutor of his father's choosing, one the old man would be paying for and, therefore, manipulating. It was just one more means in which the father could control the son and invade his privacy, Noah had no doubt.

But he could do this, Noah reminded himself, thinking of his long-game strategy to win the parental spy over to his side. The odds of that were actually in his favor, as his father had made the crucial, tactical error of hiring a female tutor. Females just happened to be Noah's specialty. Sure her name was Elaine and she was apparently some boring genius in the fields of quantum physics and biochemistry of all things, but he had high hopes he could successfully charm her pants right off once he applied himself to the matter. It was really his only hope to survive this latest hostile invasion, and to control the information flowing back to his father.

Now as he neared the corner table, Noah purposefully pasted on his winning, thousand-watt smile that had won him many an audition and female heart alike over the years. He unceremoniously plopped his brown leather messenger bag on the table, saying as way of hello and introduction, "You must be Elaine."

The girl startled and looked up at him. As her brunette curtain of hair swept back, piercing blue eyes collided with his, making his heart stutter.

With a sudden jerk of his breath, Noah realized his tutor was none other than the mystery girl from the gym, *the* girl... his girl. He stared in disbelief, his mouth agape.

She was suddenly right there, flesh and blood, front and center, as if plucked from his thoughts, his fantasies, his worries and insecurities, her eyes on him at long fucking last. For a suspended moment he couldn't form a single thought in his head let alone articulate an intelligent sentence out loud. Then finally... *oh, shit.*

She was his tutor? The bewitching sorcerer that had mind control over him and was marching him straight towards that dangerous and destructive minefield of self-examination and incrimination? So much for his long-term strategy of ignore and override. So much for charming the pants off his father's spy. All of his brilliant self-preservation tactics had just gone up in smoke, along with his whole entire long game.

He was so fucked.

CHAPTER 4

To say Noah was shell-shocked was an understatement. After all these weeks of staring at her, thinking about her constantly - obsessing about her, really - his beautiful enigma was suddenly mere inches away, her eyes locked right on him. Fear and excitement swelled in equal measure.

Noah stood there frozen, staring down at her in complete disbelief for long, pregnant moments. Finally he managed to stutter out a few strangled words of horror and awe. "I-It's you."

He flushed at his own stupidity, closed his mouth and swallowed audibly.

He's nervous, Lainee realized in surprise as she looked up into his stupidly handsome face and studied him with her own set of butterflies running amok in her gut. She noted with interest that he had only the slightest of New England accents, and his breath smelled faintly of cinnamon. It was... nice. Even when his mouth had been hanging agape like a caveman's, he'd looked really good, even better up close than he had from across the room at the gym.

Of course Lainee knew who Noah Riley was. She didn't live under rock, after all, even if she did keep to herself and stay hyperfocused on her studies and academic achievements. And, of course, she'd seen him at the gym, staring her down every single day from across the room... as if she were an oddity or a freak he couldn't pull his eyes away from. She supposed to someone like him, picture perfect with friends and fans fawning all over him at all times, she was just that.

She was his antithesis, and he hers, the most handsome and popular boy on campus. He was nothing short of her worst nightmare wrapped up in one helluva mouth-watering package. To be stared at so closely by someone so flawless and perfect, knowing he thought her a freak already, was a true test of Lainee's stoicism and inner strength.

Every instinct born and bred into her screamed at her to flee and stay far away from him. He was too good looking, too visible. He would shed an even brighter spotlight on her than she already had, while at the same time making her look even more hideous next to his pretty, polished good looks. Beauty and the beast. And she was the beast.

Noah Riley was a reflection of everything Lainee would never be. He was flawless and undamaged, confident and at ease in one's own skin and the world at large. He was beloved. Desired. Wanted. He was hands down the sum of her failures, flaws and fears encapsulated in flesh and bone, standing right in front of her, a mere inch away. Perfection personified. And utterly untouchable. He represented that invisible plateau at the top of her steep mountain that she would never reach despite her best efforts.

Even as her mind raced, Lainee forced herself to still, to stay and settle here, hanging precariously to that high cliff by mere fingertips, despite her every instinct to retreat to safety. *Stronger, smarter, better,* she all but chided herself now. *Control at all times.* She demanded it of herself.

By taking this tutoring job, Lainee had challenged herself to face both Noah Riley and her worst fears - exposure, shame, public humiliation, just to name a few. She had hesitated at first like a coward, despite his parents pushing, prodding and throwing money at her. Despite her disappointment in herself. Truthfully, she'd only had the confidence to agree to the arrangement once she'd gleaned something unexpected and disarming about Noah from his parents. It had been one surprising revelation after another. *Noah Riley wasn't actually perfect.* There was more to him than meets the eye. And he was hiding something, too...

And now here he was standing before her, seemingly just as nervous as she, if not more so, indicating she'd probably been right in her assessment. She had made the right call. This was reassuring to Lainee as, oddly enough, his obvious nerves helped settle some of her own.

As always, his gaze was laser focused on her, but this time she could return the favor.

◆◆◆

Noah couldn't help himself. He took in her every feature slowly and carefully, top to bottom, as if cataloging details to sketch later: large, almond-shaped eyes the bright blue of a sun-lit sky, emphasized by dark full eyebrows; high, rounded cheeks in a narrow face which punctuated her aristocratic bearing and consistently stoic expression; almost too-full, kissable lips; and, of course, the scar.

Slightly pink and raised against otherwise smooth, alabaster skin, it was a jagged, angry slash across her entire right cheek. Noah's fingers twitched at his side as he observed it up close for the very first time. Inexplicably, he ached to reach out and trace it from end to end with gentle fingertips, confessing all the while that he thought her completely, uniquely attractive and mesmerizing. All of her, but especially the scar.

Hell, her scar was his favorite part.

He was trying to absorb her through osmosis, to pull her in through his pupils and know each and every inch of her, inside and out. Honestly, he wasn't sure he could take his eyes off of her now even if he tried. And right about now he didn't care to try, as she was at long last front and center, her eyes locked on him in return. God, she was beautiful. Magnificent.

She was even more stunning up close, he realized with sharpening interest, though she raised her chin slightly just now in a way that made him understand she was uncomfortable under his close, piercing gaze that had lasted moments too long. Still, he couldn't look away, not even as a favor to her.

Surprising him, as if reading his mind, Lainee suddenly reached her hand up, subconsciously flitting her own fingertips along her scarred, flushed cheek. Then, as if checking herself, she quickly lowered her hand back to her lap. Noah had never seen her do that before.

She thought he *only* saw the scar, he realized in that moment, when in all actuality he saw so much more. He saw everything, and appreciated it all.

Like him, Lainee did not look away even though her cheeks were flushing hotter with embarrassment. No, his girl was much too proud and strong for that, Noah knew. The awe he'd always felt for her just grew tenfold in that moment, as did his attraction and empathy.

Noah could see the smallest nuance of Lainee's changing, hardening expression despite her best efforts to remain unaffected under his intense scrutiny. It was as if she was shoring up her defenses, awaiting an inevitable attack. It kind of broke his heart just a little.

That stony, haughty facade is just her defense mechanism, her attempt at armor, Noah easily recognized. It wasn't truly reflective of the person underneath.

He understood all too well the need for facades, defenses and armor. He slipped them on every single day, even outside the lacrosse field and theater stage. He had them in place even now as he flashed his best smile in an attempt to impress her and put her at ease. Because he *had* to penetrate that stoic surface and get to know her. He was dying to dive in deep and discover who she truly was when no one was looking. And he absolutely needed to know how she'd survived her trauma, how she could bear it every single day under the watchful gaze of everyone else around her, and somehow still thrive anyway.

If he knew how she did it, maybe he could do it, too.

With practiced patience, Lainee took in a full, indiscernible and steadying breath, attempting to pull up her dignity and pride all around her like a protective cloak as she endured the intense study of her scar by perhaps the most perfect male specimen this side of the equator.

With his thick, dark brown hair, startling amber eyes that were quite golden at the centers, and the model-like bone structure of his flawless face attached to a ridiculously hard body, Noah was quite beautiful, Lainee conceded, if only to herself this one time. But she'd already known that about him. Everybody did.

What she didn't know was what kind of man he was underneath that perfect, practiced, pearly white smile. Were her instincts right about him or had she been projecting? Maybe even hoping? He was untouchable, at least for her, but was he also unknowable? She wasn't sure because Lainee had a feeling very few actually got to see the real, imperfect man underneath the polished exterior.

She had long ago noticed from afar at the gym that Noah turned on that charming smile of his every time someone approached, but then she saw it would slip, just a degree, when he thought no one was looking. She saw it slipping away now as she deliberately gave him a penetrating, unwavering stare right back, all but daring him not to put on the same old act.

She had thought him shallow - pretty but shallow - as she'd watched him right back from the corner of her eye all these weeks at the MAC. Then she had met his parents and had learned something startling and unexpected. His slipping smile now seemed to confirm it.

We're both putting on a show, Lainee concluded with certainty in that moment, eyeing him close and seeing him perhaps for the first time. *That's why he's so nervous around me.* And then a sudden and shocking question, unbidden, on the heels of that realization...

Is Noah Riley as lonely as I am?

◆◆◆

Noah swallowed audibly. Without a hint of an expression on her sober, stunning face, clearly and remarkably unimpressed by his good looks in return, Lainee suddenly stuck her hand out to him with business-like efficiency. "Please call me, Lainee," she requested formally, breaking the now awkward silence. "And you must be Noah?"

Noah raised an eyebrow at that ridiculous question. Everyone on campus knew who he was, and many beyond, too. She needn't pretend otherwise. Plus, they literally worked out together at the same time at the same gym every single day, well except this past week when he'd intentionally been avoiding her. She *really* hadn't noticed him even once before? Noah couldn't be sure so he gave her an uncertain nod and stiffly took her outstretched hand. He slowly shook it.

And still, she just looked up at him impassively, completely and utterly unaffected by him it was evident to see. Noah wasn't sure if this was kismet, serendipity, irony at its finest or a practical joke by the fucking funny fates who often liked to laugh at his expense, but he was becoming more uncomfortable by the second under her return scrutiny. Her apathetic, all-knowing, penetrating gaze was beginning to make him sweat.

After another strained silence in which he continued to stare down at her mutely like an imbecile - he was maybe, possibly even drooling - Lainee waved a hand at a chair across from her in queen-like invitation. She was ice cold and business-like, never an expression crossing her delicate features.

So it's going to be like that, Noah thought to himself with crippling disappointment, trying to shake himself out of his frozen, spiraling stupor. *Fine by me*, he tried to tell himself as he shored up his own defenses. He had plenty of options, after all, and Lainee was just a hired parental spy at the end of the day, better to be kept at arm's length.

Despite this pragmatic, dogged thought process and the tsunami of both awareness and wariness washing over him, his every nerve ending still vibrated and sang with keen interest as he pulled out the chair opposite her.

Lainee... Noah turned her name over in his head for the first time, finally given a clue to the magical mystery that was She.

Lainee suited her, he decided quickly. It was unique and... endearing. And thank God she didn't want to be called Elaine. He didn't think even she could pull that one off.

As per usual, Noah couldn't seem to drag his gaze away from Lainee's face even as he told himself the girl could do some serious damage to his ego and sanity alike. Seriously, what *was* it about her? He was almost irritated now by the otherworldly pull of her when she was so clearly unmoved by him in return. In fact, she was being down right cold and aloof. It stung a ridiculous amount.

Lainee raised her eyebrows at him then, communicating her irritation and disapproval over his ongoing stare and stupor. *Right. Straight to the business at hand, ladies and gentlemen,* Noah thought sarcastically with more than a little embarrassment and disappointment. *Pleasantries concluded.*

He forced his eyes away and pulled out his own laptop, trying his damndest to refocus his thoughts and lift his diving spirits. But it was difficult to do. Biochemistry and applied mathematics with his completely unmoved and unimpressed tutor who just happened to be the mystery girl he'd been obsessing over for weeks. *Fucking dandy.*

Then Noah happened to catch out of the corner of his eye some turned heads and nearby stares of other students. He glanced over at the next table and all guilty occupants quickly turned away. He looked up and caught a few additional stares from the foot traffic that ebbed and flowed around the nearby stacks of books. Actually, now that he took stock of the room, pretty much *everyone* was looking at him and Lainee.

Huh. Well, it wasn't anything he wasn't used to, and he supposed if there was anyone else more infamous around campus than he, it was Lainee here with her facial scar. The two of them together seemed to be a real showstopper, at least here at the boring 'ol stuffy library. Still, the longer Noah surveyed the area, the more he realized that *every* pair of eyes kept coming back to them on repeat. Literally everyone was watching them with keen interest at some point, even as far away as the opposite corner of the long and narrow room, some craning their necks awkwardly to catch a glimpse.

Okay, this is getting weird. Even Noah was getting a little uncomfortable with the unwavering and intense scrutiny from the rest of the student body while they were just sitting there about to study. He looked over at Lainee to see her reaction.

She was staring stiffly straight ahead at him, completely still and unblinking now, her back so rigid that he could practically feel the tension radiating off of her. She was definitely picking up on all the attention. It was clearly unwanted and making her uncomfortable, too. And now that Noah thought about it, she was sitting in such a way that her right cheek with the scar was actually facing the corner, away from everyone else.

The profile she showed the rest of the room was her smooth, unmarred one. Clearly that was a strategic move on her part, though it did little to stop the gawking. Noah's heart squeezed as he clearly recognized her reality for the very first time.

Though she pretended to ignore the world around her, to be aloof and above it all, she was painfully aware and affected. The poor girl was ice cold because she *had* to be, just to get through the never ending, intense scrutiny, which he was undoubtedly compounding. Noah quickly got over himself then and there.

"Hey, Lainee," he said gently, compelled to reach out across the table for her hand that rested there, like they were long lost friends, "are you okay? Do you want to get out of here and go somewhere more private?"

◆◆◆

His question, and the grimace on his handsome face that accompanied it, almost broke her. Lainee was strung so tight from head to toe she thought she might shatter if he gave her hand even a light stroke, so she snatched it away before he could make contact.

She couldn't stand the pity on Noah's perfect face. She could endure anything but pity, especially from the golden likes of him. Her resistance to his despicable act of sympathy had her heart hardening and her walls shoring up once more, and she was grateful to him then. His pity had snapped her crumbling defenses back into place.

"I'm absolutely fine, Noah," she told him quietly, defiantly, all but daring him to disagree as she locked on and held his gaze as if they were the only two people in the room, hell, on the face of the earth, and they were right this very moment having a life-or-death stare off.

Whoever looked away first would lose and know great shame. And she did not plan on losing.

The frame of her chestnut brown hair fell in long waves, spilling over her shoulders, softening her pinched features slightly. Her raised chin, married with her prim-and-proper navy and green argyle sweater with a high white collar underneath, made Lainee look haughty and poised as she commenced with the challenge of a stare off and ignored the rest of the room.

Yep, all business and fuck-you-defiance, Noah was relieved to see, and he actually had to hide a smile just then. Damn, this girl was impressive with her inner strength of steel and voodoo-like allure. No wonder everyone was staring. He certainly was. She squinted her eyes at him rather angrily then, reminding him that this was a showdown of wills. And he was losing.

Get your game face on, Riley, he ordered himself then. *Try and remember she is the paid spy of your enemy. And she thinks you're a goddamn fool, if not a straight-up idiot.* As if agreeing with him and finding him completely lacking and unpalatable, Lainee sniffed at him, eyes further narrowing.

Nope, she didn't want his sympathy and support, clearly. And it didn't seem his strategy of charming her pants off was going to be the least bit effective due to her shifting between a complete lack of emotion towards him and sentiments of anger, irritation and disgust. So Noah decided to shift gears and go straight frontal attack.

"So you sold out to my disgustingly rich and overbearing parents, huh? Are they giving you a handsome tip if you snitch on my social activities and personal life, too?" he asked coolly, a cocky half-smile, half-smirk on his lips as he sat back in his chair and crossed his arms over his chest. He pretended to feel superior in the moment.

Lainee tilted her head to the side slightly, as if confused or surprised by the power move. Still, neither of them looked away. Game on.

CHAPTER 5

Eyes still locked on his like a heat-seeking missile, Lainee gentled slightly, thinking through Noah's telling question about his parents. *He isn't as perfect as he seems,* she reminded herself then. Maybe she did illicit stares like a freak show wherever she went, but he wasn't entirely unblemished either, at least internally. His show of superiority was a little less believable now.

Lainee answered him rather softly, "I won't spy for your parents, Noah, though they will undoubtedly ask me to." She paused, hesitating a moment, and then conceded, "When I met them I fully understood they are those kind of parents, sterile, clinical, watching from afar and yet very controlling..." She thought specifically of his aggressive, domineering father and shuddered. There was just something dark and concerning about the man...

Lainee's face was no longer impassive. Her piercing blue gaze had softened immeasurably with compassion and... understanding. "Maybe they are even worse than that."

Her eyes held the forbidden question as well as the unwanted invitation for him to open up. It was Noah's turn to go completely rigid then. His mouth was suddenly dry and he licked his lips as he tried to process this new input. "You met my parents?" he asked hoarsely in dawning horror as his sensitive stomach twisted in a knot. He'd assumed she'd just gotten a phone call or an email, but no. She'd actually met them. In person. *Fuck.* This was bad. Really bad.

That's when Noah knew with absolute certainty that he definitely wouldn't be able to hide from Lainee Reed like he could everyone else. At her spot-on description of his fucked up parents, she already knew too much and guessed at the rest.

Maybe they are even worse than that, she'd said.

Suddenly *his* scars were out there on full display for *her* eyes. And there was nothing attractive about his. Noah flushed with embarrassment and... shame. There was so much shame.

He could visibly see Lainee softening further as she easily read him, and he cursed the fucking fates for their freaking hilarious joke once more. Of course this incredible, intuitive, intelligent girl would be the one to see every one of his own scars, visible or otherwise, starting with the worst of them. It was terrifying and humiliating. And it changed everything.

Noah held himself very still then, fighting the urge to flee again even as his heart raced with fear and anxiety.

Lainee had pegged his parents instantly when they had driven over an hour from Cape Cod just to track her down on campus, right after she'd politely refused their handsome offer of tutoring their son over email and then again on the phone. Clearly "no" meant something different to these people than the rest of the world.

Merely galvanized by the word, they had driven out of their way and hunted her down on campus for a face to face as if she'd merely challenged and inspired them to hyper focus on their target. They were just that much more determined to recruit her, in fact, almost doubling their initial offer of payment.

They wanted "only the best" for their precious son, perhaps talented in other ways but "rather slow to keep up" in academics. Nothing but the best and most expensive would do for the Rileys it was plain to see from all the blinding bling and unnecessarily expensive clothes and footwear they were sporting as they waved their checkbook around so casually, spoke of their son so clinically and with absolutely no warmth or pride. Far from it, actually.

They were not good people, Lainee quickly concluded as they stood outside her dorm room. Much worse, they seemed to be horrific parents. Noah's mother had been downright out of it, tipsy and dazed in the middle of the afternoon, seemingly high or drunk or both. She'd let her husband do most of the talking. Mr. Riley was arrogant and persistent, almost bullying. At first he seemed just passive aggressive about his son's grades, all but sneering when he spoke of Noah as slow, undisciplined and challenging. Then it became increasingly, uncomfortably clear as the conversation went on that his issues went much deeper than that.

Fifteen minutes in and Lainee had identified Mr. Riley as narcissistic to a sociopathic and pathological degree thanks to her psychology courses. *This* went far beyond passive aggressive disappointment in his son's academics. This was something much, much darker. It was impaired empathy mixed with jealousy and a feeling of direct competition with his son.

Lainee quickly understood that Mr. Riley had to be the most powerful and admired man in any room he entered. He, therefore, could not abide his own son, who was nothing short of magnetic himself. In addition to that unsettling discovery, there was a rage vibrating just beneath the surface waiting to be unleashed on anyone who dared get in his way but mostly, probably, directed at his poor son.

Lainee knew with absolute certainty then that she should shut her door in the man's face but, paradoxically, she felt pulled to accept his offer for the very first time. The tipping point in her acceptance hadn't been the exorbitant amount of money he was offering, nor his persistent cajoling. Instead it had been this new information she'd gleaned about Noah himself through his parents' actions and words.

Though he seemed the perfect face of her worst nightmare, Lainee suddenly couldn't help but feel empathy towards Noah and a... kinship, knowing what she knew of his home life now.

Her view of him had forever been altered. He was no longer just a flat image of a pretty boy grabbing at attention. He was flesh and bone with hidden depths and hardships to bear, just like her. Though she typically shied away from intimacy of any kind, she had wondered if she could help him, and not just in academics. Perhaps she could aid him in a way someone else might not be able to. After all, she knew suffering more than most and, suddenly, she wondered if Noah Riley did, too.

As Lainee looked at his pale, pinched face before her now she once more had the haunting, awful feeling they'd been through something similar. His scars just happened to be hidden from view. Though she hated the very thought of that, she had a sudden longing to share the pain, both his and hers.

Her scars were drawn to his like a magnet.

She felt oddly intimate with this beautiful stranger, even as he watched her warily through pained eyes. It was suddenly imperative that he understand she was on his side and would hold sacred the gift of seeing him, if only he'd let her.

His parent's systematic way of buying whatever they wanted hadn't been effective with her. That wasn't why she was here today. Yes, she had shook hands with the devil and cashed his first check without too much guilt, sure. That was due to the fact that she'd busted her ass to get to Harvard, and she was working even harder now to stay in the top one percent and maintain her academic scholarship. She deserved that financial leg up. But she wasn't here for the money. She was here just for Noah himself.

It seemed absolutely ludicrous to say out loud now, but she couldn't help thinking again that Noah might... *need* her. How could she possibly express any of this in a rational way he'd accept? It was difficult even for her to completely understand the compulsion to be here when it wasn't logical or cerebral in the least.

It was all instinctual.

◆◆◆

Noah shifted uncomfortably in his seat, unable to read her expression even as she read him like a fucking text book. Then she surprised him by quite gently asking him the same question he'd asked her just moments before, "Noah, are you okay?"

He blinked at her, unsure of what she could possibly mean by that.

When he stayed stiff and quiet she clarified kindly, boldly, "Do you want to talk about your parents? Your dad?"

Noah swore his heart stopped beating in his chest then and there. He suddenly felt so raw and wounded, laid bare and completely exposed beneath both the blinding lights of the Widener Library and Lainee's all-seeing gaze.

Noah shook his head adamantly and looked away, the first to break eye contact. *No surprise there.*

"Noah," Lainee said gently then, bringing his eyes reluctantly back to hers.

She had more to say he could tell but his flashing amber eyes begged her not to, and he shook his head at her. He implored her to tread lightly on this dangerous minefield and not to go *there* into its deepest, darkest of corners. He couldn't face it, the ugly truth eating him from the inside out, nor the sickening certainty that she now saw it in him, too.

Oh, yes, from across the table, under the revealing sky lights of the Loker Reading Room, Lainee's piercing blue eyes saw him alright. They defined him.

Noah hated what she saw. He loathed who he really was, a scarred and broken soul who was shallow and, so much worse, hollow to the core. He couldn't bear the weight of her stare or her knowledge of his ugly truth, so he found himself deflecting and blurting out like the fucking coward he was, "Hey, how did you get that scar on your face, anyway?"

Lainee visibly flinched and pulled back from Noah, unprepared for the blunt, cutting question that came out of nowhere. Though everyone stared, thankfully very few actually had the gall, or lack of class, to ask her about it. And here she had been opening herself up to Noah like she hadn't with anyone else in a long time when he'd suddenly just... attacked.

It surprised and hurt her more than it should have. *This was a terrible mistake,* Lainee knew with dead certainty then. She'd been utterly foolish to take this job. She'd been so wrong about Noah. He didn't need her help. He just needed the upper hand at her expense, like everybody else. Her instincts about him had been way off, and now it was too late to run.

She'd made a deal with the devil and his son's dagger through her heart was the price.

Nausea roiled through Noah and he hated himself even more than he had a moment before, which had been quite a bit. He was a complete fucking bastard and he knew it. He called himself every derogatory name known to mankind as he watched Lainee try to recover from his brutal verbal assault.

He could practically see her physically gathering up her strength and self-esteem that he'd just shattered like a motherfucker, and then she said almost evenly, bravely, demanding even more of his respect if that was possible, "You don't want to talk about your parents and I don't want to talk about my scar, so we won't talk about either. Deal?"

Noah nodded once, feeling so sick and ashamed of himself, unable to speak or look her in the eye again after that.

"Let's get to work then, starting with biochem," Lainee said quietly, taking in a steadying breath, ending all personal conversation then and there.

They were in silent agreement that it would be all business from here on out. It had to be, or mutual destruction seemed all but guaranteed.

CHAPTER 6

Much later that night, under both the cloak of darkness and the oversized hood of her navy wool peacoat, Lainee walked to the Charles River which divided the main campus in two. She stood by the rippling water and closed her eyes, letting the slightest of cool breezes wash over her along with the absolute silence. She took in a deep, steadying breath and tried to clear her mind of all troubling, intrusive thoughts that had been overactive since leaving her first tutoring session with Noah earlier.

Hey, how did you get that scar on your face, anyway?

She flinched even now, hours later and all alone under the cover of darkness, thinking about his blunt, harsh question. She had seen his immediate flood of guilt and remorse so she knew he was human beneath that glossy, slick shell of his, but it still had hurt. Worse, she'd been taken by surprise.

Foolish, she scolded herself now as she watched the slightest of waves dance along the surface of the dark water. Why had she let her walls down even for a moment? She was a scarred oddity. Noah certainly hadn't hidden his intrigued stares, especially from across the room at the gym. He'd been a little more subtle about it sitting directly across from her at the library but, *of course*, he'd asked her about it. It had just been a matter of time, really.

Lainee understood all too well that Noah's exact timing of the intrusive question had been strategic in order to shut her down. It had worked beautifully.

He would never know, she vowed to herself resolutely as she stood alone by the river's edge. Noah Riley couldn't be trusted. He certainly wouldn't understand. How could she have been so foolish as to think otherwise for even a fleeting second?

Lainee was confident she wasn't wrong about his parents, but she'd been way off about him. Hell, maybe he was just like his father and had nothing to worry about from his old man. He certainly shared the same superb genes and narcissistic, excessive need for admiration of them. Perhaps they basked in the glow of their good looks and arrogance together.

Noah's precious, perfect image would stay unblemished just as he liked it and she'd stop trying to care about what lay underneath. If anything.

It must be so nice to pretend like everything's perfect, she thought with a light touch to her cheek. Lainee didn't have that luxury. Everyone could actually see she was damaged goods. She was all but laid bare at a complete stranger's first glance. All she had left as a barrier of self-protection was her silence. She wielded it like a weapon, one of the few in her arsenal besides her keen intelligence.

She vowed again that no one, especially cocky and beautiful Noah Riley, would ever know about the origin of her scar, this constant reminder of her very worst moment in life. Nor would they know that she didn't wear the scar as much it wore her. It was, after all, the most noticeable feature of her physical appearance as well as the biggest, most haggard piece of her very soul on full display.

Right on cue, a flash of her father's twisted face blared out of the darkest recesses of Lainee's brain, making her flinch. Shaking her head hard as if to dislodge the sharp, cutting memory, she refocused on what her reality was *now*, what was important *now*, in this very moment, and that was her next test in quantum physics in the morning. With focused precision she turned all thoughts back to that one safe, discernible goal fully within her control. This train of thought coupled with the quiet of the night was like a balm to Lainee's raw nerves and she took in another deep, fortifying breath.

She had needed a quick break and reset after the hours of studying and lab work which had immediately followed the two hours of tutoring Noah. Now she was refreshed and refocused, she assured herself, pulling her coat a little tighter around her against the encroaching chill of the night. Now she could get back to her disciplined studying that would cement her A+ in the challenging course.

Lainee turned resolutely and marched back towards her nearby dorm room, fingering the pocketed pepper spray she always kept on hand considering crime was surprisingly high on campus, especially in the middle of the night like this. She was still in complete control, she reassured herself, despite the dangers that existed in her environment. They would not take her by surprise, nor deter her. They certainly wouldn't stand in the way of her achieving her goals.

Absolutely nothing had changed since Noah Riley had walked into that library and into her life earlier that day. Indeed, he was just one more of those dangers to look out for.

◆◆◆

After his last class the next afternoon, Noah eagerly rushed to the library for his next tutoring session with Lainee. He'd been unable to hit the MAC at lunchtime due to a drama club meet up and he was itching to see her as soon as possible.

The irony that he was hustling now and couldn't get to Widener fast enough today did not escape his notice. Biochem studying sucked balls but he was more than willing to endure the torture to get back front and center with Lainee, who was still very much his mesmerizing mystery girl pulling at him. Plus, he may have had way too much coffee up until that point and was buzzing with both anticipation and caffeine alike. He popped a fresh piece of cinnamon gum into his mouth on the heels of that realization as he all but sprinted across Harvard Yard.

He had been quite decimated leaving the library yesterday. The pained expression he'd personally placed on Lainee's beautiful face haunted him long into the evening. He'd had the hardest time falling asleep, at least until he'd dialed one of the newer numbers in his phone for a quick booty call. Then he'd slept like a baby.

When he awoke refreshed this morning, he was more determined than ever to show Lainee the charming, irresistible and surprisingly talented bloke that the rest of campus saw. He certainly would keep his mouth shut about her scar and do what he could to make up for his hurtful deflection.

Noah was desperately eager for a second chance with Lainee. He would keep the focus on her, where it belonged, instead of on his parents or himself. *That would be no problem-o*, he assured himself now, considering his obsession with her. And just like that, he slipped back into old, comfortable habits like pretending absolutely nothing was actually wrong. He'd just been having a rare off day yesterday is all. Yep, he was merrily, gloriously back in full denial. Where he belonged.

As he pushed both his parents and memories of yesterday's confrontation completely from his mind, Noah was able to acknowledge that he was quite excited to get to know Lainee. Truthfully, he felt like the luckiest bastard on campus to have been paired with her and given this rare opportunity. He eagerly hoped they could start over so he could prove to her that he really wasn't a bad guy. In fact, he was quite debonair and dashing. Captivating even, some would say.

He climbed the stairs in Widener two at a time, a confident man on a mission once more. Lainee was all set up at the same table in the back corner of Loker Reading Room, facing away from the rest of the room, surrounded by stacks of books with her laptop open in front of her as she furiously tap-tapped away.

This girl doesn't waste a single second being unproductive, Noah realized, pulling up beside her with his infamous thousand-watt smile.

"Hi, Lainee," he said cheerily, perhaps a bit too loudly for a library, making her jump in surprise. "Sorry, didn't mean to scare you," he said with a chuckle as he quickly settled into the seat across from her. He dug out his own laptop from his messenger bag, never taking his eyes off her as he asked, "How did your quantum physics test go earlier?"

Lainee was even more shocked by Noah's question than how he'd appeared out of thin air at her elbow. He had actually remembered she'd had a test? She cocked her head to the side slightly in confusion. She honestly couldn't even remember mentioning it to him. Shaking herself out of her reverie she answered matter of fact, "I'm sure I aced it." She added almost shyly then, "Thank you for asking."

Noah nodded and smiled warmly, taking in her solid navy sweater with its white Ralph Lauren logo. *The girl obviously likes the color navy... and sweaters,* Noah noted to himself. *And she aced a friggin' quantum physics test... at Harvard.* He had nothing but awe for her.

"Did you have time to go over the study guide we prepared yesterday for *your* upcoming test?" she asked him in return, trying not to trip and fall into the warm golden abyss that was his piercing gaze. *All business today, Lainee,* she reminded herself sternly. She would not be fooled again by the disarming charm and startling good looks of one Noah Riley.

"I did," he answered her slowly, blushing a little as he admitted, "but it was hard to focus. I kind of skimmed it before I went to bed last night." *Before the booty call*, he added, but only in his head. He didn't want to disappoint her on *all* fronts.

"That's fine," Lainee assured him as if reading his mind and absolving him of all guilt. "At this point it's more about learning new study habits so that you're always reinforcing the material in your head. You will be intimately familiar with the content come test time."

Noah bit his tongue so that he couldn't ask if he'd be intimately familiar with *her* by test time, too. *Nope. Dial down both the pervert and the asshole in you today, Riley,* he scolded himself. *And whatever you do, keep it in your pants, for God's sake. This girl is different. This girl is special and deserves nothing but respect and delicate handling.*

"Let's start with biochem again today," she was saying as Noah slowly refocused, "since it's your hardest class. We'll knock out your homework and then I'll quiz you on that study guide we made yesterday."

Yep, biochem sucked balls but at least he was back in front of his girl Lainee and on his A game today. Noah was actually smiling as he pulled up the homework.

CHAPTER 7

An hour later, after a few fan interruptions and struggling through the homework, Noah was now failing every question Lainee asked as it pertained to the study guide. He was frustrated and straight back to feeling humiliated and like a fucking idiot. He was mission critical once more as his carefully camouflaged exterior began to weaken and crack under her sharp scrutiny, leaving him exposed and vulnerable.

Of course he couldn't keep his embarrassing lack of intelligence to himself, not with wicked smart Lainee Reed being his tutor and all. His pride balked. "You must think I'm such an idiot," Noah said bitterly, stabbing both hands through his thick brown hair as he hunched over the library table.

"Not at all," Lainee was quick to reassure him. Suddenly all was forgiven from the day before as she watched him struggling now. "Hey, don't be so hard on yourself, Noah. We're just getting started." She honestly couldn't remember the last time she'd tried to make someone feel better emotionally and here she was trying to do just that with Noah, two days in a row. It was a little daunting as she wasn't sure she was very good at it, nor if she'd have to pay another personal penalty for the attempt.

Truthfully, Lainee didn't have many conversations with fellow students and certainly never any centered around emotions. Her discussions were typically focused on academics. Even her side jobs purposefully kept socialization to a minimum. She did the one-on-one tutoring as well as some legal billing for a small firm back in her hometown of Blythe, Connecticut.

She'd worked part-time for the firm in high school and they'd been kind enough to offer support through remote work while she was away at Harvard. It was a relief to have the extra income and to work in seclusion from the privacy of her dorm room. Just as she preferred it.

Intimacy, emotional or otherwise, was purposefully avoided as much as possible. Lainee wasn't heartless, though, nor did she lack the capability to empathize, especially it seemed as it pertained to this amber-eyed fox sitting hunched over before her now. Even in her self-imposed isolation, and despite her carefully practiced stoicism, she was actually quite sensitive. And there was just something about Noah that tugged at that vulnerable underbelly of hers so effortlessly.

Now Lainee was instinctively responding to that flicker of shame on his handsome face as if they were... friends. Despite her determination to keep her walls up from the dangers he presented, she felt sympathy pangs deep in her gut and ached to comfort him. If only she knew how.

Noah's humiliation did not abate despite Lainee's kind words. She was clearly just taking pity on him. Self-disgust had him pointing out to her as a counter argument, "My concentration here at Harvard is theater, as I'm sure you know. I'm almost afraid to ask but... what's yours?"

"Biomedical engineering," Lainee answered him quietly. She didn't mention she was an advanced-standing student who'd be on to her Master's degree come next year, only her fourth year in.

Noah gave a self-deprecating laugh then as if reading her mind. "And you're in the top one percent. There is no way you don't think I'm a complete idiot, Lainee." He was starting to spiral again. He really wished he could crawl into a hole somewhere and have her stop peering at him so intently, stop seeing him so fucking clearly through his crumbling disguise.

First Lainee had the misfortune of meeting his dysfunctional parents - Noah hadn't really forgotten that upsetting reality - and now he was putting his stupidity on full display for her. It was humbling and humiliating to say the least. She was seeing all the broken cracks he was always trying to smooth and polish over with his talent, charm and good looks. To say it was a blow to his fragile self-esteem was an understatement.

But *of course* the one girl whom he wanted to impress above all others was the same one who'd see right through him. Noah put his head in his hands and rubbed his forehead, unable to meet her gaze. Jesus Christ, she was messing him up and always had been, even from across the room at the gym.

"Hey," Lainee said gently then, that instinct to comfort him overriding all others when his self-loathing was so evident to see, "look at me, Noah." When he reluctantly raised his head to do so, she told him sincerely, "I know for a fact you're not an idiot. All of those roles you've had to master over the years? You just need to apply those same tools here and you'll succeed, but it will take some time to develop those habits. You're going to get there, though, I have absolutely no doubt." Her eyes were soft and kind as she added quietly, "I believe in you."

Noah's heart fluttered in response to all of that. So she *did* know who he was? "You've seen one of my plays?" he asked hopefully, latching on to that one life preserver amongst his ensuing internal shit storm. For some reason it was of utmost importance to him that Lainee had seen him in his element, mastering the art of the role, at his absolute best as he stood in that spotlight up on the stage. *That's* the man he so desperately wanted her to see. Not this one.

"I... haven't," she told him hesitantly, feeling guilty at his crestfallen look. She went on to hurriedly add, "I've never had the time but, I assure you, I've heard of your talent. You're quite a legend in these parts." It was the truth and she respected the hard work he'd put in to hit that pinnacle of success. She let him in on her little secret then. "I'm not more intelligent than you, Noah. I just have a high-level strategy and effective academic habits."

He was eyeballing her as if he wasn't quite buying her ego-boosting oversimplification of the situation at hand, so she continued. "I'm here to help you learn more effectively, to help you structure your time so you get solid grades in the most efficient ways possible, and to reinforce the repetition necessary of the material."

They watched each other a minute and then she felt obliged to point out, "That same self-discipline and memorization muscle you use for acting is absolutely applicable to this area of your life, too. You can do this. *We* can do this," she promised him with complete confidence, "together."

With every word she spoke, the weight eased slightly on Noah's chest and the embarrassment let loose its grip on his closing throat. Damn, she was so kind, generous and forgiving when he'd been nothing but an ass to her yesterday. He knew he didn't deserve her kindness, but he was so damn grateful she was giving him a second chance anyway.

And he quite liked the sound of her last declaration. They could do this. *Together.*

He didn't analyze it too long, just sorted and stuffed all strange or negative feelings down and away as he always did. He felt instantly buoyed by her, hopeful even, ready to try again.

Noah flashed Lainee his thousand-watt smile. It was 100% sincere and hit its mark. "Together then."

CHAPTER 8

The next few tutoring sessions weren't nearly as stressful as they learned to settle in to the rhythm of their new partnership while focusing strictly on the work. Thankfully, Noah was beginning to pick up on some of Lainee's habits, to both his and her relief.

Her biggest trick was creating study guides for every test, big or small. He then reviewed the study guides with her during their sessions and then again on his own every day leading up to the test, both before bed and when he woke in the morning. And Lainee was right, that structure and repetition of the material was really making a difference of his handle on it.

After two weeks under her tutelage he was already feeling more confident, especially when he pulled out a B- on his biochem test. They were both ridiculously pleased with each other and themselves at that point.

Noah was beginning to relax in Lainee's company more and more, and he looked forward to seeing her every day, though he wasn't quite sure if she felt the same way.

Lainee always made him meet her at Widener, same strategic corner, even over the weekends, and she wouldn't hear of going anywhere else, or even going off to a private reading room right there in Widener. It was like she couldn't trust him to keep his hands off her or something!

Noah really didn't get it, as they were both the object of much interest and scrutiny, especially when together. Why *wouldn't* she want to go somewhere more private, he lamented, growing bored of the sterile white walls of the Loker Reading Room very quickly, despite the welcomed fan interruptions it hosted.

Often girls would come up and unabashedly flirt with Noah as if Lainee wasn't sitting right there or, rather, as if she was of no importance. Clearly they did not think of her as competition, Lainee surmised, and why would they? *Look at him and then look at her.* Still it stung just a little bit for no obvious reason beyond female pride.

Conversely, Noah basked in all the attention and was more than happy to pause studying to flirt right back with the hordes of girls and guys that flowed in and out of their tutoring sessions. Still, he was anything but "slow to keep up" as his parents had said. Lainee found him surprisingly sharp and intuitive, despite the distractions and subsequent lack of focus.

As she waited for yet another blushing fan, this one male and muscled, to get a selfie with Noah, she pulled out some fruit snacks from her backpack and eyed his schedule and work load for the week ahead on her Google calendar. Of course she'd created a calendar for him and overlapped it with her own.

Hm. Noah only had two tests this week, and one paper and lab on top of the daily homework. *Not a bad load,* Lainee thought to herself, *but we need to buckle down if he's going to master all these tasks and -*

"Are those fruit snacks?"

Lainee looked up in surprise. She suddenly had Noah's undivided attention. The admirer was long gone and Noah glanced down at the tiny bag of fruit snacks in her hand with raised eyebrows.

"Maybe," Lainee said evasively, not liking his growing smirk one bit.

"Fruit snacks," Noah elaborated then with a full-on, toothy grin, "like we used to get in our lunch boxes for elementary school?"

Lainee stiffened her back, not liking his obvious mockery one bit. "I'll have you know there is less sugar in these fruit snacks than gummy bears and other comparable candy." She'd actually traded her addiction of the latter for the former but didn't feel the need to elaborate on that right at the moment. "It's a... healthy...ish snack for all ages," she insisted haughtily. Truthfully, fruit snacks were one of the few indulgences she allowed herself. That and one hour of Grey's Anatomy a week.

Noah leaned in and peered closer, still with a shit-eating grin in place. "Are those Disney characters on your bag of fruit snacks?" He actually snorted and then outright laughed at her, offending her utterly and completely. He held his stomach and guffawed like it was the funniest thing he'd ever seen in his entire life. And it kind of was.

Prim and proper, serious and stoic, top-rated Harvard student Lainee Reed sitting in the stuffy Widener Library in her argyle sweater and penny loafers eating a teeny tiny bag of fruit snacks with Disney characters on it. It was just so incongruous with the rest of the picture that it struck him as completely absurd. And adorable.

"Shhh," Lainee hissed at him as heads swiveled in their direction in droves, "we're in the library, remember? Keep it down."

The admonishment only made him laugh harder, though Noah did clamp a hand over his mouth to muffle the sound somewhat. Still, everyone was staring. Again. Lainee rolled her eyes and sighed impatiently.

If he got them kicked out of the Widener, she swore to God and Saint Jerome, the patron saint of librarians, there would be hell to pay. There were many other libraries on campus, of course, but this was her specific beloved spot. It was so soothing and yet invigorating all at the same time. She wouldn't give it up for anyone, not even cheeky, perfect-as-a-picture Noah Riley.

"Are you quite finished?" Lainee asked in irritation as his laughter finally died off. "What exactly is so funny about my fruit snacks anyway?" She crossed her arms over her kelly-green argyle sweater and gave him her best disapproving look.

His laughter had tapered off but he still had a lopsided grin on his face as he told her, "That is the first silly and impractical thing I've seen you do," he pointed out. "It's adorable."

Lainee froze at that. *Adorable?* Had Noah just called her adorable? She blushed and didn't know whether to be flattered or offended further. "Hm. Yes, well, let's get back to work like the mature, intelligent adults we are, shall we?" she mumbled, covering the offending bag of fruit snacks with her hand and slowly moving it to the edge of the table to drop it back into her bag as inconspicuously as possible.

Noah's hand came gently down over hers then, stopping her in mid-motion, startling her in such a way that both her heart and breath stopped in unison. He was practically holding her hand at that point and she stared at their joined hands in sheer astonishment. She was a woman not used to a man's gentle touch, or any touch at all really.

Noah had a twinkle in his eye when she slowly brought her gaze up to look at him. "I'll trade you a bite of my Twinkie from my Power Rangers lunch box for some of your Disney fruit snacks," he teased her.

Lainee couldn't help herself. Her lips turned upward into a smile and she ended up laughing out loud herself. Soon, they were grinning at each other foolishly, his hand still resting over hers, warming her from the top of her fingers all the way down to the tips of her toes.

Noah felt absurdly pleased with himself then, like he'd hung both the moon and the stars with his own bare hands, and his chest swelled to max capacity.

He'd made Lainee laugh and smile, and damn did it feel good all the way through to his bleeding soul. He stared at that smile in wonder. It was a full-fleshed, honest-to-God, ear-to-ear grin on her face. And it was the most beautiful sight he'd ever laid eyes on. Noah's heart did a flip flop he would not soon forget.

There wasn't much he wouldn't do for one more of those smiles and accompanying heart somersaults. He was instantaneously an addict after that one specific, singular rush.

The chase was on.

CHAPTER 9

Besides acting, flirting was his greatest skill. Noah tried the latter out on Lainee unashamedly after that, feeling emboldened by the smile and laughter he'd inspired, but to no further avail.

He really poured it on a few times, too, the charming flirtation, the implied invitation as he tried to lure her in with his best bedroom eyes, all in the hopes of eliciting the usual female response. It would have done his pride wonders to have Lainee melting, bending, extending the invitation right back at him. After all, he had a narcissist's need to make every female within a 100 mile radius fall in love with him, or rather fall at his feet in adoration.

Instead, she would just peer at him so seriously over her laptop with those damn hooded but all-seeing bright blue eyes of hers, never blinking, never showing emotion unless it was slight irritation. A few times she even cocked her head slightly to the side as if thoroughly confused by him.

At present moment they were back in Widener - where else? - and Noah was laying it on thick yet again in order to postpone the actual painful act of studying, but she'd clearly had enough of his shenanigans, ordering tartly, "Knock it off, Riley. Leave the acting for the stage and the flirtation for the impressionable fans." Clearly she was neither impressionable nor a fan.

Noah was embarrassed of himself immediately and that quickly gave way to pouting. His ego suffered greatly under her intelligent, piercing gaze. He should have been used to it by now, but it still stung a ridiculous amount.

The timing couldn't have been more perfect as another rapt and overzealous fan walked up, slipping him her phone number on a post-it note. offering suggestively, "Call me, night or day, but especially night."

Noah felt so much better suddenly. He input the number into his phone as the girl sashayed away. When he looked back up, Lainee had her arms crossed over her chest and was giving him a disapproving arch of an eyebrow.

"What? Jealous?" he teased with a smirk. He was more and more relaxed around her, despite her refusal to succumb to his charms to date. His growing ease probably had a little something to do with the fruit snacks that were always sitting on the table between them, being shared like an inside joke or a peace offering during their tutoring sessions. They proved that super intimidating Lainee Reed was human, after all. She was not an emotionless robot that did nothing but study and work, as she'd have everyone else believe. It was their little secret.

And Noah really wanted to see Lainee smile again right about now. He was up to an average of two smiles an hour and feeling pretty smug about it. "You're still my one and only tutor," he promised her now with a suggestive wiggle of his eyebrows. "You can *tutor* me in chemistry any time, Lainee." He made the word sound scintillating.

"Noah, you need to take this work more seriously," Lainee scolded him and not for the first time even that hour, though she was valiantly fighting back a flush. She wasn't dead, after all. The guy had skills. "You need to *study*." She tried to make that word sound as sexy as he'd made "tutor," but she failed miserably.

Noah moaned loudly and dramatically then, like an over-taxed child who'd suddenly hit a wall and needed a nap. Sure enough, the whiny temper tantrum soon followed.

His head just wasn't in it today and the white, institutional walls were starting to drive him a little crazy. He itched his jaw in agitation. "Can I help it if a dozen girls walk up to me every hour when we're in this same godforsaken spot every freakin' day? Why don't we meet somewhere else - *anywhere* else - more private or fun?" He was definitely whining at this point, pouty lips and all. "This place is such a drag."

"I *love* this library," Lainee responded vehemently with a hand over her heart, personally offended by his comments, as if he'd insulted her very own private abode... *and* kicked her dog.

"Of course you do," Noah countered dryly, rolling his eyes at her. He tried arguing his case again. "Let's go to my room to study. I don't have a roommate, remember? I have a whole suite all to myself so we can study in complete isolation. We can turn on some music, sit in more comfortable chairs, avoid interruptions. That will totally help me focus." Lainee shook her head adamantly at all of that, making him whine in desperation, "What? Why? I promise to keep my hands off you, for Christ's sake. You're not in any danger here, I promise." Like a clueless caveman lumbering along, he added in exasperation, "Trust me, Lainee. You don't need to worry about me putting any moves on you. That is *not* going to happen, okay? Ever."

Lainee flinched, despite her well-obstructed walls and their growing rapport, as if he'd slapped her. *Ouch.*

"Oh, hey," Noah said, reaching a hand out, instantly regretful for the pained look on her face, "I didn't mean you aren't attractive, Lainee, only that I don't think of you in that way and you're totally safe with-"

Lainee jerked her hand away, out of his reach, when he was about to make contact. She couldn't stand another awkward word out of his beautiful mouth so she cut him off with a quiet rebuttal.

"I know I'm in no danger of you hitting on me, Noah. I'm relatively intelligent, remember?" She stated this flatly, without heat, forcing herself to keep her hand at her side and not cover her scar with it. Then she shook her head resolutely and said in a stronger tone of voice, surprising them both with her candor, "I don't want to be seen going into your room, or seen with you *at all* besides across this library table. Even this is too close. In fact, I wish I didn't have to be seen with you at all, Noah."

It was Noah's turn to flinch and think *ouch.*

Truthfully, by his side was the last place Lainee wanted to be. She didn't need any help looking scarred and disfigured, or feeling self-conscious about it. Even across this table right here was proving problematic.

Noah was still reeling from her pointed, painful words. Lainee really felt that uncomfortable with him? Even this was too close? *What the fuck?* "Lainee," he said helplessly, trying to grasp on to the right words as he floundered around in a sea of swamping emotions, all of them quite unpleasant, "You know I didn't mean-"

"Don't, Noah," she interrupted tightly, staring at her computer screen intently. She didn't want to see the pity in his eyes for a second time. And discussing her looks was uncharted, uncomfortable territory she didn't care to traverse with anyone, let alone Noah who was both the best looking guy on campus and, surprisingly, her pretty good friend now. "Please," she added quietly, "let's get back to work."

Noah stayed miserably quiet after that, feeling both wounded and guilty in equal measure. He figured his silence was the least she deserved after he'd put his foot in his mouth... again. Damn it, why did she bring out his awkward, stumbling, insecure side? He was usually so smooth and suave around the ladies but, nope, never with Lainee. He was always bumbling about and hurting her feelings quite unintentionally.

The truth of the matter was, Noah found Lainee intimidating, intriguing *and* utterly attractive all at the same time. He just had no clue how to go about telling her that without it sounding like he was trying to get in her pants, which he decidedly, shockingly, was not. He respected her too damn much to think of her like that, but he was pretty sure after this conversation she wouldn't want to hear it even in the platonic way he meant it.

She *especially* didn't want to hear that her scar was just one of the many interesting and attractive features about her that he liked. He wanted so badly to reassure her and confess that, yes, it caught his eye but in a good way, right along with her large pool of warm blue eyes, her full lips that stopped his heart when they turned upward in a smile, her adorable high-rounded cheekbones.

Truthfully, she thought of the scar much more often than anyone else did. He could tell by the way she'd touch it whenever she felt uncertain or insecure. She didn't even know she was doing it half the time he was quite certain, but a dark thought or a pang of uncomfortable emotion would have her fluttering her fingertips over it as if it were a secret message in Braille, meant only for her.

Every time her fingertips flew over the slight pink ridge, his own fingers would inexplicably itch to do the same. He felt a strange desire to scale its slight peaks himself, to kiss it even, as if he, too, could then understand its secret message, along with the enigma of the girl herself. He desperately wanted to make it less shameful for her in the process. He shook his head now, trying to end his rather romantic reverie and focus on the text book open in front of him.

Focus, Riley, he scolded himself. *Lainee doesn't want to hear any kind of commentary from you, and she isn't even your type anyway,* he quickly added as a weak defense to her stinging rejection just now. A mocking voice in the back of his brain laughed and chided immediately, *Riiiight... she isn't the type you can easily fool and fuck, you mean.*

For the first time since he'd entered the library, Noah willingly forced his brain to focus on the subject of biochemistry, trying desperately to shut every other thought right down.

CHAPTER 10

The next day, after the tenth girl in the first fifteen minutes interrupted their tutoring session, Noah somehow talked Lainee into walking to the bustling Harvard Square to study at the Crema Cafe over lattes.

Word was clearly getting around and he had his aggressive fans to thank for springing and saving him from being institutionalized one more wretched day at Widener. Noah was literally humming in happiness on the walk over to the coffee shop, smiling and waving at pretty much anything that moved along their path.

Lainee regretted immediately giving in to Noah and leaving the safe harbor of her library as soon as they set out across campus. Many heads swiveled as they passed by, and there were more of 'em out here in the wild. She slid her eyes sideways to glance at Noah as they walked, acknowledging his stupid good looks and thousand-watt smile for the millionth time. That coupled with his little bit of fame that inevitably followed him around was a nightmare for someone like her who just wanted to operate alone and in the shadows, invisible from the rest of the world.

The scar on her cheek felt even more noticeable and hideous against the backdrop of his polished good looks and glamorous life. It practically burned now on her skin as she was more aware and self-conscious of it than she'd been in a very long time. She cursed Noah then and wondered how she'd ever ended up as his bloody sidekick in the first place.

She of all people knew that fate had a cruel sense of humor but this was her biggest nightmare come to life, so many eyes on her while she was side by side with Adonis himself. If she was so smart, she wondered bitterly, how had she ended up *here*, walking across campus at Noah Riley's side?

At the library she was safer from prying eyes, or at least there were far less of them, especially if she kept her head facing the corner and bent over her books, her long hair falling forward in an attempt to keep the world at bay and minimize the impact of its reaction to her garish scar.

Still, despite her best efforts to hide away from the world, it wasn't ever easy. The scar was front and center, after all, calling out for attention wherever she went even if the rest of her wasn't. Everyone's eyes always inevitably wandered to it and lingered uncomfortably there, similar to a car wreck that came into view... fascinating and yet horrifying, too. For an insecure girl who hated to be the center of attention, it was a slow-burning kind of hell she found herself walking through on a daily basis.

As if that wasn't burden enough, her internal world and very consciousness revolved around it like the earth to the sun. It wasn't just at the center of her outer-life but at the core of her inner-dialogue as well. How could it not be when it represented her worst single moment of existence and its subsequent trauma? It symbolized a horrific moment she'd barely endured and was a badge of immense shame she'd carry with her always. She used it like a thick wall to keep her distance from others.

She had managed to get comfortable with it in a strange way, the scar, the stares, the separation. It kept her singularly focused on her studies and career path to be a biochemist. She hoped one day to be like the great Nobel-Prize winning Dr. Jennifer Doudna, the American biochemist who'd helped pioneer CRISPR gene editing and, more recently, genetic scissoring which had the potential to contribute to new cancer therapies and cure inherited diseases. Lainee longed to be a pioneer in the field herself and, more importantly, make a lasting contribution to society while not necessarily having to intimately interact with it.

Her drive to make a difference and be a pioneer in the sciences defined her, as did her need to separate herself from others. This paradox was at the crux of her very being, and just one more reason she was never quite comfortable in her own skin.

Of course, Noah with all his annoying swagger and oozing charm had talked her into coming out of her cocoon anyway. He was the exception to every rule, she was coming to believe and, truthfully, hard to resist. *Oh, he is flippin' good,* she acknowledged then with another sideways glance at him. *No wonder he can charm the pants off every girl on campus.*

Still, he'd held up his end of the deal with her and never once mentioned her scar again after their first fateful encounter. And strangely enough, when his golden eyes glanced over it, there was only a look of... tenderness... And it never lingered there. When Noah looked at her, he took in her whole face so intently and so... warmly. It was as if the scar was just a small piece of her overall countenance and he liked what he saw, all of it individually and in totality.

He really did have the kindest eyes and Lainee felt quite at ease beneath them.

Slowly, he was drawing her out of her shell despite her hard-won pragmatism and her resolve to stay at a safe distance. A couple of weeks in and she was chagrined to admit she was just another female succumbing to his charismatic charm and freakishly good looks despite her big brain and above average IQ.

Alas, she admitted to herself with a resigned sigh as he opened the cafe door for her with a grand flourish like a common-day dashing rogue, Noah was proving that she was just like every other girl on campus. *Damn him.*

As they settled into corner seats after ordering their coffees, she gratefully pulled out her laptop and bent over it, pulling down the curtain of her chestnut brown hair all around her with relief.

She jumped a fraction when Noah suddenly brushed her hair back with his hand, saying so very casually, "You should wear your hair back sometime, Lainee. You've got a beautiful face." It wasn't a come on. It wasn't a joke. He stated it as a casual, factual observation.

She blinked at him in shock. No one had ever called her beautiful, at least not after the incident. She lifted her head slightly then, something relaxing and untangling at the core of her. Noah Riley thought she had a beautiful face? She could tell he was completely sincere in his statement and there was no ulterior motive behind it. It was in the warmth of his tone and the ever-present look of appreciation in his kind eyes. He left no doubt in her mind that he meant exactly what he said.

Wow... Noah thought she had a beautiful face. It shouldn't have, but it mattered. It mattered greatly.

Noah slammed the door to his dorm room shut with his foot as he grabbed for her jacket and peeled it off over her shoulders and down her arms. It landed silently on the floor, his lips never once leaving hers. He guided her with practiced ease across the room to his king size bed, their tongues dancing feverishly and their hands grabbing greedily.

When the bed hit the back of her knees she fell into it eagerly, pulling him down with her as she held on to the front of his shirt, her lips staying glued to his despite the jostling. Noah drew back only long enough to discard his brown leather jacket and pull his white t-shirt up and over his head, then he quickly unzipped his jeans and pushed them off along with his navy boxer briefs. He was naked in mere seconds.

Excitement thrummed through his central nervous system as she undressed as hastily as he, right on top of his red plaid duvet cover, her long brown hair spreading haphazardly all around her as she squirmed out of her pretty panties and her blue eyes flashed up at him with hunger.

Finally, he thought with lust and satisfaction when they were both completely naked. His eyes roamed appreciatively down her lean, sexy frame and then he was joining her on the bed, careful not to put too much of his weight on her as he crawled up her bare form, his skin sliding across her skin. Noah shivered with pleasure and anticipation. *This was it.* This was the moment he'd been waiting for.

He couldn't remember the girl's name at the moment but he was very grateful she was gifting him with her beautiful body even as he was subconsciously fantasizing about another brown haired, blue-eyed girl with a similar athletic build. He trailed covetous kisses down her neck, across her small breasts, then down her flat stomach.

"Is this alright?" he asked huskily as he kissed the top of her pretty, hairless vagina. He always made sure to ask, and to give as much pleasure as he got. He was perhaps a promiscuous cad, but he was a gentlemanly one at that. He always asked for permission, and then left them smiling and satisfied.

"Mhmmm," she moaned pushing his head back down towards her center, which he took as a resounding yes to his question. Permission granted, he dove in with his tongue, making her squeal delightedly in shock and awe.

As she writhed and moaned underneath him, Noah unconsciously fantasized it was his favorite enigma with the serious, sad eyes and sexy scar coming undone beneath him. His cock thickened and pulsed with pounding need as he gently pressed her thighs further apart and dove in deeper yet with his scratchy tongue, envisioning her to be the most mysterious, stoic girl he'd ever come across... at least until he got his hands and tongue on her. Then he imagined she'd be a wildcat begging for more, just like this.

As Noah's lover called out his name and began to shiver and shake with the orgasm he generously bestowed upon her, his hard cock ached and jumped along the surface of his duvet in response. He licked her long moments more to prolong her pleasure, fantasizing all the while that it was his bewitching muse coming apart and calling out to him instead.

It was the first time Lainee visited him unbidden in his bed when he was with another woman, but it wouldn't be the last.

CHAPTER 11

Their rapport and rather organic, easy connection began to solidify as they each let their reservations slide away little by little. Noah had proven himself as quick-witted as he was kind, and Lainee had come to relax and really enjoy his company. In return, Noah learned Lainee was sweet as well as whip smart. He knew he was the luckiest bastard on campus to have the opportunity to get to know her like this.

Her confidence at an all time high, she let him talk her into going to dinner in downtown Boston after studies at the library the next day. This was new territory, both downtown Boston and Noah's growing influence over her. He was excited. She was extremely nervous as he pulled his BMW out of the campus parking lot in the pouring rain.

He was chatting away, completely oblivious to her mounting nerves as he jetted down the busy expressway linking campus to downtown. As he came upon a slower vehicle in the fast lane, he braked hard and eased up but followed close behind in the hopes the other driver would get the message and move over to the middle lane. No such luck.

That's when he happened to glance over at Lainee to find her gripping the console with one hand and the passenger door with the other. Her face was drained of all color as she stared unblinkingly straight ahead. She looked as if she'd seen a ghost.

Noah immediately felt guilty at his aggressive driving. "Hey, are you okay, Lainee?" he asked uncertainly. "Are you nervous because it's raining?" When she didn't answer or even blink in acknowledgement, he eased over into the middle lane himself, giving wide berth to the vehicle ahead of him. "Is this better?"

She licked her dry lips then and managed a nod but still did not look away from the road ahead or release the death grip she had on the vehicle.

He felt instantly guilty for being such an aggressive driver, especially in declining weather. "Here, I'll slow down even more. You're safe, Lainee, I promise. You can relax."

She looked over then and blinked at him, slowly registering his words. She nodded and whispered, "Thanks, Noah."

He eased into the slow lane, once again careful to give any car in front of him wide berth. "Better?" he asked gently. She nodded but he could clearly see she was still uncomfortable.

Fifteen minutes later, to both their relief, he eased off the expressway into downtown, managing to find a metered parking space on a side street not too far away from their destination. Jacob Wirth Co. in the theatre district, one of Boston's oldest and most prestigious dining establishments, was a personal favorite of Noah's. He hoped she'd like it, too.

As he slid the gear into park and turned the engine off, he told Lainee, trying to distract her, "Hey, did you know Tom Cruise and Cameron Diaz filmed a scene at Jacob Wirth in the movie Knight and Day?" Lainee had finally completely released her grip on his vehicle he was happy to see. "Maybe we'll watch it later after we eat there. Wait, do you even watch movies?"

He didn't wait for her to answer as he exited the vehicle and came around to open her door. He chatted away, trying to smooth over her nerves, as he escorted her down the block. Luckily the rain was letting up and it was just a light drizzle at this point. Lainee visibly relaxed with every step as he carried on his light, one-sided conversation. "The seafood is fresh and phenomenal. Rumor has it Al Pacino always visits Boston specifically for the oysters here. And he isn't the only celebrity who frequents the place."

A few feet away from the restaurant's door, a flash went off in their faces, stopping them in their tracks as they blinked in surprise.

"Paparazzi," Noah said in surprise, "maybe Pacino is here right now. Wouldn't that be something?" Never one to turn away from a camera, he stepped up to the photographer and gave him his best smile, then he offered up his name and resume for encouragement. He chatted with the guy for a moment, amiable as ever, while Lainee hung back underneath the canopy by the door, fighting the urge all the while to cover her scar with her hand. She prayed she wouldn't be in any of the pictures.

After a moment, Noah thanked the photographer and came back to Lainee's side, putting his hand on the small of her back and saying with a smile, "Sorry about that."

Just when he was about to open the door to the restaurant for her, the cameraman called out, "Hey, Noah, give us a big smooch for the camera!"

Caught up in the moment and needing no further encouragement, Noah threw his arm around Lainee's shoulders, dipped her slightly and planted one on her.

Completely taken off guard, Lainee froze in Noah's arms and then... she melted, moving her lips against his out of sheer instinct and desire. He tasted of cinnamon as she'd always known he would. And he was a damn fine kisser. But of course. In contrast to his oodles of practice, Lainee had had only had a few kisses before... well, before. This was the first one after. Every cell awakened, reminding her the thrill one could feel when flesh was on flesh. Until sanity came rushing back to her. She pushed at his chest in panic and Noah righted her with a wicked grin on his face. He looked like the svelte cat who'd swallowed the stupid, scared and scarred canary.

"That was fun," Noah chuckled almost to himself, completely oblivious to Lainee's stress as they finally made their way inside the restaurant and were escorted to a table for two. "I need all the publicity I can get as I'm kind of in lock down these next two years. My only creative outlet will be the theater company here at Harvard, at least until I can get my grades up." Truthfully, he wasn't all that interested in acting outside of theater but the few bit parts he'd gotten in movies would round out his resume. Noah's ultimate destination was Broadway but he had to be marketable as well as talented.

He didn't even notice that Lainee was suspiciously quiet once again as he scanned the menu and gave her food recommendations. She just nodded when he asked if he could order for them both. "Let's see if that guy gets my name right," he said cheerfully after ordering, checking his phone repeatedly as they waited for their food. "These things are instantaneous now and these days. There's a flash of an iPhone and then there's a post." He kept trolling Just Jared, TMZ and the other usual suspects, hoping he'd be tagged. He'd forgotten to ask the photographer who he was working for. *Such a rookie move*, he thought to himself as he continued his search. Sure enough, by the time their food arrived Noah saw the picture of their smooch and a few of his other poses on Perez Hilton's socials. It wasn't Us Weekly or People but it was better than nothing.

"Not bad pictures even with my wet hair," he said with a cocky grin, showing Lainee their picture from across the table. His little publicity stunt had gotten him the attention he desired and he was quite pleased with himself, he wasn't going to lie. "And you look great, even if you're not smiling in any of them."

Distracted from both Lainee and the food that arrived fairly quickly, he started to scroll through the comments on the pictures, liking and responding to some of them as he went. "At least I haven't completely lost my appeal, even though most of these people don't even know who I am," he mumbled to himself. He scrolled and scanned for long moments when suddenly his countenance darkened and he scowled.

"Jesus Christ," he whispered after a moment. Some brutal comments were coming in, and they weren't aimed his way at all. They focused squarely on Lainee in the background, or rather, her facial scar. They made cruel comparisons to his flawless looks and her lack thereof.

Noah looked up at Lainee then, quite horrified on her behalf and downright furious over the couple of negative comments that were currently posting real time. That's when he finally saw that all color had drained from her face yet again and, worse, there was a sheen of tears in her eyes. Oh, God. he'd never seen Lainee cry before.

She'd seen this coming a mile away he realized. He'd put a bulls eye right on her forehead and had been too dumb and self-centered to realize it until too late. His stomach twisted as he took in her wet eyes.

He'd done this. He'd put that look on her face and those tears in her eyes after putting a target on her. He'd railroaded her into dinner downtown, scared the shit out of her in the car ride over and then thoughtlessly pushed her into the crosshairs of social trolls. He felt like the biggest fucking bastard in the whole wide world. "Lainee," he began apologetically, reaching his hand out across the table beseechingly. "I'm so sorry. I wasn't thinking-"

"It's fine, Noah," she lied bravely, her voice only shaking a little as she stopped his words cold. "It's nothing unexpected." Again, she couldn't stand the look of pity on his gorgeous, perfect face. She valiantly fought the tears back as she pushed away from the table and stood. "Excuse me for a moment while I use the ladies' room."

Noah's heart broke clean in two as he watched her stiffly walk away. "*Fuck*," he whispered out loud, throwing his napkin on his full plate of food, knowing neither of them would want to eat a bite now. He'd ruined dinner and the whole damn evening. He'd hurt Lainee. *Again.* And in the worst way possible. He knew she hated the spotlight and he'd thrust her right into it with a target on her forehead. He was such a fucking idiot.

How could he have been so thoughtless, so careless with her? He looked around the restaurant helplessly then. What could he do? How could he make it up to her? *Could* he?

And then the most haunting question of all, *is this what she went through on a daily basis?*

CHAPTER 12

As Lainee took long minutes in the bathroom, Noah's heart sank even lower. He'd really fucked up this time, he knew, and she was paying the price. He just hoped she'd be able to forgive him... eventually. Settling the bill, he waited on pins and needles.

For another fifteen minutes he waited and all the while he suffered. Still, she didn't come back and he knew it was bad. He'd annihilated her, his proud, strong, private Lainee.

Never hating himself more, he slowly stood and walked down the long corridor to the restroom. Unsure of what to do but needing to do *something*, anything to make things right, he knocked gently on the women's bathroom door. "Lainee? Are you in there?"

An awkward minute passed and then he heard her muffled, "Y-yes. I'm sorry. I don't feel very well." In truth she felt frozen there in the bathroom, unable to face Noah, the paparazzi, the world at large. She wished, and not for the first time, the earth would open and swallow her whole. But she refused to let any tears fall. She needed to be strong, she berated herself. Why was this hitting her so hard? She hated herself for her vulnerability, her weakness. She needed to be stronger, smarter, better. How had she let that refrain slip for even a moment?

"Lainee," Noah said achingly, resting his forehead on the back of the bathroom door and closing his eyes. *Fuck!* Why did he have to be such a thoughtless asshole? "I'm so sorry. I wasn't thinking..." He trailed off miserably, not knowing how to talk with her now when there was a door separating them and when she'd banned any conversation surrounding her scar in the first fifteen minutes of meeting him.

He straightened, knowing what he needed to say suddenly. He pushed on resolutely, "Listen, I know you don't want to talk about it, but we're going to have to, just for a minute. I need you to hear this, Lainee, really hear it. You are fucking beautiful and you should embrace that badass scar. It's seriously the coolest scar I've ever seen."

He didn't hear a peep on the other side of that door but he was on a roll now and he continued with utter conviction that left no room for argument, "I don't know what happened to you, and you don't have to tell me, but that scar represents your strength and your power and no one, especially nameless social trolls, can take that away from you." *My little warrior*, he thought then with quite a bit of pride. "Hand to God, Lainee, I've always found your scar so damn interesting... and sexy as hell." He put his hand on the door, trying to transfer some of his earnest emotion through it somehow. "Your scar is one my favorite things about you, truthfully." Though there were many, many things he liked about her, and more of them by the day.

He could have gone on for hours on the merits of her good looks alone and how much he liked her whole face, including that fascinating scar, but thankfully she swung the bathroom door open right then. He was so relieved to see her he almost reached out and pulled her in for another kiss. Almost.

"Hi," he said instead, very gently, suddenly shy and awkward.

"Hi," she returned, managing a small, sweet smile which did wonders for his heart.

They stared and smiled sadly at each other for long moments as they both steadied themselves.

"Are you okay?" he finally asked her quietly.

She took in a deep breath and nodded resolutely. "Yes. I am now." Thanks to his kind, empowering words. She'd never heard such astounding accolades before. They lifted her spirits, her chin, because she knew Noah meant them wholeheartedly, and she felt ready now to face the world.

Noah let out the big breath he didn't even realize he'd been holding. "We'll leave out the back," he told her then, reaching for her hand without a second thought. "And I'll drive very slowly and carefully all the way back to campus, and we'll never leave the Widener Library ever again." As he'd hoped, this had her mouth turning up in a smile and he swore to himself then and there that she would never suffer another single second due to his thoughtlessness and idiocy. And he'd never again complain about the library.

He lead her out the back door and to his car, holding her hand all the while, careful not to say another stupid, careless word. Then he slowly drove back to campus in the rain, taking twice as long as normal.

When they were back in the parking lot near Dunster House, his dorm, he hesitated. He didn't want to end the night, not now, not like this. "Do you maybe want to study some more in my room? I think Widener is closing soon, otherwise I'd say we could go back there..." he trailed off awkwardly as she eyed him silently for long moments from the passenger's seat of his car. It reminded him of the stoic stranger he'd been hella obsessed over. She was no longer unknown to him, thank God, but he was afraid his obsession was only intensifying by the day.

She finally bit her bottom lip and nodded, making his heart flip flop. That seemed to be happening with more intensity by the day as well but, in true Noah-style, he didn't stop to analyze it. He just focused on the rush of relief and helped drag their backpacks out of his back seat.

His nerves were relatively steady as they entered his private suite in Dunster. Suddenly it didn't seem as big of a deal to either of them that they were in his room together for the very first time, not after the emotional roller coaster they'd just shared that evening.

He motioned to a couple of leather sitting chairs in one corner of his suite. As she got settled in he quickly turned on a bunch of lamps - there were at least half a dozen of them all around the room, Lainee noticed - and he grabbed some bottled waters out of his fridge as well as a nearby lighter.

He settled in the opposite leather chair from her, lighting the candle on the compact table between them, pointing out with an almost embarrassed smile, "I thought you might like this."

Lainee looked more closely at the candle and realized the scent was "Library" from the brand Magnolia. She swung her eyes up to him in surprise, her head slightly cocked to the side as she tried to remember if she'd ever mentioned how much she loved the smell of the library out loud to him. She must have. And he'd remembered... and took the time to search out and buy a candle on the off chance she would ever agree to study in his room?

Her heart warmed and started to melt right alongside the wax of the Library candle. As the soft smell of clove mixed with a slight touch of firewood wafted up, she closed her eyes and inhaled nice and deep. It was such a lovely smell and very, very close to that of her beloved Widener. Her whole body relaxed and she smiled quite contentedly.

Noah's body reflexively mimicked hers and unwound. Relief pushed some of his guilt away as he took in a deep breath, too. *Lainee liked it*, he thought with pleasure and a spark of joy. She liked the candle he'd bought for her.

She opened her eyes then, connecting with his. "Thank you, Noah," she said quietly. "This candle is amazing." What she really meant was *he* was amazing.

He nodded with a little shrug as if it was really no big deal but they were both smiling as they turned their focus to studying. He had an environmental science and engineering test the next day and she suggested running through the study guide a couple of more times, and he... well, he was just relieved she was in his room, still by his side, and hadn't walked away from his dumb, insensitive ass which would have been well within her rights to do.

He was still feeling guilty and solemn as he moved his chair slightly so that he could face her more directly. Before she even got through the first question, he blurted out, "I'm so fucking sorry, Lainee, for my spontaneous and thoughtless publicity prank back there. I-I just wasn't thinking. I didn't realize..." he trailed off miserably.

He'd soothed her raw nerves already back at the restaurant and had picked her self-esteem up off the floor after it had taken a spectacular nosedive. He'd taken good care of her, even bestowing upon her the amazing, thoughtful gift of her favorite scent, so Lainee was quick to reassure him, "I know, Noah. It's okay, really. The truth is, I can't hide..." she unknowingly touched her scar with her fingertips, "even when I try to." Her hand dropped to her lap and she took in a steadying breath.

In this gentle, safe space with Noah, which smelled an awful lot like her favorite place on earth, Lainee felt as if she could open up to him some more. "And I really can't blame everyone for thinking I look funny and curious at your side. We are a strange pair I suppose." She eyed his handsome, chagrined face thoughtfully, "I can only wonder what people think when they see us together? You're so Hollywood and I'm so... plain Jane with an ugly scar."

That is exactly how she saw herself and she'd come to terms with it long ago, and yet tonight had taken its toll on her. Her superpower was her big brain married with a singular focus and determined drive. She'd have chosen it no other way, she reminded herself, but sometimes she wished, just for a moment, that she was like every other girl at Noah's side... without scars. What she would've given for one night without hers, to feel comfortable in her own skin, perhaps to even feel a little bit pretty.

She was shocked to find herself sharing all these thoughts out loud with Noah. The fact that she was even talking about her scar at all was a small miracle that could only come about with the trust that she'd come to have in him.

He was reaching out and taking her hand then, making her look squarely into his burning amber eyes as the flicker of candlelight reflected there in his dilated pupils. "You are not plain or ugly in any way, Lainee, not one inch of you, including that scar," he said gruffly, squeezing her hand, "*especially* that scar. You are beautiful *and* badass."

That made her heart do a funny somersault and she felt absurdly light and suddenly free of the night's heartache. That's right... Noah Riley thought she was beautiful. How could she have so easily forgotten?

All negative comments about her appearance from complete strangers disappeared into thin air, at least for the moment. She shrugged off all the mean commentary then and in a much stronger tone of voice declared, "Thank you, Noah. Your opinion definitely matters more to me than any other. Besides," she added with a small, playful smile tugging at her lips, "you and I both know that I'm waaaay to smart to date a pretty playboy like you anyway."

He acted genuinely maligned by her statement, clutching his chest as if she'd pierced her heart painfully, making her laugh.

Then he was lunging and tickling her until she apologized to *him*.

CHAPTER 13

After that night, they began studying in either Noah's room or the library right at Dunster more than at Widener. They also started going to the MAC together every day at noon instead of showing up separately. Lainee even let Noah talk her into going around campus more, and getting a bite or a beer at various locations around the surrounding town of Cambridge. Not only was she growing more confident in her appearance thanks to Noah's steady stream of bolstering words, but it was also a test of sorts that she forced upon herself after coming unglued in the bathroom of Jacob Wirth. She wouldn't have that again. She needed to be stronger, smarter, better. She needed to condition herself and be in control at all times.

The varied studying locations kept the fan interruptions at a minimum as a bonus, but there were inevitably a few of them. Lainee was almost getting used to them now. Initially she'd been irritated and then, after the run-in with the paparazzi, she'd been frozen in fear whenever someone approached with their camera phone out, but Noah had learned his lesson and was quick to shield and protect her now. Truthfully, no one who approached him was interested in her anyway. The mostly female eyes were solely on Noah. And she couldn't rightfully blame them.

Lainee eventually learned to relax more and more as they went about campus or town. They didn't plan to venture back into downtown Boston anytime soon, as the car ride paired with the extra eyes and cameras were an unwanted burden to them both. Truthfully, Noah would have done anything to protect Lainee at that point, even shy away from the spotlight for the first time in his life. They were both happy to stay in their little Cambridge bubble. Together.

Soon Lainee was just rolling with Noah's "celebrity" and "fame" - his words, of course. It was such a strange life he lived, she thought at one point as she took yet another picture of him and a complete stranger posing with their arms around each other like long lost friends in front of the John Harvard statue on campus. She herself would not have been comfortable with any of that forced intimacy and yet, here she was, on the peripheral, becoming... at ease somehow. Or, at least, she was comfortable here at Noah's side anyway.

He loved it, all of the accolades and attention. He thrived on it, actually. At first Lainee thought it a bit shallow and desperate, and then she paid attention and realized it wasn't that at all. The *interaction* with others inspired him, energized and lifted him right up. And he always returned the favor. He was generous and enigmatic, always quick with a smile and a kind word when an admirer stopped him.

She was in awe, actually, of how relaxed and friendly he was with complete strangers who approached him. He seemed to light up for each and every person, making *them* feel special. After a few more weeks at his side more and more, Lainee outright envied how comfortable he was with others, and with himself. She also recognized that Noah Riley was just a really good human being.

He was nothing but appreciative and humble... well, humble to a degree. He was certainly well aware of how freakishly good looking he was and overly confident with the ladies. But even for that Lainee couldn't fault him anymore. He was just so comfortable in his own skin when she doubted she'd ever be comfortable in hers ever again. Still, just being around Noah, having him gaze upon her like she was, in fact, badass and beautiful had Lainee's confidence growing tenfold, and her equilibrium stabilizing.

Lainee was happier than she'd been in a long, long time. It was the strangest thing she couldn't quite scientifically explain to herself.

It was just... the Noah effect.

Exactly two weeks after his publicity stunt with the paparazzi had put a target on Lainee, Noah got wicked food poisoning and was barfing his guts out. He figured it was karma and he couldn't say he didn't deserve it. He always was a puker, even as a kid. Everything made him puke, nerves, anxiety, certain spices, too much alcohol, mixing alcohol, the late-night pad Thai after his first rehearsal at the theater the night before. He managed to text Lainee at some point to say he was sick and couldn't make their workout or tutoring session. Still, she inexplicably showed up at his door in the early evening.

"Go away," he moaned from the bed when there was a knock on his door. When she identified herself, this only made Noah grow more irritated and horrified. "Lainee, I'm sick. I'm not up for visitors. Go away."

And with that she inserted the key his father had given her, pushed the door open and walked right on in.

"What the hell?" he growled, embarrassed as she came over, sat on his bed and gave him a good, close look. "Go away, damn you. I'm a disgusting mess."

She pulled out a Gatorade from a grocery bag and opened it,

stating matter of fact, "Don't be silly. I'm not a *visitor*, nor one of your fangirls. I could care less what you look like Noah Bernard Riley."

Of course she had to throw in his embarrassing middle name just to really show him her utter superiority in this, his weakest moment, making him blush. Goddamn it but there was nothing her piercing, intelligent blue eyes didn't know and see.

"This isn't a movie set," she pointed out pragmatically even as he prayed the bed would crack, fold in on itself and swallow him whole so that he could hide from her penetrating gaze. "You're allowed to look terrible when you're sick. Frankly, I'm relieved to see you, too, are subject to bad hair days. I hadn't been certain until now."

Noah gave her the evil eye. She chose *now* to get a sense of humor? "Thank you for confirming I look like shit," he mumbled dryly, trying to pull the covers up over his head to hide aforementioned bad hair, but she was undeterred and stopped him from covering his face.

"You've been sick all night and now most of the day. You need hydration and electrolytes. Please take a sip and let's see how your body responds." She put a hand underneath his head and propped him up slightly without waiting for permission. Then she put the bottle to his lips.

Despite his humiliation at his weakened, unkempt state, he took a big gulp, savoring the taste.

"Easy," she cautioned, pulling the bottle away when he would have drank more. "We have to make sure your body is ready for it."

It wasn't. He ended up needing her help getting to the bathroom in time, where he weakly puked out the rest of the food poisoning and the little bit of Gatorade he'd just consumed. Now he was beyond embarrassed, raising his head from the toilet and apologizing.

"You shouldn't have to see me like this," he groaned, beyond horrified as she helped him back to bed.

She tucked him in and brushed his sweaty hair back from his forehead as a bone-weary exhaustion began to take him. "I'm glad you're human, Noah," she told him gently then. "I like you just that much more because of it. Now sleep and you'll feel better in a few hours."

And damn if she wasn't right. When he awoke four hours later, she was there in a chair pulled up to the side of his bed, doing homework underneath the soft glow of a lamp and the flickering flame of the Library candle. And he felt a helluva lot better.

He blinked at her in surprise. She'd stayed? Why had she stayed? She smiled sweetly at him then and he knew the answer to his own question. She was a fucking angel, that was why. She was an honest to God angel who didn't give a damn about his little bit of celebrity and the polished facade he showed to the rest of the world. She wanted the real man, mess and all, it seemed. It was a bit intimidating yet liberating all at the same time.

Lainee helped Noah sit up then, fluffing his pillows behind him like Florence freaking Nightingale. She had him drink some more Gatorade and when he managed to keep that down, she spoon fed him some chicken noodle soup. It was the nicest thing anyone had ever done for him.

As his stomach settled and his strength began to return, he managed to get to the bathroom to shower and brush his teeth. He still looked like complete and utter shit, pale and worn down, but he was grateful to feel partially human again with some basic hygiene back under his belt. He felt slightly less embarrassed under her scrutiny then.

He knew it would be a few days before he was back to full strength but he'd made it through the worst of it, with her help. Noah looked at Lainee gratefully now and thanked her for helping him despite his initial protests. No one had ever taken care of him like that when he'd been sick, unless you counted a paid nanny or two when he'd been a child. But there were no nannies to take care of him after the age of 5. He'd pretty much been on his own after that.

"We're a team now," she told him kindly with the slightest of shy smiles, brushing some wet hair off his forehead. "We get the rare gift of really seeing each other, of helping each other. That's how it works."

It was the strangest way to look at him throwing up in her presence but it resonated with him even as he blushed.

"You don't have to hide anything from me, Noah," she added gently, meaningfully, and left it at that.

Her words gave him pause. She was pushing him, challenging him as always to work harder, be braver and to leave his performance on the stage and to show up as himself, though it was ironically the most uncomfortable of all the characters he played.

He was more intimidated by her than ever in that moment. It wasn't just her keen intelligence and knowing gaze that cut through his bullshit so effortlessly. It was also her calm, grounding presence. She would always be the epitome of dignity and grace to him, as well as strength and bravery. She knew exactly who she was, what she wanted and her path forward. She was a strong, steadfast force to be reckoned with. And she didn't need outside validation. He was so envious of that.

He, on the other hand, *had* to have the attention, the applause, just to get by. He was insecure and unsure of himself without it. He also had to lose himself in his characters so that he could feel something, anything other than his own fucked up feelings. He preferred to be anyone but himself, truthfully, and he wasn't entirely sure either of them would like who he *really* was underneath it all.

Still, Lainee made him want to try. She made him want to try to be a better man, one who was courageous and... worthy of her. Despite his overwhelming uncertainty over that notion, he felt himself relaxing against his pillows as she intently gazed upon his pale and disheveled appearance. It was a relief to let go of the act of perfection, at least when he was sick and weak here in his own room. No one had ever taken care of him like she had today. He felt safe with her despite his growing vulnerability.

"Think you're up to doing a little homework?" she asked him then, as always ready to work. "I'll even go easy on you and give you most of the answers this *one* time, since you're having a bad hair day and all."

He huffed a laugh at her. The jokes were coming more and more frequently, he noted with pleasure. That did his heart good, along with all the rest of it.

He told her warmly then, "Whatever my father is paying you, Lainee, it isn't nearly enough." Then he remembered something and quickly added, "But I'm going to need that key back now."

CHAPTER 14

After that, they solidified as the unlikeliest and strangest of bonded pairs. They worked hard and studied daily, side by side. They seemed to always be together now when they weren't in class or he in theater practice. They were still a showstopper wherever they went but they could have cared less now about the gawking, even Lainee.

At first the other regulars in the MAC had their mouths on the floor in shock when Noah and Lainee started showing up together to workout. The girl with the scar was actually talking and *smiling*? And not just with anyone but with Noah Riley of all people? It was like a strange phenomenon they needed to study closely under a microscope. Noah, of course, basked in the stares and whispers but for a completely different reason than before. Now he felt quite cocky and downright proud to be at Lainee's side, to be the one inspiring those smiles and laughs of hers. He was the luckiest son of a bitch on campus and he knew it. His stock was going up but, more importantly, so was hers.

People were starting to approach her more and more, too, and for once she was receptive if still a bit leery and shy. When no one asked about her scar or pointed and laughed at it, Lainee found herself lifting her head up and making eye contact with the world around her, actually welcoming social interaction. It was just another anomaly from the Noah effect, she surmised rather fondly.

"Whatcha' listening to?" Noah asked now as they worked out side by side on elliptical machines, warming up. He'd always been curious about that, after all, as he'd watched her from afar not so long ago.

She still held fast to her regimented routine but he was a floater, mixing it up for his cardio and weight training. He always drifted back to her side throughout, though. He tried not to bug her too much but she didn't seem irritated as she pulled out one of her ear buds now.

"Bach," she told him matter-of-fact, gracefully climbing her imaginary mountain without needing to hold on to the elliptical's handles as she turned slightly to face him. Noah was always a nice distraction in her eyes. The time seemed to fly by when he was in a talkative mood.

"Of course you are," he replied dryly, actually rolling his eyes at her as he easily climbed his own mountain beside her. "I don't even know why I bothered asking. Is that all you listen to, *classical* music? Even while you're working out?"

She was highly offended by his line of questioning and told him haughtily, "Mozart, Beethoven, Bach, yes. You do know classical music improves spatial reasoning skills, sharpens cognitive abilities and lowers blood pressure."

"Yawn," Noah replied, quite unimpressed by any of that. "You're studying even now in your head, aren't you? Haven't you ever heard of burnout and the positive effects of taking a freaking break?"

It was her turn to roll her eyes at him. "And what, pray tell, are you listening to which boasts such great, positive effects, Noah Bernard Riley?"

"Punk rock and heavy metal, baby," he said with a heart-stopping, ear-to-ear grin. He thought a minute and then scrolled through his playlist, on a mission. "Here, listen to this."

"Fine but you have to listen to mine in exchange."

They traded ear buds and Noah had to admit he felt very energized and focused as something called "Symphony No. 41" by Mozart trilled away in his ear.

Lainee in turn listened intently to some of his classic rock gems like The Distance by Cake, Supermassive Black Hole by Muse and Seven Nation Army by White Stripes. He'd gone easy on her and had selected a somewhat tame playlist without heavy metal. He had to chuckle to himself as he watched her face now as it truly seemed she was studying every word of every song and turning it all over in her head like a new language to learn.

Ten minutes later he was starting to sweat on the elliptical machine and *still* listening to Symphony No. 41. He'd had enough. *Jesus Christ, this shit went on and on.* How could she stand it for more than a few minutes? He removed his ear buds and she did the same. "What do you think?" he asked her with a superior smile. "Good to work out to, am I right?"

"Yes, actually," she admitted. "But do you have anything... softer?" She found the driving beats stimulating and yet she couldn't sustain listening to that relentless tempo for the entire workout without becoming anxious.

Noah thought about her request and then had the perfect answer. He scrolled through his phone a moment and pulled up Taylor Swift's 1989 album. He'd deny having it in his library and listening to it with his dying breath, and yet he knew no mortal human being, even cavemen like his brothers on the lacrosse team, could truly resist Taylor's lyrical genius married to her catchy rhythms. He also bet she would rock Lainee's world.

He knew she'd heard of Taylor, of course, but had she ever *taken her in*? He thought not or she wouldn't listen solely to that classical crap. Seriously, didn't all girls of any age listen to and love Taylor with high-pitched fervor and rabid zeal? It was a no-brainer even for him.

He handed her both his ear buds and his phone then with a wink. He dismounted his elliptical and headed for the free weights, leaving Blank Space and Bad Blood to work their magic on her.

◆◆◆

There was no denying it. Noah was getting Lainee to loosen up quite a bit, to have some fun along the way and to fall madly and deeply in love with Taylor Swift. In turn, she got him to focus on academics to a greater degree than he ever had before. She was very strategic and subtle about it, of course. She'd play a game of pool with him in the common space of Dunster if he'd finish half of his social studies paper. She'd buy him a beer at any tavern of his choice in Cambridge after he pulled out a B- or higher on his tests. She'd let them skip out on Widener if he kept up with his study guides. That last one was his favorite reward as the relentless white walls of the Widener still made him itch.

She'd quickly become a good pool player and he'd triumphantly raised his below average grades to above average. As Lainee had said, they were a team now, and a good one at that. It was almost as if they balanced each other out, and Noah was really beginning to appreciate how she challenged him, inspired him, made him better in every way.

Feeling completely at ease with her now, he found himself being moody, taciturn and grumpy in her company from time to time. It was an unexpected gift that he didn't have to pretend to shine at all times with her. He could be sloppy and disheveled, pissed off and reflective. Ironically, this made him more content than he'd ever been, perhaps because he was allowing himself to process his own emotions for once.

She was forcing him to be more vulnerable and authentic, day by day, inch by inch. Still, they did not talk about his parents. Even as he pondered the cause of her scar, he honestly prayed she'd never ask him the source of his.

◆◆◆

They were in his room a few nights later, side by side in the brown leather chairs, quietly studying on their own, her ear buds in while she worked away on her laptop. Noah looked up from his Hamlet script at one point to find Lainee's eyes shining with tears in the candlelight, her fingers hovering frozen over her keyboard.

His heart immediately lurched. "Hey," he said, reaching out to touch her arm so that she'd look up and take out her ear buds. "Are you okay? What's wrong?"

She looked at him with her wet, wide, deep-blue eyes that he could easily, happily drown in. She sniffed, looking a little embarrassed. "Oh, I-I'm just listening to this song Exile by Taylor and Bon Iver and it's... gut wrenching." In fact, she could have sworn her heart just broke in two listening to it. She never knew music could do this to a person. "Have you heard it?"

He smiled slowly at her, a mix of relief and adoration flooding his system. Then it him hard all at once, like a bullet to his chest and he almost winced as his heart squeezed quite painfully. His stoic mystery girl was here in his room right now, crying over Taylor Swift songs.

Staggering. All of that.

Speechless, he shook his head. She handed him an ear bud and started the song over. As the haunting piano melody flowed through each of their ears, followed by Bon Iver's deep, heavy and pained baritone, they both became very still, staring at each other in complete rapture as if under a spell. Maybe it was the yearning strains of the song... or perhaps it was something else all together.

You're not my homeland anymore so what am I defending now? You were my town, now I'm in exile, seeing you out.

Noah swore his heart cracked just a little bit as his eyes stayed locked on to Lainee's and he listened to those heartbreaking lines. He uncomfortably swallowed the eerie words that seemed more like a premonition than random lyrics under her intense, disconcerting gaze.

Damn, he thought uneasily, *Ophelia from Hamlet had nothing on Taylor Swift in the love and tragedy department.* Both women knew how to break his heart well and truly good. And as the lyrics nudged him onward and he all but drowned in the blue depths of Lainee's bottomless eyes, he couldn't help but wonder and worry for the very first time if perhaps, one day, that sentiment might also apply to his best friend Lainee Reed, too...

CHAPTER 15

Lainee knocked loudly and decisively on Noah's door early that Saturday morning, making him groan in protest as she woke him up from a warm, cozy dream that may or may not have involved a tragic temptress with big, blue eyes.

"Go away, whoever you are," he yelled out, knowing full well who it was. She had insisted on dragging him to some boring guest lecture by some uber-brilliant scientist this morning, and on a weekend no less. It was unconscionable. Face to face with her he'd had a hard time saying no but here and now, in the warm cocoon of his covers with the solid door between them, he added defiantly, "I'm not going anywhere, Lainee. It's Saturday morning and I'm sleeping in. Go away."

"I've got a key," Lainee reminded him cheerfully, all but singing her words.

She was a clear threat to his false bravado and brittle resistance as per usual. *Damn her.* In the end, he'd never taken the key back but they had agreed she would only use it in emergencies. This didn't seem like an emergency to him.

"*Ugh,*" Noah moaned loud enough for her to hear through the door, making her smile. She heard him rummaging around inside after a moment, and knew he was getting up and around at last.

A few minutes later, after pulling on a grey shirt and joggers, he opened the door with sleepy, narrowed eyes, stabbing his fingers through his hair in an attempt to tame the bed head he inevitably had going on. "Woman," he groaned, "I was up late last night because of the fundraising party," he reminded her grumpily. "I was schmoozing alumni which is very exhausting work I'll have you know."

The school board was always tapping him on the shoulder for such things as he was the gem of their world-class theater department and all, single-handedly inspiring millions of dollars in alumni and non-alumni dollars of support yearly. Truthfully, Noah didn't mind this duty one bit. Not only was he a naturally gregarious person who loved the spotlight, the theater department there was his passion and he had no hesitation throwing his weight behind it every chance he got.

This early weekend wakeup call after a long night spent supporting that cause seemed unnecessarily cruel and punishing from his best friend. Had she no respect for him and how much money he'd just raised for their alma mater? Besides, he wasn't exactly a morning person even on a good day.

Lainee on the other hand, he noticed between narrowed eyes, looked downright perky and shiny in her pale pink button-up shirt and crisp, dark jeans and brown penny loafers. For once she wasn't wearing a sweater, but a brown leather jacket instead to ward off the cooling fall temperatures. She looked quite beautiful and polished. He scowled at her.

She wouldn't hear any of his excuses and was completely unfazed by his various dirty looks. "Rise and run, Noah," she instructed, still singing her words, tapping her watch pointedly, "rise and run."

He shot her an evil look and asked dryly, "Is that a math pun?" He was *not* amused. If she once again joked that the corner of his room was a toasty ninety degrees, he was most definitely going straight back to bed.

She was thrilled he'd picked up on a math joke and gave him an ear-to-ear grin as well as a quick, fierce hug before she could stop herself.

They both blushed then at the unexpected gesture and he cleared his throat, stepped aside and said to lighten the mood, "You might as well come in now and make us cappuccinos on my fancy new Keurig machine while I get ready. Clearly I'm not going back to bed." He sighed lustily but there was a smile tugging on his lips now. "Who is it we are going to listen to again?" he grumbled good-naturedly, going into the adjoining bathroom to quickly brush his teeth and put product in his hair.

"Oh my goodness," Lainee said with instant enthusiasm, grabbing the milk from his mini-fridge. "Cynthia Kenyon is her name. She is a molecular biologist whose genetic studies culminated in the finding of a certain hormone receptor mutation which doubled the lifespan of worms *and* mice."

She frothed the milk as he'd taught her to do the previous day, chatting away excitedly. With her back turned to him, Noah pulled on his jeans and rolled his eyes at her at the exact same time. Then he came to his closet and selected a light blue button-up shirt, subconsciously trying to match Lainee's poised and professional look.

"Isn't that exciting?" she continued as she combined the espresso shots with the frothed milk. "This could potentially lengthen the lives of humans by a hundred years."

"You had me at worms *and* mice," Noah said dryly, coming in to scoop up the cappuccino she held out to him. It had just the right amount of sweet Italian creamer in it, just as he liked it, bless her heart.

He took a big sip of the piping hot liquid, letting the warmth rush through his chest, sighing happily as he looked into Lainee's smiling, sunlit face. Maybe this wasn't such a bad way to start a Saturday morning after all, he conceded with quite a bit of joy.

◆◆◆

The following Monday after classes they met in Widener for their daily studying session. Lainee still liked to hit her favorite spot at least once every couple of weeks for nostalgia purposes, and "inspiration," of all things. Noah didn't get it *at all* but he was more than happy to indulge her and compromise every once in a while on location, anything to make her happy really.

Despite rushing today, she was there at the table waiting for him as always. *Damn.* He'd really tried to beat her here just to see if he could do it, and perhaps to surprise and please her just a little bit in the process. But there she was, his serious but no longer quite so stoic Lainee, books all around and laptop open and fired up, waiting for him.

He was grinning without even realizing it as he neared their table, but his grin slipped as soon as he was close enough to see her pale, shell-shocked features as she stared blankly at her computer screen.

"Hey," he said gently, touching her shoulder as he set his bag on the table. "Are you okay?"

She blinked up at him and his stomach dropped at the sheen of tears glistening in her eyes. "What is it?" he asked roughly through a tight throat, running a hand over her hair. "What's wrong?" Then his eyes narrowed and he asked suspiciously, "It's not Taylor Swift again is it?"

She blinked up at him a few more times and then managed to push out, "I-I g-got... a B-B- on my ph-physics q-quiz..." She was gulping for air.

Noah took a long moment to digest this, certain he was missing something key here. The sheer terror on her face did not compute with the words coming out of her mouth. "What?" he finally said stupidly.

She began to visibly shake then and it jolted him out of his open-mouthed stupor. He grabbed both of her hands in his, surprised at how cold and clammy they were. He squatted down by her side. "Lainee, hey, it's okay," he assured her, still unsure what the hell was really going on.

This reaction couldn't possibly be over a B- could it? He wanted to laugh at that and push it aside as not important, but as Lainee fell apart right in front of his eyes, he was forced to take it seriously. His high-strung, straight-A, perfectionist of a best friend put everything she had into every grade and this B- was clearly a failure of massive proportions she couldn't quite grapple with.

The poor girl could not handle a B- he was beginning to come to terms with, his stomach knotting as she literally fought for air, unable to take in a full breath. What did that say about her need for perfectionism as it overrode her ability just to breathe? He always knew she put way too much pressure on herself in an unhealthy way but this was next level and scared the shit out of him. This wasn't normal.

Noah gently rubbed her hands in his, trying to warm them and soothe her at the same time. Her eyes were wide and wild, suddenly darting around the library as if realizing there were eyes all around them that could watch her lose control and descend into madness.

He'd never seen her unravel like this. It was heartbreaking and Noah had no idea how to help her.

CHAPTER 16

"Lainee, look at me," Noah said gently, still kneeling at her side. When she brought her eyes to his he saw the sweat beading up on her pale forehead and felt the quaking through her limbs getting worse. She was still having a hard time catching her breath and it suddenly hit him that she was in the throes of a panic attack.

How had he not known his best friend had panic attacks, he wondered in disbelief, after all this time they'd spent together? Of course his proud, private Lainee would not have willingly confessed this to even him, just handling the burden in secret. Well, she wasn't alone anymore. He could and would help her shoulder this, he vowed. Somehow.

Noah knew all the people moving around them only heightened her stress level and, too, the last thing he wanted her to worry about was being watched by others. He quickly swung into action. He gathered her things, slung both of their bags on his shoulder and all but lifted her out of her chair as she stared ahead unseeingly. Arm secured tightly around her shoulder, he held her protectively to his side and walked her as quickly as he could out of the building and across the Yard to his suite.

Once inside, he settled her carefully on the edge of his bed and stood before her. Again he grabbed both of her hands in his larger ones and held fast, trying to ground her, murmuring soothingly, "You're safe now, Lainee. Look at me, please. Focus right on me now, sweetheart." Her wild, dazed eyes found his and connected. He took in deep, over-exaggerated breaths to encourage her to do the same.

"Breathe for me, Lainee. Come on. Come back to me. Breathe, baby. Breathe with me." Soon she was mimicking his full breaths and her shaking limbs began to settle some. He continued with his soothing murmurs, rubbing her hands gently to try and tether her to the here and now.

"That's right, Lainee. You're here with me, just me. I've got you. You're safe and everything is going to be alright." His eyes held fast to hers as he willed his strength, his equilibrium into her, continuing his deep breathing. "It's just you and me, sweetheart. It's going to be okay, I promise. Just keep breathing for me."

He may not have understood why a B- would cause it but he certainly understood how a panic attack could sneak up on you, ravage your central nervous system and overtake all rational thought. He'd had a few in his lifetime, though, strangely enough, never when he was about to go on stage but rather growing up, in his own home, or sometimes in elevators and enclosed spaces when his claustrophobia kicked in. He quickly pushed away those haunting memories and felt a wave of relief as Lainee's shaking hands began to still completely in his. She blinked up at him as the haze cleared, her eyes still locked on his.

"Noah," she said quietly, apologetically, still perilously close to tears. She felt humiliated over her loss of control and showing him her weakness, but she was nothing short of devastated over her academic failure. She was unmoored and couldn't possibly hide it. Especially from Noah.

"I'm right here," he promised sitting down next to her on the edge of the bed, throwing his arm across her shoulders and pulling her close to his side. He rubbed her arm gently. "You're okay, Lainee. You're safe. I've got you."

Her body fully relaxed against his then and she put her head on his shoulder, finally letting the tears come. The weight of her failure replaced the embarrassment over showing Noah she had panic attacks.

For the first time in Lainee's academic career she'd gotten a B-. She was going to lose her top-ten standing. Who was she if she wasn't top in her class, summa cum laude and a brilliant Harvard-educated biochemist in advanced standing? Who was she if she didn't have those things? She was afraid she was no one and nothing without them. She shakily voiced these thoughts out loud to Noah, who continued to hug her to him.

"Lainee," he said helplessly, at a loss. He wanted so badly to fix this for her but he knew he couldn't. He could only sit with her through it and try to show her she was fucking amazing and worthy no matter what grade she got. "You can't be so hard on yourself over one B-," he scolded and begged at the same time. "It's just not healthy." What could he possibly say, he wondered, grappling desperately for something that would penetrate her big brain. How could he make her see herself through his eyes? "You need to be as kind to yourself as you are to me, goddamnit. You're fucking thrilled when I get a B-. And you don't think what's-her-face-biologist with her worms and mice didn't *ever* get a B-? Come on."

She didn't respond for a moment as she wiped the last of her tears off her face, then she said so quietly he almost didn't hear, "I need to be stronger, smarter, better. I need to be in control at all times." She chastised herself out loud for spending too much time both listening to Taylor Swift and having fun with him. Of course her academics would suffer from that. What had she been thinking?

"You're the strongest, smartest, best person I know," Noah told her then, honestly, desperately. "You're already all of those things. Can't you see that?"

He felt her shake her head slightly from side to side against his shoulder. "I need to be stronger, smarter, better," she repeated in a low whisper, and he had the sickening feeling this was the negative litany on a loop in her brain at all times. This knowledge pierced his gut in such a physical, painful way he bent over slightly and winced.

"Lainee..." he groaned helplessly, still holding her tight. He was hurting now, too. *Fuck.* When had that happened? When had her pain become his? He rubbed his chest with the hand not clamped on to her shoulder.

He didn't know what else to say or how to help and it was the worst feeling in the world. He felt useless to the most important person in his life. Her need to be perfect and to push herself beyond what was humanly possible didn't make sense to him. Did this have something to do with her upbringing or was this all self-imposed? She never spoke of her parents or childhood and he never pushed, considering he never wanted to talk about those things either. In fact, she shut those conversations down almost as fast as he did.

All he really knew about her past was that she was from a small town in Connecticut, her mom was a bit of a religious freak, and she never went home to visit. There was still so much he didn't know about his best friend, including how she came by that scar. She was still a bit of an enigma even to him, even now, and that hurt a little bit, too, as he realized it.

She still didn't seem ready to talk about any of that and he reminded himself to be patient. He wouldn't push her, especially now, when she was so fragile in his arms. Didn't he of all people know the necessity of clinging to denial and secrets to get by?

No, he wouldn't make her talk about it and he didn't fool himself into thinking he could take away that harsh rhetoric on a loop in her head, but he could help her. Somehow. There had to be a way. His mind raced, grappled, grasped.

"Okay, Lainee," he said then, nodding his head to himself as he put together an actionable plan with step-by-step definable goals, just like she'd taught him to. "I'll help you study, too. How about that? We'll run through your study guides, too, and we'll tackle quantum physics first, before my stuff. This will be the only B- you get in that class - ever - okay? You'll still be summa cum laude. You'll still be a brilliant biochemist who makes scientific breakthroughs just like worm-and-mice lady, and Dr. Doudna."

Yes, he'd been paying attention every time she'd gone off on an excited tangent about crazy topics like CRISPR and gene splitting or whatever. He even knew Dr. Doudna's name now for fuck's sake. And he had absolute no doubt everything he'd just said about his best friend was the absolute truth.

She was *that* brilliant. And she needed him just as much as he needed her, he was beginning to realize. It felt good to be needed, despite the circumstances.

"You're going to be okay," he promised her vehemently as she turned her body into his even more and buried her head into his neck gratefully. "And we're stronger together, Lainee. Don't you forget that, you hear? We're stronger, smarter, better *together*. Me, you and Taylor. Don't even think about leaving us behind."

CHAPTER 17

They stayed that way for the longest time, her all but melted into his side as he held her up physically, emotionally and oh-so-patiently. Finally she gained control over both her rioting emotions and her physical reactions to them. She grabbed tightly on to her God-given common sense, hard-won resilience and the little bit of pride she had left, attempting to pull away with an apology for her embarrassing display of fragility and weakness.

"Don't you dare," Noah all but growled, gripping on to her so she couldn't go anywhere. "Don't you dare apologize for being human, for letting down your guard with me." He lifted her chin with his finger so she'd have to look up at him. Then he repeated some of her most illuminating words ever spoken, all but burned into his psyche, "I like you just that much more because of it. We get the gift of really seeing each other, helping each other, remember? And that goes both ways."

He waited until her lips turned upwards in acknowledgement, and then it was his turn to get down to business. "Okay, let's light up the candles and get to work, your stuff first." Only then did he let go of her and move off the bed, on a mission to help her just as much as she always helped him.

He brought their bags up on the bed and spread out their books and laptops, propping some of his overly large accent pillows along the headboard and all but pushing her into them. Then he turned on all the lamps, lit up the Library candles - which had seemed to multiply around the room she noticed - and grabbed some drinks and snacks. He placed the edible goods in the middle of the duvet cover between them like a decadent but informal picnic offering. Of course, her favorite fruit snacks were among the mix.

"Ready?" he asked as he settled onto the bed across from her, his face lit up with eagerness and a hope that he was helping her and making a difference. And he was.

Lainee looked around at all the lit Library-scented candles peppered throughout the room, then at the fruit snacks on the duvet cover in front of her and, finally, up at the kindest golden eyes framed by the most handsome face she'd ever seen. She bit her bottom lip and blushed, but not from embarrassment or awkwardness over her recent break down. No, she felt completely safe and at ease with this man. How could she not?

Noah was taking such good care of her and instead of feeling weak for needing him, she inexplicably felt stronger and braver for having asked for his help. And he'd come running, gladly, without hesitation. He'd showed up in spades, proving himself to her yet again. She was touched beyond words. Not only was Noah steadying her nerves, he was reinforcing her resolve to move forward with clean eyes and hope of her own. She knew then with certainty, too, that they were, indeed, stronger together.

She nodded to him now and a slow, sweet smile spread on her pretty face, making his heart squeeze. "Together then."

A few days later, Hamlet rehearsals began in earnest and instead of the usual mix of joy and relief when diving into the welcome distraction of a new character, Noah felt a little resentful that he had less time to spend with Lainee. Luckily she was flexible, happy to fit him in whenever his fuller schedule allowed. Sometimes he'd even find her waiting for him in his dorm room, which he'd begun to look forward to and hope for more and more. Coming "home" to all the lights on, the candles lit and his best friend waiting was the most galvanizing feeling in the world.

He managed to talk her into meeting him at the Loeb Drama Center occasionally, too, to catch thirty minutes here and there of homework between running lines. When he would wait in the wings for his next scene they would cram in a quick study session. As his brain was super-powered from running lines, he was actually benefiting from studying like this he found. It was as if acting turned on all receptors in his sleepy brain and made it super absorbent to the new information Lainee fed him. Screw Mozart. He just needed Hamlet. And Lainee.

Lainee was quite impressed with him and, he wasn't going to lie, he was a little smug about it. Finally, he didn't look like a complete imbecile and she could witness him at his best, up in the middle of the main stage of the impressive 550-seat theater, embodying Prince-turned-King Hamlet himself. It was a reckoning they had a long time coming, in his humble opinion.

For some reason, acting had always come naturally to Noah. He could slip into personas easily and without embarrassment or reservation. He had natural, emotive talent but also showed up early, stayed late and worked the hardest. It was perhaps the one thing he could be proud of. He was so happy to share that side of himself with Lainee.

The third week into daily rehearsals, as they knocked out the rest of a paper he had due in social studies backstage at the Loeb, he couldn't help but fool around and slap a mustache and a top hat on himself first and then Lainee second.

When she immediately went to take them off, he all but begged her, "Oh, come on. Humor me! Leave it on for at least a minute!" He shot her a very serious look from beneath his own top hat, expertly wiggling his mustache like a worm above his lip. "It will help me focus and work more efficiently."

She pursed her lips in doubt of this completely unscientific declaration, making her own mustache crinkle like an accordion. This made him laugh in childlike glee. He'd truly never seen anything as ridiculous, adorable and bewitching as Lainee in a mustache.

To his utter surprise, she embraced the moment, hamming it up further with a few goofy faces, making him howl. Then she winked and blew him a kiss, inspiring him to act out the part of a swooning suitor, clutching at his chest and fainting to the floor as if shot through the heart.

She giggled relentlessly, inspiring him to jolt on the ground as if being electrocuted by her mocking laughter. After a moment, he lay there still on the ground, chuckling and looking up at her. He marveled once again at how far she had come from the enigma at the gym who did not speak or make eye contact, to this magnificent creature perched high above him, now his best friend and favorite person in all of the universe, donning a mustache and top hat. He had to admit he took some credit for this wild transformation and was quite proud of both of them for it.

When some of the other thespians and crew began to file in backstage, intruding on their little corner of the world, Lainee quickly removed both the mustache and the hat, dunking her head so that her hair fell like a curtain over her profile.

"Why do you that?" Noah asked her quietly, getting up from the floor, removing his own accessories, watching her as she carefully packed herself away so others wouldn't see her. She was so funny and brilliant and he was the only one she let see it. Though he felt humbled and grateful for that, he also wanted to share just how amazing she was with the whole damn world around them. He wanted to sing her praises at the top of his lungs, in fact, so that everyone would know what a completely amazing human being she was.

Lainee looked up to see Noah's piercing amber eyes studying her carefully, kindly, all but looking right into her soul, and she blushed. How did it make sense she could show her worst and goofy sides to the most handsome, talented, amazing guy in probably all the northern hemisphere but she was shy and closed off around everyone else? It didn't make any sense at all but, nonetheless, it felt completely natural.

Before she could answer him, a pretty girl bopped over to flirt unabashedly with Noah, all but stepping in between the two of them. Lainee, of course, was more than used to this kind of interruption and she quickly focused on her laptop while trying desperately to tune them out. She was relieved to see that Noah was being polite but professional, unlike the girl who was being bold and brash and touching his thigh awfully close to his package. Personal space was clearly a notion this girl was unfamiliar with. Lainee fought back an uncharacteristic growl.

Noah tried subtly shifting away from the grabby girl and pointing out he was in the middle of something important. When that didn't work, he spelled out for her, "Shannon, I really need to get back to studying with Lainee. Have you two met, by the way?" He knew they hadn't, of course, but wanted to point out Lainee's existence and importance.

Shannon was forced to look over her shoulder at Lainee then. Lainee gave her a small smile as if to say, "yep, hello, right here." Shannon frowned, turned completely around to face her and leaned in, again with the violation of personal space. In lieu of a formal greeting, she said, "You know, we have some thick stage makeup that might cover up that scar for you."

The color drained immediately from Lainee's face and Noah swore under his breath. "Jesus Christ, Shannon, what is wrong with you? Why would you say that?" Noah called the mean girl out even as Lainee began to quietly pack up her laptop and books, outwardly composed even as she was falling apart on the inside.

"Her scar doesn't need to be covered up, goddamnit," he bit out as he all but pushed Shannon out of his way so that he could take hold of Lainee's arm and still her movements. She paused, looking up at Noah with a careful, blank expression on her face. His eyes held hers as he said with absolutely no room for argument, "She's absolutely beautiful just the way she is. Now please leave us alone, Shannon." He didn't even glance at the girl as he said this.

With a huff Shannon stomped away and Lainee slowly straightened and pulled her laptop back out.

"You okay?" Noah asked her quietly, holding steady to Lainee's gaze, waiting for any and every inflection that might cross her face. "You do realize she only said that because she was jealous of you, right?"

Lainee's breath caught at Noah's startling summarization of the situation. She tilted her head slightly as she turned this over in her mind. Was that gorgeous, flawless girl really jealous of *her*? A part of her balked at this ridiculous notion and then she remembered... Noah thought she was beautiful... and, too, she had Noah's undivided attention. So, yes, that girl hadn't said that about her scar because Lainee was a hideous freak, but because *she* felt jealous and insecure. *Wow.*

This jolting revelation had Lainee's lips turning upward into a slow, big grin. "She *was* jealous of me, wasn't she?" she said in wonder. Her face was lit up like she'd just witnessed something miraculous here today.

Noah huffed a laugh, relieved to see she'd quickly come to the right conclusion. She was beautiful and badass. "Yep," he told her with a grin right back. *Now* she was getting it... *finally.*

She reached for the mustache and top hat again then and slapped them back in place, ignoring everyone milling around and asking him, "Where were we?"

CHAPTER 18

The following Saturday afternoon, Noah decided with quite a bit of trepidation and guilt to go to the viewing party of the Pats' football game downstairs in the Dunster House common area, sans Lainee. Most of his lacrosse teammates bunked at Dunster, too, and they were riding him hard lately for being MIA the last month when it came to both hanging out and drinking. Truthfully, it had been awhile since he'd had a beer with the guys, Noah realized... or had a girl to his room for an activity other than Lainee for studying. He was quick to blame this all on Hamlet, deciding both previous hobbies were long overdue.

As Lainee packed up her things in his suite to leave him to the festivities, Noah felt an irrational surge of guilt wash over him. This had him asking rather anxiously, "Are you *sure* it's okay if I skip out on you today and watch the game downstairs?" He was legit asking for permission he realized. *What the fuck?*

"It's fine," Lainee assured him again. "I can use the rest of the day to do some legal billing I've let backslide over the last few weeks." They had actually spent most of the day together up to that point, going to the gym and then hanging out in his room for a few hours, playing card games and discussing his humble beginnings at the high school drama club in the Cape. It was definitely time for her to get back to work, Lainee was scolding herself in her own head. "I also need to study some more for my quantum physics test on Monday," she added nervously, fidgeting with her hair at the doorway, twisting a long brown

110

strand around her finger and biting her bottom lip.

Noah had never seen her fidget or look so uncertain before and he grabbed her hand in his and held on. "Hey, you've been studying all week for that test like your life depends on it. You're going to ace it. Maybe you should relax today, too. Why don't you come with me to watch the game?" Again, after he heard the words leaving his own mouth, he had to ask himself, *what the actual fuck?* What was *wrong* with him? He couldn't have one evening of fun without Lainee now? Was this separation anxiety he was feeling or premeditated guilt knowing full well what lay ahead that evening?

"No, no," she was quick to assure him, placing her free hand on his chest, right over his heart. "It will be good for you to relax and have some fun, and I really do need to focus and study."

Noah was pretty sure *not* focusing and studying wasn't Lainee's problem. In fact she'd been hyperfocused on this next quantum physics test to an unhealthy degree and he worried she was setting herself up for another panic attack. But he didn't bother pointing all that out to her right now, he just made a mental note to try something tomorrow to help her relax. He had a few ideas in mind, in fact.

For now, it was a Saturday afternoon and permission was granted - again - for a good time. So he gave her a hug at the door and told her he'd see her tomorrow. After a quick shower and change of clothes, he headed down to the common area with the huge flat screen TV used for all big games.

"Holy shit," his friend and lacrosse teammate Ryker Wallace bellowed from across the room as soon as Noah crossed the threshold, "ladies and gentlemen, look who has graced us with his presence this evening. If it isn't fucking pansy-ass Prince Hamlet himself."

"Fuck off, Ryker," Noah laughed, grabbing a beer and sauntering over. "Still jealous I get all the ladies, I see." In truth, if there was anyone who scored more on and off the lacrosse field than Noah, it was this muscled meathead with ham hands and swagger for days.

The football game hadn't started yet so they drank and ribbed each other some more as if no time had passed at all. That's what Noah liked most about Ryker. He was simple and consistent. They always had fun and never went too deep. In fact, they'd had a few epic and wild times together over the last couple of years, not that either could recall most of the details.

As the room filled to capacity, some pretty girls from Dunster sidled up to the lacrosse guys who had congregated in one corner at halftime, drinking and flirting as if it was their double major. Noah found himself relaxing and enjoying himself immensely. *Just like the old days,* he assured himself. As third quarter commenced, he pounded a few more beers and soon was lounging on the couch with a stranger in his lap, suckling his neck.

He laughed but pulled away for some reason, jostling the honey in his lap so she hopefully wouldn't feel his boner. He didn't want to give her *any* ideas. It really had been awhile, Noah was chagrined to admit. Still, he wasn't keen on the neck sucking for some reason. Nor was he looking to take her back to his room. *Huh.* He was horny *and* standoffish. That was new.

"Hey, Riley," Ryker called out from across the couch, an arm around a girl, "I don't think your girlfriend would approve. You better send that one my way."

His goading actually had Noah visibly stiffening but he threw back in an attempt to appear nonchalant, "I don't have a girlfriend, asshole. Just focus on yourself 'cause I'm pretty sure all you can handle is one at a time, my friend. If that."

Ryker barked out a laugh but didn't let it go as Noah hoped

he would. "Isn't Scar Face your girlfriend now or something?" Even from across the couch with its numerous inhabitants, Ryker could clearly see the instant flare of resentment flash over Noah's face.

Noah didn't respond to that but he awkwardly shifted the canoodling girl in his lap once more, praying she wouldn't give him a hickey. How would he explain *that* to Lainee tomorrow morning, Noah thought with quite a bit of uncomfortable guilt. Fast on the heels of that horrid flash-forward, he pushed the handsy girl away, feigning his need for another beer.

When he came back with a new refreshment, Noah squeezed in towards the middle of the couch, totally ignoring the girl that had just been suckling his neck sixty seconds prior even though she was just a foot away. Ryker was smirking at him again.

"Yeah, right, Riley. Scar Face isn't your girlfriend but you're suddenly pushing girls away." Ryker snorted and kept right at him. Of course he did when he could so easily see he was getting under Noah's skin for once. "You're with that girl every second of the day and we haven't partied with you in forever." He was shaking his head at him then in sheer disappointment, bro to bro. "Man, I hate to break it to you, but, dude, she's your girlfriend. You're obviously pussy-whipped so I hope you're at least hitting it."

"Shut the fuck up, Wallace," Noah said with more bite than Ryker had ever heard from him before. Noah was guzzling his beer to compound the buzz that was starting to take over and blessedly numb him. He felt the sudden need to be completely desensitized. He ran his hand through his hair, agitated and resentful of Ryker's commentary, but unsure at which part exactly. "Her name is Lainee, and don't talk about her like that, asshole." Ah. So it was *that* part, not the part about her being his girlfriend.

Ryker threw his hands up in surrender but howled in laughter. Thoroughly, blessedly buzzed and on a mission to prove something to Ryker and himself now, Noah grabbed on to the next flirting girl with both hands, turning his charm all the way up to a ten. He had her giggling in his lap five minutes in and fifteen minutes later they were making out hot and heavy. Noah forgot about the football game as his boner raged on.

Ryker down the way howled in laughter at him throughout his makeout session, shouting his encouragement in snide glee, "That's right, Riley! Get yourself some, boy! You remember how, don't you?"

When the eager girl stood and pulled him up to his feet, Noah knew exactly where she wanted to go. He had the wherewithal to smirk back at Ryker right before the girl walked him out of the common area and up to his dorm room. How she knew where his room was, he had no clue, nor did he care as she shoved her tongue down his throat and he led her inside.

One step into the suite with its lingering scent of Library candles mixed with Lainee's soft, powdery perfume had Noah pausing in his tracks. As the eager honey grabbed on to his shirt with both hands and made out with his neck like a mad woman he looked around his room guiltily. It was *their* room he realized with a start. His suite had turned into *their* place at some point and Lainee's smell, her very fingerprints, were all over it.

Were they all over *him*, too, he wondered with a start. Is that why this felt so different? Damn but his girl Lainee was still messing him all up inside, he acknowledged. It was her specialty it seemed.

Noah looked around the room at the empty fruit snack wrappers littering his garbage cans and side table. His sweater that she had worn just earlier today because she'd been cold lay slung over the back of one of the leather chairs, *her* chair, as she always sat in the same one and he the other. *Huh.* They were now seemingly his and her chairs. Her favorite coffee mug stood washed and waiting by his Keurig for tomorrow morning's life-giving offering. Lainee's mug had a stern image of Ruth Bader Ginsburg on it with the most appropriate caption of all time, "I'm judging you."

Guilt seared through his chest, right in the region Lainee's hand had touched not too many hours earlier in this very spot just inside his doorway, even as his present company began to unzip his pants and pull him out. He'd begun to go soft over all his guilty thoughts but the eager girl expertly began jerking him off, getting him right back up and into the game.

She pretty much led him by his dick to his bed then and pushed him in. She was on him in seconds and Noah laid back with unease and let her do all the work.

CHAPTER 19

The next morning, Noah was up nice and early despite the fact that it was still the weekend and he'd tossed and turned most of the night. His lack of sleep had nothing to do with the blowjob-girl and everything to do with the warring emotions that had assaulted him after he'd quickly kicked her out of his room, without returning the favor of an orgasm mind you.

He felt embarrassed he'd let the girl down and damaged his sterling reputation as a giving and worthwhile lover, but more than that he felt chagrined that he'd had such a hard time partaking in his favorite past time of unencumbered and utterly fulfilling one night stands. He hadn't even been able to enjoy himself because of his guilt over - *what exactly,* he asked himself with rising resentment - disappointing Lainee? Seriously, *what the fuck, Riley? She isn't actually your girlfriend, asshat,* he reminded himself. He conveniently blamed such erratic and irrational thoughts on Ryker's effective jabs.

So why was he chewing down an entire tin of cinnamon Altoids, tearing around his suite, changing the sheets, and deodorizing the place before she got there, as if he'd done something wrong? As if he'd *cheated* for fuck's sake?

Whatever. What was done was done. He'd blown a completely decent opportunity to have a good night punctuated by multiple orgasms. He'd also blown the chance to have a relaxing night in with Lainee. The latter seemed to be more enjoyable than the former now and these days but, regardless, he'd blown both options. And had been blown in the process. He winced.

"Stop it, Riley," he chastised himself right out loud then as he finished straightening the place up. "You did absolutely nothing wrong. You are a free fucking agent." He was just out of practice, that's all. *Yeah, that was it.*

As if mocking his flimsy excuse accompanied by the slight mental break down he was currently having at the moment, his heart leapt into his throat when the knock came on his door. *Lainee.* Right on time. He looked around the room nervously. Had he covered all his tracks?

Satisfied with his clean-up job, he threw the door open with a pasted-on grin and all but shouted in her face, "Cheerio!" Lainee's eyebrows rose at that strange, over-the-top greeting and Noah unceremoniously pulled her inside to cover up his embarrassment. "How was your night? Did you get the legal billing done? Did you study for physics? Do you want a cappuccino?"

She set her bag down by her leather chair and looked around the spic and span room, then over at him.

Does she look suspicious, he wondered, pulling up the collar on his button-up shirt to hide the hickey he'd gotten from one of the two suckling girls the evening before. *Or do I look guilty?*

Lainee eyed him for a second and he swore she looked right through him into his blackened, sleazy soul. This, too, seemed her specialty. He may or may not have blushed.

"Sure," she finally said, "a cappuccino would be lovely."

He all but sprinted to the Keurig. "One capp coming up. Sit. Relax." He whipped up one for each of them, all the while babbling about how he'd watched the game with his buddy Ryker and admitted he may or may not have had one too many beers. He didn't mention any of the girls, again not wanting to disappoint her on *all* fronts.

As he handed her the RBG mug after adding a dash of Italian sweet cream for her, he said over-enthusiastically, "Oh, hey. I've been wanting to try something for you."

He brought over his one plant in the place, setting it on the compact side table between their chairs, and then pulled out a small sound machine of some sort with accompanying wires. Lainee cocked her head to the side and watched as he began hooking up the little machine to the plant leaves with wires that had suction cups at the end. Electrodes, she realized with growing interest.

She sat back in her chair, sipped her heart-warming cappuccino and waited quietly with growing anticipation. *What was Noah up to now*, she wondered with a smile touching her lips. He was always surprising her in the most delightful ways, she realized. Then she glanced over at his bed and her smile slipped clean away. It was the well-made elephant in the room today.

The bed was made to Martha-Stewart standards, with all four corners tucked in very precisely, she noted. She'd never seen it made so perfectly before. It was probably safe to assume he'd had a girl over last night. He was still ladies' man Noah Riley after all, though the exchanging of phone numbers with random girls had all but died out the last month now that she thought about it.

That was none of her business or her concern, Lainee reprimanded herself sternly, focusing back on his large, capable hands as they finished hooking up the electrodes to the plant. Then he plugged his phone into the small machine, too.

"Okay, do you want to do the honors and turn it on?" Noah asked her with a genuine smile, his nerves finally settling some. This was his favorite thing to do, after all, hang out with his best friend and bring a smile to her face.

When she tapped play on his phone, there was an instant humming noise that gently floated out of the small speaker. As Lainee took in the soothing analog symphony, then the plant, wires and speaker, she looked at Noah in wonder and asked, "Is the plant *making* the music?"

He grinned and nodded, immensely pleased with himself over her wide eyes and wonderment. "Yup. Pretty cool, right? So this is the MIDI sprout which, along with an app on my phone, measures the rate at which the plant is conducting electricity." He touched the wires. "This, in essence, closes the circuit and the mini-machine analyzes the waves and assigns sound values to them."

Lainee's eyes were still wide as she looked from the machine to Noah. Then she laughed with pure, simple joy, making his heart leap once more back up into his throat, but now for an entirely different reason than guilt. "Noah, that's ingenious! We're *listening* to the plant! It's communicating with us!" She reached over and hugged him where he sat. "And it sounds absolutely beautiful. Thank you for showing me this. It's amazing." *He* was amazing.

He'd actually bought the MIDI sprout machine - and the plant - just for her and had been trying to figure it out for a few days now, but didn't mention that. He was definitely blushing this time as he tried to humbly play it all off. "It's nothing. I figured this would be better, more soothing music to listen to than that classical crap as you cram in the last day of studying for your big physics test." Anything to deter her from the fuckin' endless monotony of Mozart and Bach.

They grinned at each other, listening to the synth-symphony created by the plant's humming electricity. Lainee's ear-to-ear grin gave Noah that rush and chest flip flop he'd long ago become addicted to. Inexplicably he thought to himself, *this is way better than a blowjob.*

That thought was disturbing on so many levels so he quickly pushed it aside and finally sat back in his leather chair, enjoying his cooling cappuccino as they listened and chatted, easing into the morning together.

CHAPTER 20

The next afternoon, Noah felt a burst of happiness when he unexpectedly caught a glimpse of Lainee across the Yard. He was eagerly headed for Widener to meet up with her and find out how she did on her physics test. He prayed it went well for her sake, but he was more than prepared to help her through the fallout if it didn't. She seemed more relaxed yesterday going into it, which was a good sign he hoped.

He was actually surprised Lainee wasn't already inside the library waiting for him like usual. Instead, she was standing around socializing, he realized with a smile, making a beeline for her. That was a nice sight for sore eyes. Or at least it was until some tall, gangly bloke sauntered up and put his arm around her shoulders.

Noah slowed and scowled. *Who the fuck was this guy,* he wondered with more than a little rising irritation. *Was this asshole* hitting *on her?!* Hadn't the gangly string bean seen Lainee and Noah hanging out? Like all the time now? It was just bad form to hit on someone else's... friend... Noah thought with growing agitation, picking up his pace.

The asshole walked away just as Noah approached and he couldn't help but blurt out rather irritably and unceremoniously, "Who the hell was that?"

Lainee jumped, a little surprised as Noah appeared out of thin air at her side. Again. He had a knack for that. "Noah, oh, hi. That guy? Someone from my engineering thermodynamics class. He just asked me out." She looked and sounded surprised.

"Presumptuous asshole," Noah said to that, not very happy about the situation whatsoever. So what the fucker was super smart like Lainee? He clearly wasn't good enough for her. Period. End of story. "We both know you don't have time to date," Noah pointed out irritably, still scowling. "Can we just focus here and get to the library to study already?"

She looked at him strangely then and asked in return, "Who are you and what have you done with my reluctant pupil and best friend Noah Riley?"

He rolled his eyes, a little chagrined at his own behavior. "Come on already. I can't believe I'm saying this, but let's get to Widener for some studying action." As they made their way there, he couldn't help but inquire as a follow-up, "So... you didn't say yes, did you? You're not going on a date with that guy, right?"

"Hm?" Lainee said, obviously distracted and deep in thought still. "No, I'm not. You're right. I don't have time for silly shenanigans."

Noah had to laugh as he opened the library door for her. "Of course dating is equivalent to hijinks and shenanigans in your mind." It was quite the relief to have it confirmed for some reason. They scanned their school ID's and walked up the stairs to her favorite reading room. "Hey, how did your test go?" He'd almost forgotten in all the unexpected excitement.

"Fine," she said nonchalantly, as if suddenly the test was no big deal. "Great even." Settling into their usual table in the corner, she sighed then and told him in a total change of topic, "Your father keeps calling me, asking really inappropriate questions that have absolutely nothing to do with your grades."

Noah stilled in his seat. They hadn't talked about his father in a long while, at Noah's request. He hadn't realized the old man was frequently reaching out to Lainee, and an instant knot formed in his stomach. "He's calling you?" Noah asked her quietly, trying to process the tsunami of uncomfortable feelings washing over him as she nodded.

Noah didn't like that one goddamn bit. He was agitated his father was being pushy, controlling and manipulative as per usual, but the overriding emotion was actually acute concern... for Lainee. Noah needed to shield her from that motherfucker immediately.

As if he could.

With a sinking heart he inquired, "He's asking you who I'm sleeping with, isn't he?" His fucking controlling, nosy, sick, sadistic father... "Wait," Noah said slowly as a terrible thought occurred to him, "he didn't ask you if *we* were sleeping together, did he?"

"Yes," Lainee admitted uncomfortably to him now. She looked at him with her kind blue eyes and added, "He's so awful, Noah. Cold and... controlling." His dad never called Noah, only her, and the sordid questions he had started to pose, focusing on Noah's personal life, made her feel slightly queasy.

It confirmed to her that his father was capable of some really dark and despicable things in order to overpower and control him. "How is that man your father?" she wondered aloud in sympathy. "You two are nothing alike, thank God."

Animosity pounded through Noah, beating at him like a relentless high tide, punctuated by a fair amount of humiliation swimming in his gut. These two emotions were always invoked by his father but this time it was tenfold because his dear old dad was fucking with Lainee now. She deserved way more respect and reverence than this. Noah had to protect her at all cost... *but how?* As always, his dad was reminding Noah of his sheer and utter powerlessness.

Noah shook his head in disgust and looked down rather helplessly at his hands gripping the side of the table, turning white from the tight pressure. "I'm so sorry, Lainee. He has no right to speak to you like that. I'll talk to him." Even as he offered to intervene he knew it would be ineffective at best. At worst, it would encourage his sadistic father to target Lainee further.

He had learned in high school never to show interest in a girl, or bring one home. If he did, his father would eventually leer at her suggestively, chase her away or sleep with her himself. Or any combination of the three.

Noah knew full well he couldn't protect Lainee even if he wanted to. It was the worst feeling in the world because she was so very precious to him, sacred even. But he was supremely impotent against his father's twisted power. Waves of shame washed over him, making him feel even sicker to his sensitive stomach. God, he wanted to puke. And strangle the motherfucker.

"Hey," Lainee said then, reaching over and peeling his fingers off the table to hold his hands in her own. His eyes were dilated in a suddenly pale face. She didn't know the exact thoughts playing behind those haunted eyes of his but a sympathy pang gripped her and she squeezed his hands in response. "Don't worry about it," she implored, quick to console him and dismiss his father. "I told him not to call me anymore. I said your grades would tell him all he needed to know and if he didn't like it he could quit depositing money into my account."

Noah released a pent-up breath he'd been holding in his tight chest and huffed out a laugh. A slight smile that was more like a grimace played on his expressive face. "You told my father that?" Lainee nodded rather matter-of- fact, like it was no big deal she had stood up to his intimidating and aggressive, power-hungry father. God, she was amazing. Noah's muscles slowly released their tension as she continued holding his hands over the table with steady warmth. He squeezed back in gratitude.

Oh, his father must have turned all kinds of shades of red and purple when she'd told him to fuck off, Noah thought as he looked at Lainee in pure awe. No one spoke to his father that way, except this incredibly brave girl sitting before him now. She had more strength and integrity in her little pinky finger than the whole army of men at his father's employ. She certainly had more of it than Noah himself. *My little warrior,* he thought with quite a bit of tenderness then. His small smile slipped a little as he thought of the ramifications of her taking this stand on his behalf. "But what if he stops paying you?"

She was smiling at him then, conspiratorial and heedless of the heaps of money she was potentially throwing away. She shrugged as if she could have cared less. "Then I pick up more legal billing or another student to tutor. I'd get by. I always do. In the meantime, we're going to keep this up either way and you're going to prove to him that you are an intelligent, hard working and multi-talented man. You are Noah freaking Riley and you can do anything you set your mind to." Noah wondered if he was blushing. He was definitely grinning like an idiot suddenly. "Deal?"

Noah all at once felt buoyed, his confidence restored. Only Lainee could lift him up like this after his father had knocked him down once again. She believed in him and was willing to tutor him even if his father stopped paying her. *She wasn't in it for the money.* He had known this all along, of course, and yet this was irrefutable proof that had his heart swelling in gratitude. She did wonders for his flagging spirit and wounded soul, as always. "Deal, Lainee," Noah said with a wobbly smile. "Thank you."

She gave him a wink then that had his heart stuttering in his chest cavity. "We'll show him," she promised vehemently, squeezing his hands. "Band-Aids don't fix bullet holes. When you live like that, you live with ghosts."

"Oh. My. God," Noah said in pure disbelief of what was currently unfolding and the incredulous corner they had just turned. He blinked at her. "Are you quoting Taylor Swift at me right now?"

Lainee wiggled her eyebrows at him and confirmed, "Darling, I'm a nightmare dressed like a daydream."

Noah put his forehead on the table then and laughed himself silly. Damn, he loved this woman. And thank Christ he'd had the wherewithal not to introduce her to the likes of Justin Bieber or the Jonas Brothers.

CHAPTER 21

After a few hours of studying, they decided to walk into Harvard Square and grab a beer and a bite to eat at their favorite tavern, Brew Hall. They toasted her successful day, handling both the high-stakes pressure of her quantum physics test and his obnoxious father like the amazing warrior she was.

"Beautiful and badass," Noah said with such sincerity and awe that she blushed. He said this to her more and more often and she was beginning to believe it herself.

They made plans to meet in his suite after classes the next day and order in sushi for dinner. He didn't have to run lines for a few days while the props department fleshed out the rest of the stage design and Noah was looking forward to spending the extra time with Lainee.

He was strangely excited about it when he awoke the next morning, though as per his usual MO, Noah didn't stop to analyze it. They met in the gym at lunch time and then he waited eagerly as his afternoon classes dragged on, oscillating between coffee and cinnamon gum like an agitated addict.

Finally, Noah was through with classes for the day and he rushed back to his dorm room to shower again and ready for the evening ahead with Lainee. There was a knock on his door about thirty minutes before she was expected and he smiled. She was early. He wasn't the only eager one obviously. He quickly swung the door open with a beaming grin.

His smile instantly fell when he saw his father standing on the other side of his threshold instead of Lainee. In conditioned response, like one of Pavlov's fucking dogs, Noah's stomach tightened and razor-hot nerves shot through his solar plexus.

He took a staggering step backwards and asked weakly in shock, "What are you doing here?"

His father raised a black eyebrow and pushed his way inside the room. "I am checking in on you since neither you nor that over-paid, insolent tutor of yours deign to call or text me back. It is my money paying for all of this, need I remind you." Richard Riley could not abide disobedience. He *would not* tolerate it. Obviously his ungrateful, challenging son needed a reminder. And a not-so-gentle one at that.

Noah took in a steadying breath, telling himself to get his shit together, to ignore the mounting fear gripping at his throat and stand his ground. He was a grown ass man now with his own success to speak of, he reminded himself rather desperately. Hell, he was even an inch taller than his old man now and he sure as hell was stronger. Still, the confidence, the bravado was more of an act he was putting on for show rather than his true feelings.

"You could give me control over my own money that I've earned in my acting career, then I could pay for all this myself," Noah reminded him quietly, his voice shaking slightly with loathing and, yes, trepidation. Of course his controlling father saw to it that he had legal conservatorship over his finances even now. It was just another way for him to control and bully him.

His father took a sudden step toward him as anger flashed in his dark eyes and Noah instinctively flinched and took a step back. It was another conditioned response beat into him at a young age that even now he seemed unable to reverse.

Suddenly, he was five years old again, helpless and alone, locked in the dark closet of his childhood bedroom, petrified and ashamed.

◆◆◆

Noah's little body trembled as he fought for air in the dark closet. He prayed for light, for rescue, for love and gentle hands. Sometimes Mother would come, throw open the door and pull him out of the dark abyss. Sometimes she wrapped her arms around him and comforted him, chasing the shame and fear away, even if it was just for a few fleeting moments, gone all too soon.

Sometimes she smiled down on him and saved him from himself and the monsters all around. But those reprieves were fewer and farther between now and as the slow, agonizing minutes ticked by and the walls began to close in on all sides, that small hope was extinguished along with the light.

There was a whimper then, but it was low and soft. At only five years old, he'd learned that crying out loud only made it worse, only made the hands that much angrier when he was pulled out, so he stayed quiet even as he gulped for air and squeezed his eyes shut, trying desperately to keep the overwhelming blackness from assaulting his senses. But the dark was an all-consuming, relentless force pushing at him from every side and all but collapsing him in unto himself.

Soon the darkness was a tangible weight that sat so heavy upon his heart, his small chest, pushing and squeezing, making it harder and harder to breathe. It made the gasping and whimpering more erratic even as Noah fought with himself to stay hushed. He had to be silent. He had to disappear. He tried not to exist whatsoever.

He curled into a tight little ball on his side, shrinking as far into the corner and into himself as his traitorous body would allow, wishing he could evaporate entirely into thin air. If he could become the air itself, he wouldn't suffocate... he wouldn't be cursed... he wouldn't be shoved into the dark void of cages, closets and crawl spaces. He'd no longer be imprisoned by four tight walls or his small, shrinking chest cavity. He'd finally be light and free...

As the long minutes dragged on endlessly, he began to shiver in distress as he fought another battle, this time with his bladder. A slow, agonizing hour past and he could no longer hold it. As he peed himself and the warm, odorous liquid slid down his backside and legs, into the carpet, he began to softly cry. He knew then with absolute certainty that it was all true. He was bad and hard to love, and he would be punished for it.

CHAPTER 22

Lainee approached the inviting, slightly ajar door to Noah's room with a smile. She was about to push it open and announce herself when she stopped cold, seeing through the crack that Noah's father was in there. *What was Mr. Riley doing here*? she wondered as her stomach completely bottomed out. He was standing too close to Noah, toe to toe, eye to eye, looking very menacing and threatening.

She remained hidden behind the mostly closed door, frozen in fear. At first she couldn't hear what they were saying but she could certainly discern that his father was unhappy as he all but hissed in Noah's tight, pale face. And then he raised his voice and she could hear the hideously ugly words spewing from his father's mouth, making Lainee instantly sick to her stomach.

"You could never make it on your own, you ungrateful piece of shit. You think it was your miraculous 'talent' that got you where you are today?" His father's surprisingly loud, bitter laugh made both Noah and Lainee outside the door flinch. "It was my money, you moron, paving the way for your education and 'career' both. Besides," his father sneered then, suddenly reaching down and grabbing on tightly to Noah's bulge in the front of his pants, making him jump and take in a sharp, audible breath, "you don't have the balls to walk away from me and my money, *son*." He spat the last word out as if it tasted foul and dirty in his mouth. Still, he gripped tightly on to Noah, who was in obvious pain and demoralized to his very core.

"Then again, you've never really had any balls have you?" his father hissed, squeezing him punishingly through his pants, making Noah call out in agony despite his resolve not to give the bastard the satisfaction of a reaction. Then his father did the unthinkable and began massaging him through his jeans, hissing in his ear, "Look at you... pathetic, weak, disgusting. It's no wonder you can't even close the deal with that disfigured tutor of yours."

And still Noah just stood there without saying a word, now visibly shaking from the horror and humiliation of it all. Lainee didn't know what to do but she knew he needed her in that hellish moment. She couldn't stand by another second just watching his punishment. She quickly stepped back and yelled out, "Noah! Can I come in? It's time to study!"

She'd given them just enough time for his dad to drop his hand and take a step back before she pushed her way into the room. She'd never know how she managed it but she smiled at the sadistic, frightening bastard as she literally wedged herself between him and Noah, saying in a high-pitched, sugary-sweet voice that didn't even sound like her own, "Well, hello, Mr. Riley. I didn't know you were visiting today. I'm sure you've seen that Noah is working hard and hasn't gotten anything below a B- on his tests and assignments these last few months. You must be so proud. I certainly am."

She was babbling, a bit too loudly and quickly, terrified herself of what this man was capable of. But she wasn't going to give that bastard another moment alone with Noah. She would get him away from him no matter what it took. She forged on despite her burgeoning fear and bouncing nerves.

"I'm so sorry but we have to get to the library now. We have prearranged plans to meet the Assistant Professor in Noah's chemistry class for extra help." The lie came out quite easily as she grabbed Noah's arm. She shook him slightly, making him look down at her as she added forcefully, "It's time to go and study now, Noah. No excuses. Come on now. We can't keep the Assistant Professor waiting."

Noah blinked down at her. His eyes were dazed and unseeing. Lainee wasn't even sure if he recognized her in that moment. He hadn't snapped out of the living nightmare he was sleep walking through, so she hooked his arm with hers, grabbed up his nearby backpack and gently began to propel him forward and out of the room. She needed to get him away from his father as soon as possible and nothing would deter her, not even Noah's seeming inability to move.

"Goodbye, Mr. Riley. Rest assured Noah is working hard. He's very self-motivated." She made it to the doorway with Noah and called over her shoulder pointedly, "Don't wait for us. We will be gone all evening."

Then she was all but pushing Noah down the hallway, out of the building, and toward the safe haven of the library. She kept babbling the whole entire walk across campus as she both lead and pushed him forward, looking over her shoulder. "It's okay, Noah. It's okay. He's not following us." She still held his arm and helped steady him as he tripped over the ground periodically. "We're getting far away from him," she reassured him. She was walking quickly as if trying to outrun a bad guy, which, of course, she was.

"It's okay, Noah," she was quietly repeating without even realizing it, glancing over her shoulder and then back up at him every few seconds in concern. Noah looked shocked, shattered, and hadn't yet said a word in return. "You're okay, Noah," she kept on telling him, praying it was true. "You're safe now. I'm here. I've got you." These were the same words he'd said to her not too long ago when she'd had a panic attack, but these were much worse circumstances.

As she pushed open the huge and heavy double doors to the

library, Noah suddenly groaned beside her, "Sick." It was a deep, guttural grunt and she looked over at him in confusion. "Bathroom," he said louder this time, and then more clearly, "I'm going to be sick."

Quickly she scanned her ID and navigated him towards the closest men's bathroom. She charged in with him without hesitation. There was one guy washing his hands at the sink and she ordered, "Out." He bolted and she locked the three-stall bathroom behind him.

Then Noah was stumbling towards the toilet and he landed hard on his knees despite Lainee's attempt to try and brace his fall. She went down on her knees right beside him.

He threw up then several times and she rubbed his back and whispered achingly, "It's okay, Noah. I'm right here with you. Everything is going to be okay. You're safe now."

When he had nothing of his breakfast and lunch left in his stomach, Noah brought his head up and looked at her with tears in his golden eyes. She gently wiped his mouth with her sweater sleeve and pulled him to her until he was laying on her, his head on her chest. She wrapped her arms around him tightly, securely. "It's okay, Noah," she whispered over and over as he shook in her arms. "You're okay, sweetheart. I've got you." And then he was sobbing.

She held tight and rocked him fifteen minutes, twenty, until he didn't even have any tears left in him. He felt completely gutted and hollowed out. They stayed that way for long moments more. Finally Noah managed to whisper against her chest, "You saw?"

She knew it was the last thing he wanted, for her to witness his most humiliating moment and the shame of it, but she knew he needed a friend by his side more than preservation of pride and privacy. She would share this burden with him. She insisted on it. "Yes," she said simply, gently. "I saw what your father did to you, Noah. I'm so sorry."

He buried his head deeper into her chest, wanting to disappear from her knowing, all-seeing gaze at the exact same time he was gripping on to her, desperately in need of her. He was totally and utterly ashamed of himself. "I didn't say a word," he said with despair and self-loathing. "I couldn't even say anything. I just let him say those things to me. I let him touch me like that. And I didn't say a fucking word." He hated himself more in that moment than even his father. "He's right. I don't have any fucking balls. I'm pathetic, weak and disgusting."

Only then did Lainee pull away, and only enough so that he was forced to look up into her eyes. "*No*," she said with a sudden heat and anger of her own. Unlike Noah, she knew exactly who deserved it and where to rightfully channel it. "*He* is the despicable coward, not you Noah." She shook his shoulders then as if trying to snap him out of it. "He is a monster and an abusive father. You realize that's verbal, emotional and sexual abuse don't you? *He's* pathetic, weak and disgusting. Not you, Noah. Never you."

Noah couldn't quite believe her, though, not after all the years of hearing those exact things about himself and *knowing* them to be true, deep down to his core. He dropped his gaze to the bathroom floor in shame. *Oh, God.* Lainee had seen. How could he possibly look her in the eye? How would she ever see him as a man again? How could she ever think of him as strong, as desirable, as *good*?

The person he respected most in this world had witnessed his worst, most shameful moment. He didn't know how he was going to bear it. He felt like throwing up again but he had nothing left in the contents of his stomach.

She shook him harder then and demanded, "Look at me, Noah, goddamnit. Look at me." When he didn't, couldn't, she gently cupped his face and forced his gaze up. As always, her bright-blue eyes shown with her intelligence, her kindness and *goodness*. She was pure and strong, magnificent and powerful, everything Noah wasn't, but she wouldn't let him look away.

She gently cradled his head in her hands and insisted, "Don't you dare believe him, Noah. He doesn't even know who you are, but *I* do. You are the most courageous, talented, enigmatic man I have ever met. My respect for you has only grown tenfold since seeing that, knowing what you come from and what you've had to endure. Do you realize that?" She fought for the words, and for *him*, as her heart swelled to the point of bursting. "It's true, Noah. I only respect you *more* now. You're an amazing man, my absolute favorite person on this earth. *I* know you so believe *me*, not that sick bastard who is in no way a real father, or even much of a human being."

She knew it wasn't quite that easy to flip the switch on self-loathing but, still, she willed Noah to believe her, even a little bit. She still framed his beloved face, staring deep into his wet amber eyes and right through to his very soul, trying to transfer some of her strength, her love into him. She was desperate for him see himself through *her* eyes, not his father's.

But Noah couldn't. His shame was just too great, too ingrained and beat directly into the fabric of his being. It would not release its stranglehold on him easily. If ever.

He looked away and Lainee knew she'd failed. She was losing him.

CHAPTER 23

Lainee pulled Noah to her in a fierce, desperate hug and just held on tight. She wouldn't be letting go without a fight, she vowed to herself. He always called her his brave, resilient warrior and she was more than ready to prove it again to him right here and now.

Noah held on, too, there on that cold bathroom floor in the library for many long moments more, trying to gather some strength. Finally, he forced himself to sit up and pull away. He was quite numb from head to toe, but one emotion rose right above: unadulterated horror. Lainee had seen. *Now Lainee knew.*

She was the one person he respected and cared for most in his world, and now she knew. He was disgusting and defiled, weak and worthless. She'd seen it for herself with her own two eyes. How could she *not* think less of him now and always? Now that she'd witnessed him reduced to that helpless, broken victim, how could she ever see him as anything but?

Noah wasn't sure he could ever get past it even if she could. He looked beyond her shoulder then and whispered achingly, "I wish you hadn't seen, Lainee." Any of it, all of it. Not her. Especially her. But of course his smart, intuitive best friend would have to see him for what he truly was. Broken. Damaged. A victim and a fraud. He wasn't sure how he'd ever be able to look her in the eye again.

Suddenly, Noah realized with startling, painful clarity that he could never see Lainee again after today, not if he was going to survive it. He fought back another wave of nausea as he acknowledged his father had done it. His tormentor had *finally* succeeded in taking absolutely everything away from him, his last small remnants of dignity and self-respect, his desperately-carved out safe space... and now his best friend. Noah was stripped bare and had absolutely nothing left for his dad to take. His old man had won the war over his soul with final, brutal cruelty.

Noah's shoulders sagged and he choked out on a defeated whisper, "He broke me, Lainee. After all these years, he finally did it."

"No!" she cried out in protest, desperately grabbing on to him as her own tears began to spill over. "You aren't broken, Noah. You aren't what he says you are." Noah was scaring Lainee now. She was absolutely terrified of what he was implying and the rippling ramifications of such a definitive, horrific declaration. "Look at me, Noah, please," she whispered through her tears. "Why won't you look at me?"

She felt him pulling further away by the second. She was losing him, she thought again in a flood of panic. Without her even articulating it to herself until now, Noah had become her *one* thing. He mattered more to her than even her scholarship and academic standing, she realized suddenly. *He* was the one and only thing she couldn't really live without. It was an alarming realization especially in the context of the present moment. She couldn't just sit here and watch him slip away.

"You aren't broken, Noah," she begged, admonished and wept. "He hurt you, yes, but you're not broken. You're just scarred, like me."

Still, he wouldn't meet her gaze and she didn't know how to get through to him. He was vanishing right before her very eyes. *I can't lose him,* she thought rather hysterically as she fought back the rising tide of panic that threatened to engulf her, overtake her, drown her whole.

No, I can't lose him, too!

Suddenly, Lainee realized what she had to do. She had to lay herself bare, just like him. Noah couldn't be alone in his shame and despair right now or ever again. She had to go there with him, or lose him forever.

She snatched his hand up and placed his palm over her scarred, wet cheek, saying quietly when he glanced at her in surprise, "Car accident."

After a silent, tense moment, Noah's hand relaxed against her beloved scar and he cupped her cheek as he stared deep into her eyes. "Car accident?" he repeated gruffly, finally seeing and hearing her through his own pain. He had little choice. His love for Lainee trumped even his own self-hatred. Gently, he brushed his thumb over the raised ridge of her scar, just as he'd always wanted to.

She leaned into his warm, loving touch. "I was sixteen and I had just gotten my license," she told him quietly, giving him insight into her own trauma, her own shame for the very first time, leveling the playing field. Bravely but reluctantly she continued, "I... I was driving. It was cold... raining... and the road had black ice." A flash of metal and glass imploding made her grimace even now. She'd never get the brutal, black-and-white images out of her head. They would haunt her for the rest of her life. She felt sick and shaky as she pulled the barbed words out from the pit of her bleeding soul and gave them over to him.

"I-I lost control of the car, slid off the road and smashed into a tree going 60 miles an hour. My dad, h-he was with me." She gulped, trying to steady her racing heart and get a full breath. "He grabbed the steering wheel and turned the car... s-so his side would take the brunt of the impact." She was lost in the painful memories for a second, seeing her dad's beloved, bloody face in those last terrifying moments before she blacked out. Then she shook her head, came back to the present and continued shakily, "I-I broke my pelvis and femur. The windshield exploded into a million pieces..." She rubbed her scar against his gentle hand that was still cupping her cheek, as if he could make it all hurt way less. She'd had cuts all over her face but this one was by far the deepest and would remain with her forever. It would never heal, just like her soul.

Mere inches apart, face to face as they sat there on the bathroom floor, Lainee looked at Noah with wide, wet eyes and admitted *her* greatest shame, her heaviest burden to bear, so that he would no longer be alone with his. "My father died on impact," she whispered as the tears rolled down her face. The next words were the hardest ones she'd ever spoken out loud to anyone. "I killed my dad, Noah. I killed him."

"Jesus, Lainee," Noah, whispered in horror, his heart squeezing painfully in response. He grabbed on to her then and pulled her to him roughly, forgetting his own humiliation and pain instantly in a way he wouldn't have thought possible just a minute before. "I'm so sorry."

She took in a shaky, fortifying breath and gave him the rest of her living nightmare, saying quietly in his ear, "So this scar disfiguring my face... it's the least I deserve. I'm grateful for it, really, as it's a reminder of what I did..." She closed her eyes and whispered achingly, "I killed my dad, Noah, and every day since I've wanted to kill myself, too. "

Noah flinched as pain clamped down on his chest again, making it hard to breathe, overwhelmed by the hideous truth she'd just laid bare at his feet. He was in awe of her strength to be able to say the words out loud, to give them over to him so bravely when he needed them the most, even as he loathed them with every fiber in his being. He wished to God it wasn't her burden to bear, her reality to suffer through, but it was. And he'd gladly share it with her. His own horrors from the hour before were suddenly put into painful perspective.

Noah was so damn grateful for Lainee's love, trust and honesty. He was no longer all alone, sitting in the dark despair of his childhood closet. Lainee was right there with him, cracking the door open and letting the light in. Though he never would have wished her reality upon anyone, especially her, it was changing *everything*, because he was no longer sitting there alone in his shame.

Noah was no longer alone in the overwhelming darkness. Lainee was right there with him, his little warrior, his best friend. She wasn't giving up on him or leaving his side, despite what had transpired an hour prior. Because of her, he was feeling stronger by the second.

"Lainee," Noah choked out then, pulling away slightly to look at her in vast empathy and burgeoning love. He understood her guilt but couldn't abide her suicidal thoughts filling the space between them. "It was just that, an accident," he told her gently. "And it was your father's instinct, his *choice*, to pull that wheel. Don't you see? He was happy to make the ultimate sacrifice in order to save you." That's what a *normal* father was like and Noah envied her that love even as he mourned the loss of it with her now. "You didn't kill him, sweetheart. It was an accident."

Lainee searched Noah's eyes in desperation, as if he alone held the answers to the universe and could judge her level of guilt. She felt cracked wide open and completely vulnerable. Oh, God. *Why had she shared her worst thoughts and hideous truths with Noah of all people?* She cared what he thought way too damn much. She couldn't lose his respect and friendship. Her own mother had never looked at her the same way again. She'd pulled completely away and all but disappeared into her church community. How could Lainee expect anything different from

Noah?

But he was cupping her cheek again and his amber eyes were so warm and kind even now, especially now, as they held fast to hers. That look of adoration and awe he'd always held there just for her was still miraculously present in their golden depths. Lainee felt the band around her chest relaxing and she remembered then exactly why she'd told him. So he wouldn't be alone. Nor would she.

She was right there with him in his dark place, scarred and damaged, too. Maybe that's why she'd always been drawn to him, and him to her. They were a mere reflection of each other's pain.

Lainee remembered, too, that she could trust Noah absolutely. In fact, he was the only one who could even remotely understand the depth of her damage, embedded right into her very flesh and bones. He was also similarly branded by trauma and shame. It was like looking in a mirror as they gazed upon one other now. Their ripped-apart souls had always recognized the other and reached out, begging to unite and become whole.

Noah gently brushed the curtain of Lainee's chestnut brown hair back from her face. Then he shocked the hell out of her by leaning in and running gentle lips over her beloved scar, asking in an almost indiscernible whisper, "Does it still hurt?"

She shook her head no, mesmerized by his gentle, fluttering lips on her most hideous, disfigured part. No one had ever touched her there besides doctors. His kiss on her scar felt completely cathartic. She had laid herself wide open and he was soothing her deepest pain with his gentle, accepting touch. Of course he was. He was Noah. That's just what Noah did.

"I've always loved your scar," he reminded her quietly then. "It makes people want to know you because it hints at incredible strength and resilience. They want to be just like you, Lainee. *That's* why they stare. Because you're a warrior, a survivor. You're beautiful and powerful, and everyone can literally see it written all over your face."

Noah's gaze was intense, the golden centers practically aflame now as they bored into her with fierce compassion. It was his turn to reassure her now, and he was more than up for the challenge, forgetting himself easily to focus on her. "That scar isn't something to be ashamed of, Lainee. It's a badge of honor and, yes, a reminder of your father, but not of his death. It's a reminder of his gift to you, the gift of another day, the gift of *life*. He gladly gave that to you, I have no doubt." He ran his thumb over it gently once more.

Lainee broke down then on instant surge of emotion, tears spilling over in tempest waves. She was nodding but crying so hard she couldn't speak. Years of shame and guilt were being purged now that she had unburdened herself to her best friend and he still thought of her so kindly and lovingly. She was all but choking on the overwhelming emotion as her chest tightened and her breathing hitched. Lainee suddenly had a hard time drawing in a full breath of air and panic began to rise. She gulped for air, desperate to fill her lungs but all at once unable to.

She gripped Noah's forearms then in fear, latching on in need of his help as the panic attack bore down on her out of the blue. He saw the panic flash in her eyes and gripped her forearms in return, steadying her, tethering her to him and to a kinder reality. He held on tight, reminding her he was right by her side.

"Shhh," he whispered soothingly. "Your body knows how to breathe, remember. So just relax, Lainee. Just relax and let it breathe." Somehow Noah was reaching through all the rioting internal chaos and pulling her out.

He took in deep, steadying breaths for her to mimic and soon her body was instinctively mirroring the action, filling her lungs with life-giving air. As her chest filled to max capacity, her heart rate began to settle. She felt every inch of him beneath her hands as they held on to one another and locked gazes. Lainee felt Noah's solid tendons married to strong muscle, hard and warm beneath each of her ten fingers as she gripped his forearms. She felt his deep, full breaths rolling in and out of his body through each of her fingertips as his broad chest expanded each time.

As their breathing synced into a calm and steady rhythm, the tenderness in Noah's gaze washed over Lainee warmly. He saw completely into her soul and knew the worst of her now, and *still* he looked at her that way. Still he stayed. She wasn't going to lose him, too.

Lainee *felt* Noah in that moment with every atom, every fiber of her being. For the first time in five years, after the psychological distress and the subsequent social reclusion, Lainee was fully and completely connected to another human being and anchored by him in this moment. Of course it had to be this incredible man right here.

No one else but Noah could have gently, systematically broken down each and every one of her walls and then built her back up into someone capable of confidence, connection and joy. There were no secrets or barriers between them now and she discerned this was unique and special to them, to *him.* No one would ever know her and understand her like Noah, and vice versa.

It was intimacy personified, flooding her whole system and her every atom with dopamine and... love.

The Noah effect.

CHAPTER 24

As always, Lainee was having a chemical and physical reaction to Noah, responding to him at a cellular level. He was rearranging the very structure of her DNA, rewriting her base sequences and eradicating the sickness there as effectively and precisely as any gene editing tool known to man. This made him even more amazing to her than Dr. Doudna and all the pioneering scientists in the world put together. She blinked at him in awe then.

Somehow through the tsunami of reactions and emotions, Noah was making sense of the madness in her memories, coloring in the startling black and white images from that horrific day with the pretty yellow of the sweater she'd been wearing and the bright blue of her father's eyes as they rounded with realization and he looked over at her a second before impact. Her father had been wearing his navy coat that day, Lainee suddenly recalled. She'd forgotten that until now. *He'd always looked so handsome in that color.* It brought out his eyes... the same eyes he'd given her.

Noah was inspiring a paradigm shift that suddenly had everything coming into Technicolor focus in her mind's eye. Her father had shouted out that he loved her as he grabbed that wheel and viciously turned it. She gasped then, eyes still locked on Noah in wonder. She had forgotten that, too, along with the color of his coat. How had she forgotten *that*, her father's last words to her? They were words of love... and hope, so much hope, that she would survive and go on to live another day, just as Noah had said.

She would always feel guilty over her father's death and it would always feel like a tragedy but suddenly she could see it also as his willing sacrifice, his beautiful and loving gift to her that he had handed over so easily, without hesitation. Suddenly she could see what Noah saw when he looked at her.

The scar was her talisman of strength and resilience. It was her reminder to *live*, fully and completely, with every ounce of her being every day. It was also her permanent connection to her dad and that life-changing, life-giving moment at his loving hands. For once it represented her starting point, not just his end.

For the first time since the accident five long years ago, Lainee could see that not only was a life taken in that pivotal moment, but a life had been given as well. As her father had grabbed and turned that wheel, he had once again chosen to give his baby girl the gift of life. He had given her life not once but twice. How beautiful and pure a love was that, and how lucky was she to have been given it?

The last piece of Lainee's remaining wall came crumbling down even as Noah was putting her back up on a pedestal, even more in awe of all she'd survived and her subsequent strength. He was so fucking grateful that she had come into his life. She'd saved him from his father this day, and from himself, too. Every day.

"Thank you, Noah," she whispered then, inexplicably saying the very words he'd just been thinking he should give over to her. She leaned in and touched her forehead to his, no longer afraid of intimacy. It was just more of that magical Noah effect coming to fruition in her being. "Because of you, I can see things more clearly now."

They stayed that way for a long, tender moment, not in a hurry to move apart or face the world outside. Then she was crying again because it had been so damn long since she'd allowed herself to freely do so and she had to complete the metamorphosis. Noah pulled away then, just enough to wipe her fallen tears away.

"Don't cry, Lainee," Noah begged achingly after more time and tears had passed, "I don't think I can take it anymore." He could tolerate his own pain way better than he could hers he was coming to see.

His tender words only made her cry harder and he pulled her to him in a fierce, tight hug, holding on for both their sakes. He let her just cry then, to get it all out, to purge as much of the pain away as she could.

Slowly, she ran out of tears, shedding some of the burdensome guilt and sorrow along with it. She began to pull herself together as he wiped the last of the tears from her face with such gentle hands. She looked at him then with nothing but love and wonder. How could such kindness and empathy come from such darkness and torment?

There was simply no more amazing of a human being on the planet than the one before her now. She was only more certain of it after today. She had only to convince *him* of it now. It was her turn to ease Noah's burden and eradicate some of the sickness his father had injected into *his* DNA. It would take time. It was a long process, but it would start today and she would never, ever give up on him.

"Noah," she whispered, holding fast to his gaze. "You have been through hell and your father has hurt you terribly, but he has *not* broken you. You are still standing, and you're still so *good.*"

Noah completely froze in her arms but this time his eyes locked on to hers and would not let go. He was listening to every word with bated breath.

"You are not broken, sweetheart," she repeated gently. "You're just scarred. Like me. And if I'm brave and resilient than so are you. If I'm a survivor and a warrior than so are you. If I'm good and worthy of love even with my scars, *than so are you with yours*. You can't say these things about me and not apply them to yourself as well." She was ripping him open again but pouring warm, liquid sunshine into all of his rough, ugly, and filthy cracks. "*Noah, I see you,* all of you, and you are *beautiful*, even more so because of your scars. Like me."

Noah took in a slow, shuddering breath along with Lainee's every gentle, loving word. And he had no choice but to believe her, just a little bit. She was Lainee, after all. She was the most honest, intelligent, warm and intuitive person he'd ever met.

He had never respected or loved anyone more, and he was pretty damn certain he never would for as long as he lived. Surprisingly, Lainee wasn't turning away from him in shock and horror even knowing the worst of it. In fact, she had just the opposite emotion pooling in her eyes and pouring from her lips. And if Lainee said it, felt it, believed it, there had to be some truth to it.

Maybe... maybe he *wasn't* broken. Maybe he was just scarred, like her. Noah blinked at her, processed. He *loved* Lainee's scar. Only more so now knowing the horrific trauma behind it. So maybe... maybe he could be loved with his scars, too?

Maybe he wasn't such a disgusting, damaged, hopeless human being, not if Lainee could look at him quite that way and say such kind things. Maybe, just maybe, he could look at himself in the mirror when he got back to his room and not loathe what he saw, even as the ghost of his father lingered there and everywhere he looked. Perhaps, with Lainee by his side, he could face himself and the whole godforsaken world even after today.

He nodded slowly at her then and reiterated quietly, as if needing to repeat it to subscribe to it, "Not broken, just scarred." He desperately needed to believe it, just a little bit, to get up off that floor. "Like you."

"Yes," she whispered lovingly, "you're like me, Noah."

She thread all of her fingers through his then and he inhaled a shuddering breath of relief as she anchored him to her again. *Lainee still wanted to touch him.* She still looked at him as if he was good and... worthy of her. Maybe... maybe he could believe her over his father. Just a little bit. In time.

"Superimposable," Noah said on a whisper then, bringing her hand up to kiss it, remembering the term from their earlier biochem studies. It had struck him as prophetic, resonating and staying with him as he'd gotten to know Lainee more and more. *Two overlapping objects containing an internal plane of symmetry with no perceptible difference.* He had known with one look that the two of them were not the polar opposites they would appear to be to the outside world, but could he dare to believe, to hope he was like her even a little, and not *him*, that sick and twisted bastard whose DNA had built him and shaped him?

"Yes," Lainee agreed with a watery, loving smile, as if answering all of his unasked questions of the universe. She leaned in and kissed him gently on the lips then as if it was the most natural thing in the world and his heart took flight. "You and me, Noah. We're the same." She needed him to see himself through that kinder, more truthful lens than that of his father's. She touched the side of his handsome face and it was his turn to lean into her palm gratefully. "And I *need* you. I could never be this clear-eyed, brave and strong without you."

Noah turned to kiss her palm with tenderness even as he wondered how any of that could possibly be true. How could someone as magnificent, strong and talented as Lainee need *him*? Still, if she said it, he had to believe it. Just a little bit. And if Lainee needed him, well, he wasn't completely worthless after all.

She held out her just-kissed hand to him then, asking quietly, meaningfully, "Together then?"

Noah took in a deep, steadying breath, grabbed on to her and nodded. He would be brave like her he vowed, his amber eyes flashing with resolve. He would be brave *for* her. Hell, there wasn't anything he wouldn't do for Lainee. Even face the cruel world outside, and his reflection in the mirror. "Together, my little warrior."

They slowly helped each other up off the floor and stood. With threaded fingers, they left the safety of the locked bathroom, both inexplicably lighter than when they'd entered. They were purged of all their secrets, and that was no small thing.

They were an army of two, wounded and weary, but still standing and ready to fight. Side by side, they were coming out of the darkness and into the light.

CHAPTER 25

They were inseparable after that, always together, as if magnets pulled through space and time. Sometimes they even held hands without even thinking about it. It just seemed a natural extension to their solidified connection.

They got more stares than ever before but Lainee smiled at those people gawking at her now. She felt different somehow. She felt open and... brave. She was suddenly proud of herself for being a survivor, a warrior, as Noah always said, and she was damn proud of him for being the same.

He was the most impressive man she'd ever met, besides her own dad. It now felt like a privilege to be at his side, not because of his good looks or his irrefutable talent, but because of his amazing heart and soul that had somehow persevered amidst all the trauma he'd endured. She would always hold sacred the gift of seeing him and truly, deeply knowing him. It was changing her, and had been for awhile now she realized. Their connection was now complete. She wasn't alone anymore, and neither was Noah. They would keep each other's secrets and when one went to war, the other would go right alongside them.

They quickly eased back into their routine, their studies, even their playfulness, but it was different after that fateful day. There were no walls dividing them, no facades to hide behind. They were cracked wide open and laid bare before the other but there was no pain or worry, only extreme devotion and... relief.

If Noah had to sum up his feelings for Lainee in one word it would have been tenderness. Extreme, undiluted tenderness. It was a pure, raw, almost aching in his gut that he'd never felt before except perhaps for maybe his mother when he'd been just a child, before she colossally failed him by pulling away from him and turning to her daily medications to numb herself from *his* pain. Yes, he imagined *this* was the feeling parents felt for their children in return, when they were normal and healthy, anyway: aching, unconditional, and extreme tenderness.

It was such a simple, pure sentiment embedded deep in his core now. It wasn't dependent on what Lainee could give or do for him, nor was any action or word from her required at all. This deep-rooted sentiment did not require a thing from her. It just was.

Born out of the sharing of their parallel pain, followed quickly by the understanding and acceptance of one another in their totality, this warm, tender feeling now existed in his gut with a great amount of joy and comfort exuding outward to all extremities. Noah was certain that no matter what actions either of them took from that day forward, nor what the forces of the outside world threw at them, his devotion to Lainee would hold. It would just be, like a permanent physical trait such as his sandy brown hair and height.

It was certainly the key to his emotional recovery, though his default setting was still very much stuck on avoidance. He could only bear to speak of his father and the abuse he'd endured for more than a few minutes at a time, but looking at himself in the mirror had been surprisingly easy after Lainee had rewired some of his thinking.

Still, he was grateful for the looming opening night of Hamlet and the subsequent hectic schedule that would follow. It was a welcome distraction from the emotional upheaval but it also reminded him of his talent, his worth in and of himself. Acting had always provided him with purpose, fulfillment and a much needed confidence.

Noah asked Lainee to run lines with him a couple of days before opening night. She had heard him practice here and there at the theater, of course, but in its totality tonight Hamlet - Noah - had her in tears. From Hamlet's grief over his father's death, expressed without reservation by Noah himself, to Ophelia's heartbreaking suicide, it was actually quite gut-wrenching for her. Lainee fought tears throughout, unexpectedly overwhelmed and moved by Noah's immense talent. He had the rare ability to become completely vulnerable and emotive, without any fear or hesitation. He never held back, even from the extremely unpleasant emotions that came with the man that was Hamlet.

She'd truthfully never appreciated the art of acting before now, until Noah miraculously morphed into another man, carrying himself completely different, no longer even sounding like himself, shape shifting before her very eyes. The bravery and boldness required to do so was suddenly not lost on her.

"Noah, you're amazing," she said breathlessly when they were done with the last act. She was almost looking at him like she'd never seen him before. "I'm speechless."

The tone in her voice, the look on her face had Noah actually blushing. He cleared his throat and said almost shyly, "I reserved a front row seat for you, in case you wanted to come to opening night."

"You saved me a seat?" She wasn't at all surprised by his thoughtfulness but she was honored and touched. She could have paid for a ticket like everyone else, but she probably wouldn't have gotten a very good seat, especially front row.

"But don't feel as if you *have* to come if you don't want to," he rushed on to say. "I mean no pressure but, of course I'd love to have you there." Damnit, was he still blushing?

"I wouldn't miss it," Lainee assured him, flashing him a big smile, the ear-to-ear one which made his heart flip flop.

Noah smiled in relief. "Yeah? You'll come? I mean, truly don't feel obligated but... I'd really like you to see me..." he trailed off helplessly, thinking, *I'd like you to see me like that, whole and in control and shining in the spotlight up on the stage versus on the dirty bathroom floor crying and puking my guts out after my father molested me...* He lamely concluded out loud, "on stage."

Lainee looked closely at him, always so kind and understanding. "I wouldn't miss it, Noah," she restated sincerely. "Thank you for being so thoughtful and reserving a seat for me. And front row? I'm so excited!"

He smiled, chagrined, and waved off her last comment. "It's nothing. I mean, I'm the star of the show so I could reserve the whole front row if I wanted to. I have that kind of power, you know. In case you haven't noticed, I'm kind of a big deal around here." He gave her a playful wink.

She had to laugh. "And yet somehow you remain so humble. It's really quite commendable."

A cocky grin lit up his entire stupidly handsome face and Lainee's heart gave a funny little hitch. She hadn't seen that thousand-watt smile of his in quite awhile she realized, and it did her heart so good to see it now.

There he is, she thought then with love, relief and an answering smile, *my sweet and playful Noah.* Her smile quickly fell away. *Wait, what?* Her *Noah?*

Easy there, Lainee, she warned herself then. *Don't cross that line or you will be in serious trouble.* She wondered why it seemed that dangerous line got closer and closer by the day.

When they were studying in Crema Cafe the next afternoon, a long-legged blonde sidled up with a latte and a lazy, seductive smile. Both Lainee and Noah bristled as the girl presumptuously plunked right down in Noah's lap and threw a possessive arm around his neck.

"Hello, lover," she whisper-purred, loud enough for Lainee to hear. Noah felt a flush of embarrassment and... shame. His long-standing, old friends. They never went too far, always sure to make a frequent appearance. "Last night was *fun*, Noah. Am I right?"

Lainee's heart squeezed and she went completely still, unable to divert her eyes from Noah as she processed. *Last night?* Noah had been with this girl *last night*? After Lainee had spent all evening with him, running lines, sharing sushi and secrets? After she'd left his suite late into the night, utterly content with the world and... *happy*, Noah had called this girl over and slept with her? Lainee shouldn't have been shocked, or completely gutted, but she was inexplicably both.

That line she was trying her hardest not to cross over was all but wrapping itself around her throat and strangling her right now.

Noah stiffly pushed the unwelcome girl out of his lap and sent a tentative glance Lainee's way. Her face seemed flushed with his embarrassment. He glanced up at the very beautiful and sexy girl whom he'd tumbled in his room last night and wished she'd just fucking disappear. Under Lainee's piercing gaze, Noah felt like the dirty, disgusting bastard he undoubtedly was. Through a tight throat he said, "I'm studying, Amber. Now is not a good time."

Amber was undeterred and actually grinned at him, as if she was accepting his implied challenge. She threw a dismissive glance at Lainee, acknowledging her for the first and last time. Then she leaned over, bracing her hands on Noah's thighs, giving him a nice, clear shot of her cleavage, whispering a secret and naughty invitation right into his ear.

Though Lainee couldn't hear the specific words coming out of Amber's mouth, she nonetheless understood the seductive invitation pouring into Noah's ear at that exact moment as she sat a mere foot away in stunned silence. She couldn't help but admire the girl's bravado and sex appeal even as she felt sick to her stomach over it.

Lainee took a crushing moment to admire Amber's flawless profile and long, lean body encased in a low-cut t-shirt and tight jeans. For a fleeting, stinging moment, Lainee wished she could *be* her, hanging all over Noah, utterly beautiful, effortlessly sexy, and completely confident. Fresh from his bed.

Lainee's heart cracked then and a rush of pain made its way into her chest, making her wince and look down at her laptop in confusion. She touched her scar unknowingly, despising it again for the first time since Noah had kissed it in the bathroom of the library. How could she forget it was there, separating her from everyone around her, even him? Especially him? *Foolish,* she hissed at herself as she kept her gaze downcast.

Noah was on edge with raw, fraying nerves stinging with shame. When he saw Lainee flinch and touch her scar, his heart cracked. She hadn't done that in days. He understood all too well that he'd made her do it now. He was making her feel ugly and less than, flaunting his sordid sex life right in front her face like she meant absolutely nothing to him. After what they had been through together, after they'd both been laid bare and her sweet, life-giving kiss in the midst of his bathroom breakdown, it was the epitome of insensitive to flaunt his new lover in her face. He felt sick to his stomach as he glanced uncertainly her way.

In truth, Noah had always been slightly ashamed of the revolving door to his well-traveled bedroom. He knew it would surprise most people to know he'd never been particularly proud of the fact that he was so sexually active with countless one night stands. It had been fun for awhile and then... it had stopped being as fun. Noah could only admit to himself now, after sharing the truth of his past with Lainee, that his overactive sex life was less about fun, freedom and opportunity and more a symptom of sexual depravity, his father's and now his own.

In the honest, darkest moments of the night, while every light in his room blared and his skin still stung from his third or fourth too-hot shower of the day, Noah glimpsed at this ugly truth. He acknowledged only then and only fleetingly that he needed the non-stop parade of nameless lovers to prove something to himself, and to his father. He had to show them both that he was in control of his own body, his own bedroom. That he was a desirable, viral, healthy, and whole man no matter what his father had always said about him, or done to him. That he wasn't a fucking head case with a history of abuse, mostly physical and psychological but also a little something even darker and more perverse at times. That's what he'd been trying to prove to himself even last night with Amber, but it had been more out of habit and desperation than passion and interest itself. And it had come inexplicably with more guilt than pleasure from start to finish.

It was hard to wade through and dissect all the uncomfortable emotions swamping his system at the moment but, in addition to the usual embarrassment and shame over being a man whore, Noah felt a healthy dose of stabbing guilt. What he and Lainee shared was so... sweet and intimate. Much more intimate than sex. He never wanted to disrespect that, or her, but he was uncertain of what she expected of him now, of what the new rules of their relationship entailed. He could sense he was hurting her in some new way now, and it only added to his remorse and confusion.

Noah saw Lainee as nothing but good and strong, brave and kind. For some reason she had deemed him worthy to stand by her side, to know her and see her in totality like no other. He never would take that gift for granted. He wanted to tread lightly and respectfully but he felt so clumsy and unsteady instead. He was hurting her *right now* despite his best intentions.

All of these barraging thoughts slamming into him at once, Noah stiffly removed Amber's fingers from his thighs and pushed her away yet again. "I'm sorry, Amber, but I really need to get back to studying," he said as subtly as he could, shooting another guilty glance Lainee's way.

Amber shrugged without internalizing one iota of rejection but finally getting the message. She turned on her heel with a sultry, "Call me," over her shoulder and then she walked away and straight out of the cafe.

An awkward silence befell Noah and Lainee.

CHAPTER 26

Noah cleared his throat and turned back to Lainee, who was staring intently down at her laptop, though he assumed she wasn't reading a thing as she was completely still, not even blinking. Her fingers weren't even at the keys, but instead lay limply in her lap.

"I'm sorry about that," he murmured quietly, honestly, not knowing how to proceed. He would have given ten years of his life right about then to know Lainee's thoughts. "Amber and I..." he trailed off miserably. What could he say? They fucked in his room last night after Lainee had left? That he'd hastily called the first name in his phone out of sheer habit after the insomnia married with the heavy darkness started weighing him down, suffocating him? That he'd used the girl as an easy distraction and a cheap means to feel better about himself for about thirty minutes, then he'd tossed her right out without a second thought? All of that was true, but there was no way in hell he would share any of it with his sweet, innocent best friend sitting across from him now, though he worried she discerned most of it anyway.

Lainee lifted her piercing blue eyes to his, looking at him with such heavy sadness that his heart sustained another crack. *Fuck. What was she thinking?!*

Had he disappointed her, hurt her? With their new closeness and tenderness came an unfamiliar responsibility and a still unknown rippling of side effects. What did she want him to say and do? Whatever it was, he'd say it and do it without hesitation but, unfortunately, he had no clue what that was. He had no fucking idea how to chase that sadness away from her eyes even though he'd been the one to put it there.

As always, Lainee let him off the hook gently, seeing the regret and uncertainty stamped on his handsome face. "It's okay, Noah," she said with a small smile that was soft and kind but did not reach her eyes. "I understand." Truthfully, she thought it was quite normal that he was having sex with beautiful women. Why wouldn't he? He was young, gorgeous, in demand and uncommitted. She just wished... *what,* she chided herself. That it wasn't so many? That it wasn't directly in her face? That it had been *her* in his bed last night instead of Amber?

Lainee felt a growing sense of protectiveness and, yes, possessiveness over Noah that she had to work her way through now. It was uncomfortable and... painful. But he'd done absolutely nothing wrong in actuality. He had not violated his existing commitment to her. This last simple truth finally brought some clarity and resolution to her troublesome examination. Their friendship was beautiful and intact. His romantic escapades need not negatively affect them in any way. She tried to just let it go then, reassuring him half-heartedly, "I just want you to be happy, Noah. And Amber is very beautiful."

So are you, Noah thought instantly but didn't say. She was acting as if Amber was his new girlfriend when in truth he would never call her again, or even see her again if he had anything to say about it. But he thought better of voicing those truths, too. He nodded instead, wanting to leave the whole uncomfortable and confusing situation behind them.

Her happiness was way more important than his own when it came right down to it. Noah would always choose Lainee's needs and wants over his own. If only he knew what the hell they were...

◆◆◆

When she saw him up on that stage for the first time the next evening, Lainee couldn't drag herself back from that line any longer. Noah was nothing short of magnificent and mesmerizing. And she was most definitely in trouble.

He'd looked for her from behind the curtain before he'd gone on stage, and when he saw her there, in the best seat in the house that he'd picked especially for her, he'd lit up like a Christmas tree. He killed it that night, he made sure of it, for her.

Afterwards, she tried to find him backstage as he'd put her name on some special list granting her access. Just as their eyes found each other across the crowded greeting room, a gaggle of girls pushed their way in past her, all but running her over in their haste to accost Noah. Apparently, she wasn't the only one on that special list. Really, she should have known better.

Noah laughed and peeled the girls off him, happy to take pictures and sign playbooks. He kept an eye all the while on Lainee across the room, who stood back and watched with an expression on her face that he couldn't quite read.

As more girls came running up to him, forming a long line, Lainee smiled sadly and shook her head at him, turning to leave. She was finally beginning to understand there would never be an end to the fangirls. Really, *she should have known better.* Where was her keen intelligence now, she chided herself as she swiftly exited Loeb feeling crestfallen.

Noah's heart had dropped to his feet in disappointment as Lainee turned her back to him and walked away. He wanted her eyes on him still, damnit. He wanted her nearby within range at all times, if he was being honest. He'd tried to call her name out to stop her from leaving but it had been swallowed up by the squeals and cacophony of backstage noise.

As the door shut behind her, Noah tried to push Lainee from his thoughts all together. He was a professional and had a job to do. *Focus and finish, Riley*, he scolded himself, trying to get his head back in the game. He turned to his fans with a forced but charming smile.

As was his usual routine, Noah ended up escorting one of the more aggressive and good looking female fans back to his dorm room afterwards, closing out the night with a couple of orgasms, one for her and one for him. But as he quickly showed his latest, loudest and rather perverse lover out the door not too much later, Noah felt that overwhelming guilt and remorse grip him once again. He felt quite weary from it as he jumped into a scalding hot shower.

His stomach was in knots as he changed the bed sheet and lay down. He begged his mind to quiet, to let him sleep, but instead it replayed over and over for him the profanity his recent lover had spewed the entire time they were having sex. She had even asked, ordered really, that he spank her and squeeze her neck. And he'd done it, harder at her behest, hating every second of it even while he was helplessly driving towards his own orgasm. He wasn't sure why he'd given in to her uncomfortable demands. He should have stopped, pulled out, told her to leave. But he hadn't. He'd been utterly submissive, acting powerless against her domineering commands.

Because I have no fucking balls, just like my father said.

Noah got up then, walked to the bathroom, fell to his knees in front of the toilet and threw up. He knelt there weak for a quiet moment and then stood, brushed his teeth and took another scalding hot shower. Still, as he lay exhausted in bed, he felt dirty and disgusting as he replayed his father's words, his father's touch, over and over again in his mind like he hadn't since the day it had last happened. The victory of opening night was a long lost memory, overshadowed by the last dark hour filled with nothing but twisted, terrifying ghosts.

If Lainee was here I wouldn't feel like this. The thought echoed through the chambers of his rioting mind with absolute certainty. Lainee only brought the light, the good, the safe and steady. She was comfort and joy, loyal and loving. *My homeland,* he thought with extreme tenderness.

She was where he needed to be. She was what tethered him to sanity and hope. She gave him a strong foundation on which to stand, heal and grow. She steadied him, then saved him.

All the other girls have to go. Noah knew it then and there with absolute certainty. For his sake, and Lainee's.

He wasn't sure what her kiss on the lips in the Widener bathroom had meant, if anything, nor why the look in her eyes was changing. But he did know one thing with clear finality. His old coping mechanisms weren't working, if they ever had. They weren't healthy or effective. Worse, they seemed to be hurting Lainee now, too.

I can't lose her, Noah thought rather desperately, and not for the first or last time. He wanted to respect and honor Lainee, to infuse nothing but joy into her life like she did for him. He certainly never wanted to put that sad, hurt look in her eyes ever again. It was time to get rid of all the other girls because Lainee was the only one that really mattered.

With warm thoughts of Lainee pushing away the horrific ones of his father, Noah finally, gratefully, slipped into oblivion.

Lainee rushed across the dark campus, back to her dorm room as tears blurred her vision. *So stupid*, she hissed to herself as she desperately tried to flee from Noah's growing grip on her. It was a useless and futile effort.

Like an insipid, stupid fangirl herself, she had found herself outside Noah's door just now, over an hour after she'd left Loeb, as if she couldn't stay away from his overwhelming talent and magnetism. She hadn't known what she was doing but she was compelled to go to him nonetheless. She couldn't seemingly wait another second to see him, and she couldn't talk herself out of it. It really wasn't a choice. She had to see him *now* or her heart would burst. Lainee's whole body seemed swollen with something sweet and yet strangely bitter, a yearning like she'd never felt before growing within her gut and then consuming her entirely. She was just a slave to it as it pushed her out of her room, across the campus and to Noah's front door.

Just as she'd lifted her hand to knock, she'd heard them.

"Harder, Noah! Fuck me, harder! Yes, make it hurt, goddamnit! Choke me! *Harder!*"

Lainee literally gagged on her own heart then, taking a step back in the hallway in horror.

She heard Noah's grunting and moaning and it was like razor blades dragging slowly across her nerve endings. Above it all she heard the girl's repeating chant, "Hit me, Noah! Harder!"

Some semblance of sanity and common sense returned in a rush, infiltrating Lainee's own raging, rioting need of Noah. She turned and fled. As she stumbled into her dorm moments later, she knew she would never go to his room again.

CHAPTER 27

"Well?" Noah asked Lainee anxiously the next day when no praise was automatically forthcoming. They were squeezing in a quick homework session in the Widener library before that night's performance. She had been disappointingly, disconcertingly distant and quiet.

"Do you really need me to say it?" she responded quietly, the sadness back in her eyes today, painting him with it, too. She found herself melting towards him despite the haunting memories of the night before. In the end, she just could not stay a safe emotional distance from him it seemed. It was Noah, after all. He pulled her in like a magnet.

They were just friends, best friends, she repeated pragmatically on a loop, trying to get back to where they'd been right before she'd about knocked on his door last night. She desperately wanted to get back to that safe place so that they wouldn't lose each other completely.

She took in a deep, steadying breath and told him honestly, "Noah, you're incredible. I've never been so riveted by a performance in my entire life. I'm in awe of your talent."

A slow smile spread on his face, because no one's opinion mattered more to him than hers. He purposefully ignored her sad eyes and the shadows across her face indicating she, too, had a long, sleepless night. "You'll come see me again tonight?" he urged like an insecure nitwit. She looked at him a long moment as if considering, her piercing, serious gaze making him squirm a little in his seat.

"Yes," she finally answered quietly, loyally, though that part of her desperately fighting for self-preservation protested. "I'll come support you tonight." And she would come to almost every performance after that, too, without him even having to ask.

◆◆◆

A couple of weeks later, after the band around her chest had finally begun to loosen and things felt more normal between them, Lainee and Noah were at their bar Brew Hall blowing off some steam and getting drinks. As yet another groupie came up to interrupt them, though, Lainee was beyond perturbed. Noah had a rare few nights off from the play and she greedily wanted him all to herself for once. *Was that really too much to ask?*

"Could you not encourage them?" she asked in annoyance as the female admirer walked away after getting a photo with Noah. "I mean, seriously, does every woman want to sleep with you in every room we enter? It's ridiculous."

Noah chuckled at her then which made her want to rip out his perfectly coiffed hair. "*You* don't want to sleep with me," he pointed out.

That was debatable at this point she admitted only to herself, not saying a word.

"Besides, it's my duty to thank the fans for their support, don't you think?"

That was also debatable but she merely responded grumpily, "It's rude they all just overlook me and assume I'm not your girlfriend."

Noah took stock of Lainee's usual uniform of prim and proper sweater with a high white collar underneath, dark jeans and brown penny loafers. "It's a safe assumption," he concluded absentmindedly.

It was like a slap to her face and Lainee immediately flinched and stood up on shaky legs. Before she could take a step, however, Noah was up on his feet, too, grabbing her shoulders and adding desperately, "Lainee, that's not what I meant, goddamnit." He stood in her way as she attempted to walk away.

"Why are you always so quick to believe you're not good enough?" he shook her shoulders then in frustration. "You're *too* damn good for me. I just meant that you don't act like you're interested in me. You certainly aren't dressed like you're on a date, like you know, you're trying to impress me."

She met his eyes then. "What does that mean?" she asked quietly, still hurt beyond reason.

"Well, look at all the other girls here at the bar. They are wearing sexy tops and flirting with everything that moves. Some are even going the extra mile and wearing high heels. *You* look like you're about to go to church." And she never, ever touched him, flirted or went to his room anymore, but he didn't mention that part.

Lainee looked down at her kelly green sweater that covered her completely from chin to wrist. She loved that sweater but she supposed he had a point. "I can be sexy," she threw back, feeling ornery.

He huffed a laugh, relieved she was no longer trying to walk out on him. He pulled her back to her seat. "I have no doubt about that," he told her truthfully. She looked at him with a scowl, as if he was making fun of her. "Lainee," he said helplessly, "don't you get it? You're beautiful, breathtaking even. Do you really need me to keep pointing it out to you? Have you really not noticed all the guys around us always checking you out despite the church getup?" Noah certainly had noticed all the intrigued looks, and he scowled at one now a seat over in warning.

Lainee tilted her head at him in consideration then and it was a sweet, familiar gesture that made his heart do a funny flip. She did that when he said something especially stupid or thought-provoking that she had to take further time to process. He adored that little tic.

He brushed her hair back from her face as he often did and said gently, not for the first time, "You should wear your hair back, Lainee. You've got a beautiful face. And those eyes..." He was suddenly staring into her large, almond-shaped eyes the color of a sleepy sea on a clear, sunny morning, and he was happily drowning in them.

Those damn all-seeing eyes that he couldn't hide from, even as he was in awe of their depth and intelligence. *And those full, promising lips...* He was suddenly looking down at her lips quite unintentionally and his brain started humming, buzzing really, as he dangerously admired their pink fullness for long moments like never before. She really had fantastic lips. He'd noticed them before, of course, but now he stared and continued staring, visualizing his own lips brushing over them, practically feeling their welcoming softness all the while.

Lainee licked her bottom lip as he stared at it and Noah felt himself harden instantly in response. Startled by his strong physical reaction to her, his eyes darted up to her eyes. Her pupils were dilated in the dark bar and her cheeks flushed. Was that in response to *him*, he wondered incredulously, even as an invisible force was pushing him toward her. They both slowly leaned in to one other.

Noah was in a hyperfocused trance, looking from her eyes to her lips and back again as if utterly mesmerized by her and what was transpiring between them in this suspended, electric moment.

The background completely melted away.

He kept leaning in, his eyes once again fixated on those full, beckoning lips, his mind buzzing in anticipation, his body tightening as he came closer... closer... almost close enough to touch... his lips a mere breath away from hers...

Noah was suddenly jostled as three girls rushed in between them, all but knocking Lainee out of her chair. He reached through the girls and grabbed Lainee's arm to steady her as she was forced to her feet, asking in concern, "Lainee, are you okay?"

He tried to push the enthusiastic crowd out of the way with one hand even as Lainee was pulling out of his other hand's grasp. She was shaking her head at the groupies, or maybe him, or possibly all of them, he wasn't sure.

"I've got to go," she said, looking almost... panicked. " I'll see you tomorrow." Then she fled.

Noah stared after her in shock and dismay. *What the fuck had just happened, or rather* almost *happened?*

Lainee ignored his texts all night and into the following day. She didn't even make it to the gym at their normal time. Noah was beginning to outright panic. Had he screwed everything up once and for all by almost kissing her, by *not* kissing her, by something else all together? He was going a little nuts, he wasn't going to lie.

She'd been disturbingly distant these last few weeks and had seemed to be avoiding his room at all costs, *their* room, damnit. It left an uncomfortable knot in his stomach and a rising tide of panic that threatened to overtake him at any moment.

He didn't know what the hell was going on but, in his true cowardly nature, he was too afraid to face it head on and ask her. Now today she was blatantly ignoring him, avoiding him even, and it hurt, goddamnit. It also scared the shit out of him.

Then he finally got a text back in the late afternoon. *Meet me at our bar @ 7p.*

He read the text several times suspiciously. No studies today? Why would there be no studying today? She insisted on studying every day. Then he looked up and searched about his empty suite as if it would hold the answers sprawled out on one of its walls.

Noah honestly had no idea what to do with himself and his freed-up afternoon. He had no performance tonight and now no tutoring session. *What the hell am I going to do with myself?* He was lost and floored to admit that he'd rather be studying because that meant he'd be with Lainee. What the hell had occupied his time before her? It was honestly hard to recall.

It was a slow crawl of four hours until 7p and he decided to work out alone - again - to pass the time. Then he did his homework... on his own. *What the hell is happening to me,* he wondered again as the minutes slowly ticked by. Then, still feeling uneasy and unsure of the situation, he entered Brew Hall a full half hour early, with an eye to their usual spot at the bar. Hell, they'd been there just last night, so why did this feel so alien and unnerving?

Because something is changing between the two of you and you're afraid of ruining what you have, you idiot, and losing her forever. That was now his biggest fear he admitted to himself, still standing in the entrance of the bar like a moron, looking around like a lost little boy. *I can't lose her.*

This was the downside to being known and seen, accepted and cared for. If Lainee was to ever look at him in disgust or walk away from him indefinitely, he didn't think he'd be able to recover, at least not for a long, long time. Yes, he was growing more and more terrified of losing her every single day. The last few weeks he'd felt her pulling away and it had been brutal.

Now, with a knot in his fucking sensitive stomach, he wondered nervously, *where is she?* Was he the only one early and over-eager here?

Apparently so because there was someone else in their usual seats at the bar, a brunette with her hair pulled up in a high, flirty ponytail. She was wearing a tight crop-top and black leather pants which even from across the room accented a nice round bottom.

Some tool was coming up to flirt with her as Noah watched, making her turn sideways ever so slightly on her bar stool. That's when Noah saw that the sexy brunette sitting in their usual seat was, in fact, Lainee, his sweet, innocent, prim and proper Lainee. With her hair up and her bottom half wrapped in black leather.

His mouth fell open and his heart plummeted to his feet as she smiled at the tool encouragingly.

CHAPTER 28

"What the fuck?" Noah growled out loud without even realizing it. As the stranger ordered Lainee a drink, Noah quickly shook himself out of his stupor and walked up to her, saying pointedly, "Sorry I'm late, *dear*." He gave the guy a heated look.

"Oh," the other guy said, having the decency to look chagrined, "I didn't realize you were here with someone."

The dope looked at Lainee with big, sad puppy dog eyes and she was quick to reassure him, "Oh, he's just a friend." She looked at Noah and smiled sweetly. "We're not together, are we?"

"Oh," the buffoon standing between them said again, visibly relaxing. "Cool. Hey, man, I'm Brian." He had the gall to stick his hand out at Noah then.

Noah looked from his hand to Lainee's sweet, smug smile. She batted her eyelashes at him and he saw for the first time that she had a ton of makeup on. She had outlined her eyes dramatically to stand out like a freakin' sexy model's and her lips were a seductive dark red. That's when he took in her full attire from the front. Her midriff was showing - so much skin! - and her leather pants were crazy tight. She was even wearing high heels. *What the actual fuck?*

Noah was flabbergasted and more than just a little peeved. Why was she dressed so provocatively? Was she actually there to pick up guys right in front of him? Noah would rather have punched

Brian in his stupid face than shake his hand, so he left the guy hanging awkwardly.

Suddenly, like a gift from the gods, Noah's first fan of the evening flounced over at that most opportune moment and gave a high-pitched squeal, kissing him square on the lips in lustful delight.

With that telling introduction, Noah finally took Brian's hand and gave Lainee a smug smile in return. "Noah."

Noah spent the next fifteen minutes gushing right back at his very handsy fan even as he pushed her fingers off his uninterested crotch. He couldn't remember her name but he offered to buy her a drink, which is how he and Lainee inexplicably ended up on a double date with complete strangers in their usual seats at their favorite bar as they glared angrily at each other.

In truth, Lainee was barely giving Noah the time of day throughout the next round of drinks, which had his pride and anger smarting and taking a dangerous turn. Brian had the unfortunate timing of putting his ham hand on the small of Lainee's back just then.

Noah instinctively reached out and smacked Brian's hand away, warning him with a low growl, "Watch it, buddy."

Brian looked shocked and then confused, glancing at Lainee. "Sorry, I didn't mean to offend you-"

"It's fine," she reassured through gritted teeth, tossing an angry eye dart Noah's way. "You can put your hand on me, Brian."

Brian looked at Noah uncertainly and slowly moved his hand to the small of Lainee's back.

That fucking did it. Noah pulled Stacie - he thought her name was Stacie - hard up against him then and nuzzled her neck making her all but swoon in a very loud, theatrical manner.

"Brian, will you kiss me?" Lainee suddenly demanded, making both men look at her as if she'd grown a second head.

"Oh, well, sure," the tool said with a rather attractive blush.

When Brian leaned down, Noah leapt out of his seat, unceremoniously pushing Stacie out of the way and angrily shoving Brian backwards. He growled, "Don't even think about it, asshole."

Brian was finally perturbed himself now and looked in confusion from Lainee's flushed face to Noah's scowling one. He shook his head and threw in the towel. "Man, forget this. This is just too weird." Then he walked away.

Lainee stood up then, confronting Noah in anger. "Are you serious right now?" she asked heatedly. "You can flirt with hundreds of girls every night and nuzzle this tart two inches from my face and *sleep with them all* but I can't have one decent guy give me a kiss?"

"The short answer to that is *no*," Noah bit back, his anger on par with hers. "The long answer is *hell no.* You don't know that tool from a hole in the wall and you shouldn't be throwing yourself at him in the first place."

"And *her*?" Lainee asked, looking Stacie up and down with obvious distaste as the clueless girl stood mere inches away scrolling on her phone with one hand while the other lay claim to Noah's bicep. "She's okay to throw yourself at? I bet she's even okay to take back to your room to have sex with tonight, huh, Noah?"

Flabbergasted, Noah looked from Lainee to Stacie and then back again. When he had no immediate answer for her, Lainee turned and began walking out on him for the second night in a row.

Noah called out her name as she exited the bar. "Lainee, wait!"

Tonight he had the sense to throw some bills on the bar and race

THE HIGHER EDUCATION OF NOAH RILEY

after her, completely forgetting about Stacie in an instant.

"Lainee, will you stop, goddamnit?" he yelled after her as he followed her down the sidewalk. He couldn't help but notice how hot her ass looked in her tight black leather pants and high heels as she marched away from him. "My car is the other way. Let me drive you back to campus."

She completely ignored him and his very existence as she sailed on, making him swear under his breath and take after her in an easy jog.

He grabbed her wrist and she whirled around on him, all female wrath and ire. "You just couldn't stand someone flirting with me for once, could you? You couldn't let me enjoy feeling pretty and desirable for one night. What gives you the right to act like a jealous boyfriend while feeling up a complete stranger right in front of my face tonight, and every other night for that matter?"

Noah ran a hand over his face in frustration, "I-I don't know. I just... I didn't want him touching you."

"And why not?" she yelled, pushing at his chest in anger. "You're always being felt up by strangers and feeling them up in return. You're always taking them back to your room for sex. You don't think I know about all of them, do you?" She pushed his chest again, harder, in fury. "I came to your room after opening night and *I heard you.*"

Now her eyes were sparkling with what Noah could only assume were unshed tears. Guilt twisted like a knife in his gut.

"I heard you in there, having sex, if you want to call it that. It sounded horrible and debasing to me, but what do I know? Always having a one night stand and meaningless sex with stranger after stranger, aren't you? Does that feel *good* to you, Noah? Is that how you prefer it, with girls who will never really know you, girls who won't ever really care about you, girls who want to be choked out and smacked around? Does that actually feel good to you?" Her voice cracked on that last question, and his heart right along with it.

"Lainee," Noah said helplessly, her accusations hitting like rapid-fire stab wounds to the heart, making him quickly bleed out. They pained him to his soul because they were both truthful and laced with her pain. *Oh, Christ.* She had come to his room opening night? *Why had Lainee come to his room that night?* She'd heard him having sex with that sadistic girl whose name he couldn't even remember now. The girl had been loud and profane, and he'd been weak and submissive, powerless to her distasteful biding. *Jesus.* Lainee had been standing on the other side of his door, listening to that? A wave of nausea poured over him.

It sounded horrible and debasing to me, but what do I know?

Oh, God, she'd heard it all. As always, Lainee knew his darkest secrets and all of his worst sins. He felt so dirty and defiled then, like he'd prostituted himself in desperation for a little bit of a distraction from a complete stranger at the sake of Lainee's sweet and dignified friendship.

"Jesus," he whispered in horror out loud, stabbing all ten fingers through his hair in horror. He realized *that's* why she'd been pulling away. And why wouldn't she? He was thoroughly disgusting, nothing short of a male whore, really, sleeping with absolutely everyone he possibly could just to feel relatively normal and healthy. He could see the sick irony in that now.

He felt tears burn his own eyes then as he looked upon her beautiful countenance. She was so good and pure and innocent, and he was so... not. "I didn't know..." he choked out miserably. "I didn't know you were coming to my room. If I had known, I wouldn't have..." *fucked that depraved stranger...* "I-I just..." *want you...* "Lainee..."

She took in a shaky, fortifying breath then, followed by a telling step backward. "I don't know what I'm doing," she said with a rather hysterical laugh. "I'm acting crazy and I look absolutely ridiculous."

"No," Noah protested, shaking his head now, reaching out to her. "You look beautiful and sexy as hell, Lainee." *Too* sexy.

She eyed him a long time then and it reminded him of the first time she'd sized him up in Widener, seeing straight through to his blackened soul even then. And now she knew every dark and sullied spot, every ripped and haggard tear. What must she think of him now?

"You wore your hair up," he pointed out stupidly, desperately. She'd never worn her hair up before. He was proud of her because he knew how much courage it took for her to do that. "You look so pretty, just like I knew you would."

She looked close to tears again and Noah felt like a helpless bastard as his chest tightened painfully. Why was he always hurting Lainee? Why was he always selfishly keeping her from other guys and cock blocking them when he pretty much jumped on every female in sight *except* her?

He didn't have any of these answers. He didn't understand any of it, but he didn't want to share her. *She's mine*, he suddenly thought out of nowhere, scaring the hell out of himself. He shook his head at that invasive, crazy thought. *Fuck, where did that come from?* She already had too much power over him and here he was fighting the urge to hand himself over to her completely, heart, body and soul, as if she would even have him. *Would* she even have him?

Lainee reached her hand up then and unwound her hair. It fell seductively down around her face and shoulders and his whole body tightened in physical response. "I'm not sexy," she told him then, truly not knowing her own beauty, her own worth. "I'm just a foolish girl pretending to be in the dim light of a dark bar." He started to protest again but she cut him off quickly. "Do you know I haven't kissed anyone since the accident... until you kissed me."

Noah looked at her in confusion. He hadn't kissed her, except for that silly one for his paparazzi prank... Then realization hit him and he cursed under his breath. *Goddamnit.* That had been her first kiss in five years since the car accident? He'd been so careless, so stupid with her all along, he realized. She was too innocent, too good for him... but then *she* had kissed *him* on that bathroom floor... What could *that* possibly mean?

Lainee looked at him expectantly then. Noah's gut twisted in fear and his shoulders hunched slightly at the sheer weight of the moment that was suddenly thrust upon him and resting squarely on his weak back like an uncomfortable albatross.

She was in his head, in his heart, always, but he wasn't sure what to do with it, what to do with her and her kiss. He was so fucking afraid in that moment of ruining everything that he completely froze.

I can't lose her, he thought in desperation once again. And yet, he suspected he was perilously close to doing just that.

CHAPTER 29

Noah was practically choking on all of his bad decisions leading up to that moment: all of the throw-away girls just to prove he was a man; that stupid, careless kiss he'd planted on Lainee for attention from complete strangers; all the recent tender but unspoken emotions.

No one and nothing mattered like Lainee did right now. She was the one thing he absolutely couldn't lose. She was the one person who saw him, knew him, and really cared for him anyway. She was a merciful angel who actually made him feel something good among this shit show of a life.

Did she even *want* him to kiss her, after seeing him with all those other girls, after hearing what she'd heard that night after the show, after watching his father touch him like he had? Noah honestly couldn't see how she could find him desirable in the least. He was dirty and defiled and she was so good and clean. She couldn't possibly want him to touch her... could she?

So now here he was, standing uncertainly in front of her, speechless, helpless, petrified of the suddenly shifting plates beneath his feet. The very foundation of his world was cracking. He was afraid to make even the tiniest move for fear it would all come crumbling down around him, for fear he'd be demolished right along with it or, worse, exiled from this his homeland. And so he did nothing. He didn't even fully breathe.

When Noah didn't respond for long moments, Lainee gave up. "This," she said, gesturing at the small space between them, "this can't happen. This has to stop or we're going to ruin everything." It was a vow she was making to herself more than him. She had to stop this madness *now.*

She turned and began to walk away from him then and Noah felt an instant tide of hysteria swell up in his chest cavity. She was slipping away from him once and for all. "Lainee, please, let me drive you back to campus." *Don't leave me,* he screamed in his head.

"I'll walk," she told him flatly, not looking back. "I'll see you tomorrow in the library."

"Lainee, please," he called after her a few times but she was clearly done waiting for him to catch up and be a better man.

Still, he followed her in his car all the way back to campus, slowly creeping a few paces behind her in his BMW. She did an amazing job of ignoring both her aching feet and his very existence despite the obvious crunching of the earth beneath his car tires a few feet behind her.

Once on campus, she walked off in the direction of her dorm room without a backwards glance and he let her go without a word, completely and utterly out of his league with this girl and the whole damn situation. *But that is really nothing new, is it, asshole,* he thought with quite a bit of self-derision.

When she was safely inside her dorm, Noah turned his car around and drove straight back to the bar.

Noah rarely drank to excess, partially because of his proclivity for puking but mostly because he was unable to push the tide of horrific memories back into the recesses of his brain when he was straight-out drunk. Still, he planned on getting shit-faced now and damn the consequences that followed.

He ordered a shot, a beer and then another shot within the first fifteen minutes as he sat in their usual seats at Brew Hall, all alone, nursing another beer and contemplating the ridiculous scene that had unfolded right there not even an hour ago.

Noah stabbed his fingers through his hair and was annoyed for once when a girl approached him asking for a picture. He gritted his way through it and got rid of her as quickly as possible, not his usual bombastic, flirty self. Then he flipped up the hood of the sweatshirt he was wearing in an attempt to hide from the rest of the world.

As the drunken distortion began to mess with his mind, he ordered another beer. He was a lousy, miserable drunk and he knew better but he couldn't stop because he couldn't cope. Images flooded through his mind of Lainee's hurt eyes and direct words. He'd been her first kiss since the accident? He'd been the only one to kiss her in *five years*? He fucked that up royally, carelessly planting one on her without a care in the world. She had paid a price for his stupid publicity stunt in more ways than one. He was such a callous fucking idiot. It was a bloody miracle she'd put up with him this long, actually.

Noah put his head in his hands and wondered in frustration, *but what the hell does she want from me now?* He had obviously hurt and disappointed her - again - but he had no clear idea what she expected of him now. Did she *want* him to kiss her, for real this time? Was she feeling a pull like he was? And, if so, was it really a good idea to even go there? His instincts forewarned him it would ruin everything because he would certainly fuck it up. He clearly wasn't the steady-boyfriend type and he'd rather cut off a limb than ruin their precious friendship. Or taint her.

All he knew for certain as he threw back another shot and the room tilted on its axis was that he didn't fucking deserve her. He was... corrupted... stained. He was also good and drunk now and in no shape to drive back to campus. So, of course, who did he call for help? Did he call Ryker or one of his other lacrosse teammates who were surely up and out this time of night? Nope. He called Lainee, and she picked right up even though they'd had a fight and she'd clearly been sleeping.

"Noah?" she whispered groggily. "Are you alright?"

"Laineeee," he drawled out in answer, "I'm druck." He sighed and said her name again, struggling to remember what else he wanted to communicate. Oh, yeah, he fucking loved her. "Sooo much," he slurred. *My fucking sexy warrior*. He closed his eyes and rubbed his aching chest then.

With that, he hung up and ordered another shot but the bastard bartender wouldn't serve him another one. He got a fucking water instead and he hung his head, sipping the clear liquid and feeling sorry for himself.

Unwillingly, as his defenses went down, those dangerous memories from the dark past began to push their way forward to the present. Noah shook his head now, trying to dislodge them, but it was impossible. They were embedded in his brain matter now.

No, he didn't want to think about it, any of it, that closet in his bedroom where he frequently was imprisoned, his fucking father's sadistic mind games that only got worse and more humiliating the older he got, his father feeling him up while Lainee watched from the doorway. But they were all right there, tormenting him and demanding his attention, especially now that his mind swirled out of control into dizzying drunkenness.

The beatings with a wooden paddle and leather belt in elementary school combined with being locked in closets and crawl spaces for hours at a time had conditioned him to fear his father's wrath, but it was the mind games that dear old dad would deploy later on that would really have Noah loathing his guts and, worse, so much worse, despising himself, too.

These evil remnants of horrors past slipped through his shaking grasp now as the room spun around him and he was assaulted once again.

◆◆◆

He was in middle school and his father came into his bedroom and demanded he undress. Noah stood there completely exposed for the first time and horrified as his father took his time studying him. His dad walked around his naked, pubescent body, looking at the progress of his genitals then and intermittently as Noah struggled through the phases of adolescence. His father had plenty of commentary but didn't touch. Noah supposed he should have been grateful for small mercies even as the humiliation occurred repeatedly as he grew up.

Then he was in high school and his father's cruelty seemed to know no bounds. As Noah had morphed from boy to young man, suddenly he found himself growing taller, stronger, more muscular. His startling good looks made him the center of attention wherever he went. It was quite unintentional and unnerving at first. Soon, he began to revel in it, though, crave it even, both positive affirmation from females and audiences alike.

He threw himself into theater as that came quite naturally to him and the accolades on the side were very much needed to survive his harsh and humiliating home life. Noah also treasured the escapism of it all. He was grateful to shed his own skin even if just for a few hours while he morphed into a character. Ironically, it made him feel less distorted to be someone else, anyone else, and to have an audience clapping their approval all the while. Unfortunately, his popularity also incited jealousy and more cruelty in his old man.

Noah tried so damn hard to pretend like he was just a normal, happy-go-lucky high schooler, pasting a smile on his face for the outside world and trying to take advantage of his popularity to make himself feel just a little bit better. He threw a couple of pool parties his freshman year and valiantly tried to ignore the fact that his father leered suggestively at every bikini-clad teenage girl in his class. Then his father coerced a few of the girls into his bed to Noah's utter horror and disgust. And he stopped having pool parties after that.

His junior year, he made the crucial mistake of bringing his first girlfriend home after school one day. He tucked her away in his bedroom, having no intention of introducing her to his parents. He did this for several weeks and they simply did homework and kissed, fooling around with clothes on. Then, finally, Noah found the courage to ask her if they could do more, if she was ready, and she all but leapt at him, ripping both his and her clothes off eagerly.

It felt so good as they lay in his bed and pressed together naked, skin on skin for the first time. They touched each other carefully, exploratory, excited they would lose their virginity to each other. They were kissing, him on top as she opened her legs for him.

Nervous but excited, Noah clumsily attempted to slip on a condom, just like he'd practiced. After a few fumbling minutes, his girlfriend offered her eager but equally inexperienced assistance. It took both of them a few more minutes to get the damn thing on. Then, about to burst at the seams after just having her hands all over his hard cock, Noah slowly, carefully inserted himself inside her, again needing quite a bit of her eager help.

He took in a huge, shaking breath once sheathed inside and had the wherewithal to ask her, "Is this okay?"

She nodded and thrust her hips up, making him about come right then and there.

"Jesus," he bit out, trying desperately to hold his orgasm at bay. He had no idea what he was doing but he knew coming two seconds after entering a girl was not a good experience for her.

She moved her hips again and Noah was lost despite his best intentions. He couldn't pull the thundering tide back as it crashed over him and had him shaking and moaning helplessly between her legs. He poured himself into the condom inside of her.

He laid over her panting after the orgasm had ravaged his body, careful not to put his full weight on her. Slowly the embarrassment crept up, making him apologize profusely.

She was sweet and told him it was a compliment he had come so quickly, then she guided his head down between her legs and encouraged him to use his tongue. Again, he had no idea what he was doing so it took longer than it probably should have, but eventually she grabbed on to his hair and called out his name and her *body shook this time.*

After she had quieted, Noah looked up at her from in between her legs and grinned in satisfaction. He was pretty proud of himself, he wasn't going to lie. They immediately made plans to do it again the next day after school.

After she dressed, she kissed him goodbye with a satisfied smile at the front door and he wore a matching one.

After she'd gone, Noah decided to get a sandwich from the kitchen as he was suddenly ravenous. But as he made his way through the house, he heard his dad calling out for him from his first-floor office, making Noah's steps falter and his smile slip clean away.

Reluctantly but dutifully he walked to the office. He stood in the doorway, not wanting to venture in any further than he had to. He was always leery of getting too close to his father, though the physical beatings were now few and far between, probably because he surpassed his father's height now at 6'2".

"Yes?" Noah asked stiffly from afar. His father sat behind his desk, watching something intently on his computer screen.

Then Noah's ears picked up on a strange noise coming from the speakers. Was that panting, and groaning? What the hell was his father watching, he thought in disgust. Porn? Why the hell had he called him in here if he was watching porn? Warning bells were starting to clang in Noah's brain and he took a hesitant step backward.

The he heard it. His own voice, coming from the computer speakers, "Is this okay?" Then after a few more seconds he heard himself calling out "Jesus!" The stark sounds of his climax followed.

Noah's face blanched and he thought his knees might buckle right then and there with the dawning reality of what was happening. Right now on his computer screen, his father was watching him and his girlfriend's first sexual experience that had just taken place in his bedroom a few moments before.

CHAPTER 30

"Y-you have cameras in my room?" Noah whispered in horror, already knowing the answer, already pushing back the nausea that threatened to have him vomiting right there on the threshold of his father's office.

His father tsked as he continued watching the screen with singular focus and he simply responded, "Better luck next time, son." He finally looked up and snickered at him. "Maybe I'll give you a few pointers so that you won't embarrass yourself again and ejaculate as soon as you stick your dick in her."

Noah's head was spinning then and he stumbled backwards. Oh my God. His father had been watching them the whole time. His father had seen his girlfriend's naked body, had watched him struggle through his first time. He'd had eyes on him when he'd lain between her legs and gone down on her.

Noah knew he was going to be sick then and he stumbled back to his room and made it just in time to the toilet in his adjoining bathroom. He was done emptying his stomach but still kneeling before the toilet weakly, in a daze, when his father appeared in the bathroom doorway, actually laughing at him.

"You're so weak and pathetic," he told him then, and not for the first time. "Get your shit together," he ordered. "For God's sake, masturbate before she comes over tomorrow so you can actually hold out longer than a fucking second. " He shook his head at him. "It's

almost hard to watch but I guess I can suffer through it one more time." With a smug smile, he turned and walked out.

Noah had no doubt his father was going right back to his office to watch it again, his most private, intimate moment displayed across the bastard's computer screen. Then it dawned on him, all of the times his father had been an invisible voyeur inside the sanctuary of his private bedroom, seeing him naked frequently, masturbating quite a bit, crying occasionally, and now his first sexual experience. His father had pulled up a front row seat and had been watching him this whole time without his knowledge.

Noah laid his head on the toilet seat and cried.

He never invited his girlfriend back again, or any girl after that.

He searched and found several cameras in his bedroom, his bathroom even. He angrily ripped them all out but he never felt safe again. He assumed his father would just put up new cameras and he made it a daily routine to look high and low. Sure enough, from time to time he'd find new cameras, rip them out, only to find new ones again.

Noah thought that was the worst of it, that gross violation of his privacy, and his girlfriend's, but there was still more mind games to be played, more torture for his father to bestow upon his favorite subject.

Not long after Noah started ripping the cameras out, his father started showing up in his bathroom when he was mid-shower. Noah would freeze in horror and humiliation, turning away from his leering eyes.

But his father would just stand there, arms crossed, watching him in what appeared to be disappointment, looking him over head to toe, his eyes lingering on his genitals. Noah would quickly finish up and grab a towel, wrapping it around his waist as he dripped water all over the floor.

His father would let him pass by into his bedroom but not without a brush of his hand, and Noah would stumble hastily into his room to pull on boxers underneath the towel, followed by a shirt and pants. Noah couldn't get dressed quickly enough as his clothes stuck to his dripping wet body. Then his father would leave without a word. This repeated until eventually Noah was taking his showers only in the gym locker room at school.

And then, of course, just weeks prior, his father grabbing him, rubbing him, while Lainee watched.

◆◆◆

Now in the bar, Noah put his spinning head in his hands as these horrific, defining moments brutally assaulted him once more. Fuck his life. He didn't think he could bare it another goddamn moment.

"Noah."

Suddenly Lainee was there, touching his arm, looking at him so tenderly as she took in his wet, red eyes, his disheveled appearance, his haunted features. How had Noah been reduced to this in just the few hours since she'd left him, she wondered sadly. She was heavy-hearted as she recognized that she'd had something to do with it. She immediately felt remorse for changing the rules on him earlier that evening and acting not quite like herself.

She sat on the bar stool next to him then and touched his cheek tenderly. "Are you okay?" She had nothing but love for him now and always. She shouldn't have pushed for more because what they had was already enough.

"Lainee?" Noah asked, blinking in surprise. Was she really there or a figment of his desperate imagination? He felt her gentle fingertips on his cheek. He reached up and covered her hand with his and acknowledged, gratefully, that she was real.

He was so relieved he wanted to cry. She was here suddenly as if dropped from the heavens out of pure pity for his poor, stained soul. He was just sober enough to take stock of what she must be seeing as she looked at him now.

He pushed his hood back and ran his fingers through his hair as if straightening his appearance would make him seem less pitiful. He knew it was a lost cause, *he* was a lost cause, and asked quietly, brokenly, with a great deal of shame, "Why do you always have to see me at my worst?"

She ran her fingers gently through his hair then, as if trying to help him straighten himself up.

"Why do you have to see me at all?" he asked rather angrily then, only slurring a little bit now as the couple glasses of water the bartender had shoved at him began diffusing the alcohol in his veins. Noah was suddenly furious that Lainee was looking at him and seeing into his bleeding, hideous soul yet again, that she'd insisted on it from day one. "I'm a fucking mess."

"I see you," Lainee confirmed quietly, standing up and taking two steps towards him until she was standing between his legs, a mere inch away. She framed his face and told him gently then, "I see you and I love what I see, Noah Bernard Riley. You're a beautiful man, inside and out."

What was left of his heart shattered into a million pieces. *How could that possibly be true,* Noah wondered as he pulled her to him in a fierce hug, his face resting on her chest.

"Lainee," he whispered with rising panic, his voice cracking as he remembered all of the haunting memories again, always there circling his thoughts like vultures waiting to dine on the scraps of goodness he managed to carve out with her help, "I'm a fucking shadow. Who am I when no one is watching?"

She pulled back then to kiss him on the lips, in empathy, in love, because she absolutely had to. Heart, mind, body and soul demanded it of her. "You're a human being just like the rest of us," she insisted, "scarred but still beautiful. You're my best friend, Noah, and hands down my favorite person on the face of this earth. *That's* who you are." She was more than happy to remind him.

He looked up at her in sheer disbelief, wondering once more how any of that could possibly be when he so obviously wasn't anything special. Just the opposite, in fact. He was a piece of shit and didn't deserve her. But he was buzzed and needed her so fucking badly right now, so he pulled her down for another kiss, telling her desperately, "Ditto, Lainee. Ditto." He laid his forehead on hers and tried to breathe her in, her sweetness, her goodness, her kindness and love. "Help me feel something good again," he begged her on a whisper.

And then she was kissing him hard and passionately, taking what she had wanted to take since she'd put her hair up and slipped on tight leather pants that she'd borrowed from her roommate earlier that evening. She also gave him what he so desperately asked for in return, something good, so damn good, it pushed the haunting memories away slowly but surely.

As they kissed for long, hungry moments, their hands grabbing on to each other rather desperately, the ghosts finally began to retreat back into the recesses of his brain. Noah was so damn grateful. He knew then that he'd be able to get through the next few moments after all. He hadn't been so sure of his survival before Lainee's arrival.

She paid his bar tab then and helped him up off the stool. He flung his arm across her shoulders and she half carried him to his car, where she awkwardly shoved his heavy weight into the passenger seat.

She drove him back to Dunster and half dragged him up a couple of floors, avoiding the elevator on his behalf, though using it would have been much easier on her. She unlocked his door with her key, then gently helped him into his bed. She made him take an Advil and a few sips of water before he passed out.

CHAPTER 31

Noah overslept and missed his first two classes the next day, still hung over even after puking several times throughout the night. He was completely miserable, especially as Lainee was nowhere to be found and wasn't responding to his texts. Again.

He slipped on sunglasses, took some more Advil and then headed to the library early for their tutoring session. For once he arrived before her and he waited on pins and needles. He was beyond relieved when she came marching in, prim sweater and penny loafers, and said casually but meaningfully, "Shall we get back to work?"

He nodded, letting out a breath he didn't realize he was holding. He didn't say much throughout the next two hours but neither did she. Both of them were processing, avoiding, afraid and unsure of what was changing between them. Finally, as they stood to gather up their things and leave, Noah touched her hand and asked quietly, "Will you still come tonight to the show? Please?"

He knew it was totally unfair of him, that he asked for far more than he gave, yet he couldn't help himself. He just didn't like who he was without her at his side. And what he was really asking her to do was not give up on him.

She held his gaze for the first time since she'd arrived and slowly nodded. She could never deny him her support and friendship, nor would she ever completely give up on him, but she quickly declined coming backstage afterwards.

She didn't come to his room later that night either, though Noah waited alone, worrying and hoping in equal measure.

As the days went by, fall commenced and turned the Cambridge air crisp and clean. The leaves became strikingly colorful across campus and Noah and Lainee slowly eased back into their partnership with more defined boundaries. They eventually met in Noah's room again versus the library but Lainee didn't go to the bar with him anymore. She'd play cards in his room but she wouldn't play pool in the common area, where his admirers were sure to flock to him. She came to most of his performances but she never came backstage.

Noah understood and respected these new boundaries. Though his heart ached a little from the distance she was putting between them, he was just grateful and relived to have her in his life at all. For now it was more than enough, more than he deserved, and he never pushed. He also never brought another girl back to his room again.

Soon Thanksgiving break was upon them and Noah felt ill as he got the royal family summons in the form of a hissing, venomous voicemail. His father was pissed he'd been ignored as long as he had by both Noah and Lainee. The old man made it perfectly clear it was mandatory for Noah to come home for Thanksgiving. There would be dire consequences to pay if he didn't, his father threatened, and Noah believed him without question. His father never bluffed, after all, and punishing him was his favorite past time.

"I don't know if I can face him," he told Lainee quietly in his room after listening to the message, his gut twisting in that all too familiar response of loathing mixed with genuine fear that his father invoked.

They were sitting cross-legged on his bed, facing each other and having an informal picnic of fruit snacks, popcorn and hot tea while listening to the soothing synth-symphony of the MIDI sprout and doing homework.

"What's wrong with me?" he asked quietly. "Why can't I stand up to him?" All awkwardness over the last few weeks since they'd kissed in the bar was completely forgotten by them both in that instant. They were still in the foxhole together, and that's all that truly mattered. "I'm a fucking conditioned coward," he bit out angrily.

Lainee reached across the small space and grabbed both of his hands in hers, telling him vehemently, "That isn't true, Noah! There's absolutely nothing wrong with you. He's a sadistic monster and you have the keen intelligence and honed survival instincts to stay away."

There she is, Noah thought in sweeping relief as he squeezed her hands gratefully. *There's my girl. Beautiful and badass.* Lainee was back to holding his hand and coming to his defense. Damn if he didn't love her for it. He'd missed his champion, his little warrior, though he'd known even in the more awkward, quiet last few weeks that she was always ready by his side for when he really needed her.

"Don't go," Lainee said then, still clasping his hands. "We can go anywhere, you and me, Noah. Let's go to the west coast, or south, where it's warm. We'll go to the beach." That appealed to her for so many reasons. Lainee could keep Noah safe that way, and spend one on one time with him. She could also strategically avoid her mother and her intrusive, extended religious "family." Besides, her mother was going on some kind of spiritual retreat day of. She was going to be alone and turkey-less unless she stuck with Noah. And Lainee was more than happy to be stuck with Noah if she allowed herself to admit it again. Whereas before alone and lonely had been her favorite place to be, now it was at Noah's side. Still. Always.

Noah looked at her and his heart leapt at the idea. Thanksgiving with Lainee, just him and her on the run, far away from all that haunted and persecuted them. It would be a dream come true. Then he remembered sadly, "He controls my money and pays for all of this. I just need to get through college and then..." he trailed off miserably. He knew he needed to take his father to court to get control over his own finances and yet he never took that first step. "I'm such a coward," he whispered again with self-loathing. It was the tape on loop in *his* head since he was a kid. He was weak and pathetic. He wasn't a man. He was no one and nothing. It went on and on, in his father's voice.

Lainee could not bear to see him beaten down by his dad yet again and she jumped in with conviction, "You are not a coward in any way. I'll go home with you and we'll face him together, you and me, Noah. You go to war, I go to war, remember?" She squeezed his hands reassuringly. "And after the holidays, after New Year's, you will file those legal papers to get emancipation. If you need money for a lawyer, you can borrow some of the money your father has been paying me. There's some kind of cosmic justice in that, I'd say. We could probably even use the lawyer from my hometown that I do billing for and get a nice discount." It was what she was good at, a step by step plan that allowed them to meet their objective, together. "That's what we'll do, okay?"

Because she said "we" Noah nodded. He could handle anything as a "we" with his best friend who was so brave and fearless at his side. "Okay," he said quietly. "Thank you, Lainee." How had he ever survived without her? He honestly couldn't remember.

She leaned over and pulled him in for a fierce hug then,

finally forgiving him for his insensitivity and the pain he'd unknowingly caused her these last few weeks. She let go of all the unanswered questions that swirled between them. This right here, what they already had, was more than enough. It was everything.

Noah held on to Lainee and breathed in fully for the first time in days, weeks really. She was hugging him again, and thank God for it. He had missed her so damn much even though she'd been right there beside him the whole time. He knew then that they would be okay. She was still in his corner. She was still his rock. They were still a "we."

He acknowledged as he held on tightly to her that he was so fucking heavy and she carried him too often. It was unfair of him to ask this of her and yet he couldn't seem to bear the weight of his life all on his own. He didn't think he could go home without her.

"Noah," she said softly then, "how bad did it get growing up?" She needed to know the extent of what he was dealing with, if not necessarily the specifics, so that she could help protect him from his father when they walked into that house of horrors soon. And she just wanted to share his pain, whatever he was willing to bring out into the light of day.

Noah pulled away to look at her. Lainee's kind eyes reminded him that he could trust her, always, with anything, even this. Especially this. Still, he licked his lips nervously and tried to be matter-of-fact while sparing them both some of the more unpleasant details. "He... locked me in dark closets all throughout my childhood, beat me frequently. He always berated me, telling me I was worthless and hard to love." He looked away then. "When I was in high school, he... he hid cameras in my room. I didn't know at first that he was watching me, and after I ripped them all out he'd just put more in. H-he'd come in and watch me shower. " The bile rose in the back of his throat as he added, "He started... touching me a little like... when he came here a few weeks ago. Usually, though, he just gets off on humiliating and controlling me from afar."

Lainee took in a shaky breath, threading her fingers through his in support. Now all the lamps always on at nightfall, his claustrophobia and the three to four showers a day made complete sense. So, too, did his pension for sex without any real intimacy.

"He's a legitimate sociopath utilizing psychological warfare on you," Lainee pointed out quietly as a fury like she'd never felt before began to take hold of her on his behalf. "Your father's tactics are so insidious and undermining." It was almost brilliant, actually, in the worst, most hideous and perverse way possible.

She gripped his hands tighter. "He's cruel and abusive, Noah. The evil, the broken humanity lies within *him*, not in you. I hope a part of you has always recognized that to some degree?" She thought of Noah having to deal with this kind of abuse all throughout his life, even as a little boy, and she wanted to cry.

He kissed her hand, relieved once more that she wasn't turning away from him in horror, that she was trying to reassure him after his uncomfortable confession.

"I'm trying to, Lainee. I'm trying to separate myself from him and what he did to me. It's not always easy." Noah needed her to know something else. "I-I haven't had a girl in my room since opening night." He looked down at their interlocked hands in embarrassment. "I've been trying to prove I'm a man, you know... in control... but it wasn't helping. It wasn't... meaningful or fulfilling, really. So I'm not going to do that anymore." He looked up, his face flushed, his eyes eager and apologetic, "I just wanted you to know."

They stared at each other for awhile, both of their hearts in their throats, as they waded through what was being said, what was being felt. Something was shifting between them again with Noah's last confession. He was pushing aside something unhelpful, unhealthy and rather hurtful to make room for... something else. What that something else would or could be, neither of them knew quite yet. Still, Lainee felt hopeful, loved and respected by Noah. She felt valued by him in a brand new way.

She nodded and whispered with butterflies in her stomach, "Okay, Noah." Then a smile slowly grew on her flushed face, making his heart flip flop. "Thank you for telling me."

They were staring at each other smiling then, both light-hearted after a long, stressful two weeks of walking on egg shells around each other. Then Noah thought about Thanksgiving with his father. The old man was always close by, ready to ruin any peaceful reprieve.

Noah's smile slipped and he said, "I swear my father is always here, hanging over my head. I know it sounds stupid but I swear I can still feel him watching me sometimes-" Suddenly Noah stilled, his whole body tensing, as he slowly replayed his own words over in his head very carefully. *I can still feel him watching me... he usually just gets off on humiliating and controlling me from afar...*

Then a recent memory scratched away at him uncomfortably, making him search and grasp for it. What had his father said about Lainee when he was here last?

His father in his room, in his face, his hands on him, hissing, *"It's no wonder you can't even close the deal with that disfigured tutor of yours."*

Noah surged off the bed then and dove for the bookshelves butted up against the opposite wall, facing them. He threw every single item off each of the shelves searching like the madman he was fast becoming once and for all at his father's hands.

"Noah?" Lainee asked uncertainly, still sitting on the bed, her head cocked to the side in confusion. He was ripping books off the shelves at a frantic pace, throwing aside his many theater awards and plaques as if they were meaningless. What was going on?

Then suddenly Noah found it, as he knew he would. He ripped out a camera from the corner of the middle bookshelf and laughed bitterly as he threw it down on the floor and crushed it into a dozen pieces underneath his foot. "Motherfucker," he growled as he kept stomping away on the shattered camera.

Lainee came to his side then, touched his arm and asked in horror as she glanced down at the mangled electronic, already knowing and dreading the answer, "Is that... is that a camera?"

Noah laughed rather hysterically then, feeling dangerously close to losing his shit. Once again he was as angry at himself as he was his father. That was the ultimate magic in his father's fucking mind tricks. At the end of the day, Noah had no choice but to hate himself, too. "I should have known he'd put hidden cameras in my dorm room, too," he spat in disgust. "I am such a fucking idiot."

Then he was tearing through the rest of his room and his adjoining bathroom, upending every single item, looking through every single nook and cranny, even light fixtures and switches. Lainee helped him with his methodical search but, surprisingly, neither found another camera. There was just the one, on his bookshelf, pointing straight at his bed.

CHAPTER 32

Lainee looked uncertainly at Noah as they stood in the middle of the trashed suite. She didn't know what to do or say. He was panting and looking around with wild eyes, ready to murder in cold blood. She wasn't scared of him in any way, she just didn't know what he needed from her in this unprecedented, brutal moment.

She couldn't fathom how violated he must be feeling *again*, and all those poor girls that he'd had in his room... being watched by his father... Lainee felt sick to her stomach. She knew Noah with his sensitive gut would be feeling much, much worse. She suddenly rifled through her memory files trying to recall what she had done and said unknowingly in front of that camera herself.

Luckily, she and Noah had never even kissed here in his room. Still, they'd shared many private thoughts, feelings and secrets, sitting on that bed as they'd studied and hung out. And she'd taken care of him there when he'd been sick, too. That was all almost more intimate than sex. The thought of his father watching them, listening in on their private, vulnerable moments, made her ill. He tainted the sweet, joyful memories instantly and invaded their private sanctuary, stripping them of its safety in an instant. His psychological warfare tactics were beyond ruthless and effective.

"Oh, Noah," Lainee whispered achingly then, touching his arm, at a loss for words. "I'm so sorry."

Noah felt like screaming and raging and wrapping his fingers around his father's fucking throat and squeezing until all of the life went out of him. He'd fucking kill him this time. He would. He couldn't go on like this another moment or he'd lose his goddamn mind.

"We'll go back for Thanksgiving," Noah vowed quietly, "and I'll finally face him and demand control over my own money. And then I'll kill him."

◆◆◆

Three months after meeting the distasteful and extremely expensive Rileys, Lainee was walking up the sprawling white porch steps of their mansion on the southwestern tip of Cape Cod, about to have Thanksgiving dinner with them.

No one could have been more surprised than she at this turn of events, though his parents were plenty taken aback when she followed Noah through the front door and stood at his side in the expansive, white-marble foyer underneath the grand, glowing chandelier.

His flaky, tipsy mother recovered nicely, giving her a rather overzealous embrace. His father, on the other hand, was clearly none too pleased to see her. Not only did he dislike surprises, he disliked her specifically. He was scowling at her like the menacing bully he was.

Lainee only stood taller, boldly looking him in the eye as she stood by Noah's side and held his hand. She could practically read the arrogant man's thoughts as she evenly held his angry stare.

This audacious fucking imp always has the nerve to disobey me, with an infuriating knack for interfering in my *business with* my *son.* That's what Richard Riley was thinking. He was really beginning to dislike the bitch, and now he had to stare across his Thanksgiving table and look at her disfigured face? It was unforgivable. He began to rue the day he'd tracked her down and hired her.

"Don't you have somewhere else to be?" he asked Lainee pointedly with a frown. "With your own family perhaps?" *Or could they not stand to look at her either?*

Lainee smiled rather smugly at him, feeling some nervousness in the evil man's presence and yet quite giddy that she was clearly getting under his skin. This was their own undermining psychological warfare tactic in defense of his, and it was working just fine. She explained to him rather cheerfully that it was just her and her mother, who'd be at a church retreat, so she was taking advantage of Thanksgiving break to help Noah prep for upcoming exams.

"I just want to make sure you're getting every cent worth of what you're paying me to tutor your son, Mr. Riley," Lainee pointed out with a sugary-sweet voice that no one in that sterile foyer was buying. "Besides, I enjoy Noah's company so much." She laced her fingers through Noah's then, making him glance at her for the first time since they'd crossed the threshold. "We've gotten quite close and there's no one I'd rather spend Thanksgiving with."

Noah had been stonily quiet since nearing the vicinity of his hometown and all of his bravado from the previous night seemed to be slipping away in the seething presence of his father. Not for the first or last time, Lainee cursed the bastard in her head. She pointedly added, "Noah is the most talented, enigmatic man on campus, after all, and probably in all the east coast if I'm being honest." She was really trying to goad the cocky, narcissistic man for some reason. She wasn't sure it was the smartest idea she'd ever had but she couldn't seem to stop herself. She had the overwhelming need to defend Noah as she eyed his father through narrowed, scornful eyes.

Richard Riley took in Lainee's persistent praise of his son along with her hostile stare. He understood then. Lainee had learned of his special parenting tactics, and she had to be brought under his control, too. Immediately. He'd use the most effective tools in his arsenal, he decided then and there: intimidation, fear and sheer brute force. "Yes, well, need I remind you that I'm not paying you to kiss my son's ass or suck his dick, Ms. Reed," he spat out unkindly, managing to startle her despite her mental preparations for this confrontation. "I'm only paying you to tutor him in academics, so perhaps find other plans for the holidays."

The change in Noah was instant. He went from quietly subdued to sprung tight and he took a step forward, clenching his teeth. "That's enough," he said quietly, his voice vibrating with barely controlled fury. "Don't you dare speak to her that way."

"Noah, it's okay," Lainee told him gently then, grabbing his arm and pulling him back to her side. Though she appreciated that he was coming to her defense and relieved to see him standing up to his father, Lainee didn't want a physical altercation between the two of them. She couldn't stand the thought of Noah getting hurt. And she had a sharp, uncomfortable feeling his father was capable of physical violence to an extent Noah, and any normal person, wouldn't be.

His father looked from him to her and then back again, scoffing, "Isn't this cute? I guess I also bought you a girlfriend, Noah. You're welcome. I hope *you're* getting my money's worth because God knows you need the help in all areas, especially the bedroom."

With that he turned on his heel and left them staring after him in stunned silence. A strained couple of minutes slowly ticked by.

"I'm so sorry, Lainee," Noah finally pushed out through gritted teeth. "This was a bad idea. We should go."

But Lainee protested, not about to throw in the towel just yet, and his mother was weeping and begging them to stay, making Noah feel guilty for leaving her alone with his brute of a father for yet another night. When he reluctantly agreed to stay, his mother immediately headed straight up to her room in her own wing of the house, far away from his father, to "retire for the evening."

"She's going to self-medicate and drink herself into a stupor," Noah said bitterly, "as she does every night." It was hard to blame her for wanting to numb herself to his father's existence but she'd been doing this since he was born, when he'd been small and helpless and had needed her so desperately.

"Hey," Lainee said gently, still holding his hand and pulling on it so he would look at her. "I'm here. You and me. We can do this. We have a plan, remember?"

Noah nodded, still feeling sick and nauseous about what they were walking into, but he resolutely grabbed their bags at his feet and lead the way up to their rooms. Because they *did* have a plan and it would result in his eventual emancipation. That truly couldn't come fast enough.

"Stay close while we're here," he ordered quietly as they walked up the winding staircase. "I'm putting you in the guest bedroom right next to me and I'll search for cameras, but just assume there are cameras everywhere, and be sure to lock your door whenever you're inside."

And as Noah said this they both had the sinking feeling that this had, indeed, been a hideous, disastrous idea.

CHAPTER 33

The next afternoon Lainee came around the corner in the large mansion, searching for Noah and trying to remember her path back to their rooms. It was too easy to get lost in this cold fortress with nothing but white at every turn. She would bet no one ever called this sterile structure "home." It was more like a creepy institution. *No wonder the white walls of Widener drove Noah slightly crazy.* It reminded him too much of this awful place.

Lainee was still trying to reconcile this empty house of horrors with the warm, charming smile that always lazily adorned Noah's handsome face back on campus. She knew with one glance, of course, that he had come from wealth like most of her fellow students. Then she discovered at that first meeting with his parents that he came from the extremely dangerous kind. In this family, money equated to power, isolation, control and cruelty. And that was just scratching the surface.

Lainee had accurately envisioned a "home" just like this one the first time she'd met the Rileys. It was stunning in its grandeur with its white marble floors and two-story -high ceilings, its sweeping staircases and over-priced sculptures and ornate artwork placed about so carefully and strategically. It was all breathtaking, overwhelming and completely void of warmth and humanity. It made her practically shudder as she walked through the cold and barren museum-like hallways.

Lainee ached for Noah the young boy who had been born into such privilege and yet deprived of all that actually mattered in childhood, security, safety, love, and acceptance. She forgave him his every fault right then and there, though truthfully they were few and far between. It was a miracle, really, that he was such a damn good man and friend considering all that he'd had to endure within these cold, heartless walls.

An hour prior, they had eaten his mother's omelets and drank cappuccinos on the enclosed veranda overlooking his vast, landscaped lawn that hugged Cape Cod Bay. His mother had quickly made herself scarce afterwards, as per usual. Noah had been quiet, subdued and solemn in some new way Lainee had never seen before. It seemed as if a dark cloud had descended over his handsome head as soon as they'd walked through the door last night, and his mood was only getting worse by the minute.

She was so used to seeing him vivacious and *on*, every head turning as he walked into a room, his thousand-watt smile always generously on display. It was like a switch had been flipped when he'd been forced to return here, the light extinguishing from his eyes and the curtain falling over his features as if hiding his true self from one harsh, abusive critic of one.

Lainee understood the urge to hide more than anyone, but over breakfast she'd encouraged Noah once again to face his father, sooner rather than later, and demand he hand over control of his own money. She doubted it would be effective, of course, but they could and would take legal action afterwards, and get the heck out of Dodge for good. For now she intuitively sensed Noah had to face his father and stand up to him once and for all, or forever regret not doing so. As it was, Noah was growing more despondent over the memories of abuse and, much worse, more spiteful towards himself. She feared he would self-destruct at some point if he didn't properly channel the hate and horror. He needed to place it all squarely where it belonged, at his father's feet.

She assumed and hoped that's where Noah was now, confronting his father and getting the painful confrontation over with. He hadn't been in his room when she'd finished showering and dressing after breakfast. She was desperate to find him as she wandered the halls, wondering if her advice in the end had been foolish and potentially dangerous. Maybe she should have told him to stay as far away from his fucked up father as he could. She should have at least insisted she be at his side at all times.

Lainee turned a corner on the first floor and saw for the first time a massive library with 2-story bookshelves that rivaled a few of the smaller bibliothecas at Harvard. It was too alluring to pass by so she took a quick detour and entered inside, admiring the nearest column of ancient spines.

She was running a finger across a row of old tomes when suddenly she heard footsteps behind her. She turned in eager anticipation but her heart fell to her feet when she saw it was the elder Riley, not the younger one. Instinctively, Lainee took a step back as Mr. Riley hovered in the doorway and eyeballed her.

She tried to school her face so as not to show any emotion whatsoever even as she was remembering Noah's orders to stay close to him while they were under that roof. How could she have been so stupid as to end up in a room in a corner of the house alone with this hideous man?

"Ms. Reed," he said coolly, glancing around to see if his son was also about. He felt a thrill of satisfaction when he discovered he was not. He was alone with Lainee for the first time. What a fortuitous opportunity.

"Mr. Riley," Lainee countered rather weakly, forgetting her usual bravado as he came closer. "Noah will be here any minute," she lied, trying to keep him at bay.

"Undoubtedly," he responded dryly, "as you two seem inseparable these days. In fact," he said, slowly closing the small distance between them, making her bump into the bookshelf behind her, "he seems quite attached and ridiculously fond of you. I wonder why that is?"

He looked her over closely, now an inch from her face, taking in her scar for long moments and then dropping his eyes to her small breasts. For the life of him, he couldn't figure it out. Noah had dated much more beautiful women than this one. That's what made the older Riley so damned intrigued.

He reached out a hand then and grasped her chin with tight, pinching fingers, making her flinch. She attempted to pull her face out of his hands but only succeeded in smacking the back of her head into the books behind her rather painfully.

"Maybe it's because you're disfigured and he takes pity on you," Richard said thoughtfully, squeezing her face and staring intently at her scar. This brought instant hot tears to Lainee's eyes, both his bruising actions and his cruel words. "Or maybe because you're an oddity that has him curious? Or, more likely, you pose a virginal challenge to conquer?"

Finally finding her voice, Lainee looked him in the eye and returned quietly, "Or maybe he's just a really good man and not a sick, sociopathic sadist like his father."

The rage was instant and Richard didn't even bother to hold back now that they were alone like this. "You insolent, ugly child," he bit out between clenched teeth. He smacked Lainee across her smart mouth with so much force her whole body slammed back into the bookshelf behind her. Then he backhanded her right across her cheek, the one with the offensive scar, jarring her head to the side and making her see instant stars.

He grabbed her face again, pinching her jaw painfully once more even as he leaned in and pressed his mouth to her ear. Lainee cried out then in both pain and fear. It was music to his ears and he greatly looked forward to teaching her this lesson and reminding her of his power. He whispered into her ear, "You *will* respect me, fear me and learn to watch your smart mouth around me, you damaged freak-"

Suddenly Noah was there and ripping his father away from Lainee, sending him flying back with so much force that Mr. Riley landed hard on the marble floor behind them with a loud thud.

Noah's eyes were wide and wild as he looked Lainee over and took in her bloody lip, the torn skin on her cheek, the tears magnifying the sheer terror in her eyes. He roared then and rounded back on his father who'd managed to get up to his feet.

"I'm going to fucking kill you," Noah seethed a mere second before his first punch landed squarely against his father's nose, crushing cartilage and blood instantly spurting. Surprised and stunned by the unprecedented attack, his father stumbled backward. Noah advanced with singular, cold focus and determination. He pulled back his fist and punched him again, this time right in the mouth, unleashing all of his strength and power, sending the elder Riley right back to the hard marble floor once more.

Mr. Riley was scooting backward on the ground as Noah kept coming for him. With more than a little satisfaction, Noah saw that his father had fear in *his* eyes for once as he came to hover over him. His old man threw his arms up across his face in protection, so Noah kicked him hard in the ribs and heard a satisfying crack followed by an immediate howl of pain.

"You shouldn't have touched her, you sick fucking bastard," Noah growled then, kneeling over his father and holding him up slightly by the front of his blood-soaked shirt. "You shouldn't have fucking touched Lainee."

Then he was punching him in the face over and over again as all the years of pent up rage and impotence, shame and helplessness poured out of him. It was cathartic vengeance at long last and he wasn't sure he'd ever be able to stop doling out his retribution, it was so long overdue. "Don't ever fucking touch her again. Don't ever touch *me* again."

Noah was panting, punching, lost in the violent fugue that was for once his own doing, when Lainee suddenly cried out his name. Somehow her sweet, high-pitched call managed to penetrate his haze of bloodlust and rage.

He turned to look at her over his shoulder, wild-eyed and panting, chest heaving, still holding the front of his father's wet and bloody shirt, his arm recoiled about to throw yet another fist in fury.

Tears were streaming down her battered face as she came closer and begged, "Noah, stop. You're going to kill him." She didn't give one good goddamn about his father dying but she certainly didn't want Noah to throw away his future on the monster. "He's not worth it."

Noah stared at her, blinked, and slowly came back to himself. As always, Lainee's voice of reason brought him back to rational thought and sanity. He looked back down at his father whom he'd effectively beat into a bloody pulp and threw him to the floor in disgust, moving off and away from him.

Noah went to Lainee then and she reached for him gratefully, still crying and shaking. They both grabbed on and pulled each other in tight for long moments. Then Noah pulled away slightly so he could rightfully take in her bruised and tattered face. *Oh, God, her beautiful face.* His father had hit her. He'd *hurt* her. Made her precious scar bleed. How could Noah have let this happen? How could he have brought her here, near that monster of a man? What had he been thinking?

Noah protectively turned her away from his immobile, collapsed father and half-carried her out of the library so she wouldn't have to be near the fucker one second more, or ever again. He took her up to his bedroom, still holding her against him, holding her up really. She sobbed against him and this pain felt so much worse than taking a beating himself.

God, he wished he'd taken the punches she'd taken. He wished to God he could absorb her fear, her bruises, all the abuse she'd just endured and take them away from her so that she was clean and untouched once more. But all he could do was helplessly hold on to her after the damage had already been done.

Eventually, Lainee quieted and Noah kissed her forehead, her temple, the top of her head. "Are you okay?" he asked gruffly as he smoothed her hair back from her face with his bloody, throbbing hand. "I'm so sorry, Lainee, so fucking sorry."

She was calming now, trying to gain the last of her equilibrium through steadying breaths as she gripped on to Noah. "I should have listened to you and not gone wandering." She buried her head in the crook of his neck and whispered, "Thank God you came when you did. I was so scared." She felt nothing but love and gratitude for him coming to her rescue but Noah knew better than to feel good about himself.

A wave of nausea hit him and he pushed it down even as he pulled her in tighter, picturing what his motherfucking father would have done to her had he not stumbled upon them when he had. He shuddered at the thought. Thank God he'd been alerted by the noise. He'd never in his life forget the sound of Lainee calling out in pain and fear.

He could have so easily killed his old man then. After enduring all of those years of abuse and the endless mind games and intimidation, the bastard hurting Lainee was what had finally broken him. Oh, yes, he could have easily killed his father in that moment if Lainee hadn't stopped him. A part of him would always regret not doing so, despite the consequences.

Noah promised her vehemently then, "We're going to get out of here, Lainee, and I swear to God you will never have to see that man again. I'm never going to let him near you." It was his solemn vow to her and to himself. For once Noah felt strong enough to see that promise through.

CHAPTER 34

They quickly gathered their things and headed out, running to the car mere minutes later.

Noah knew he was never coming back and he felt freer than he ever had as he raced down the driveway for the last time, holding fast to Lainee's hand. He gladly, purposefully, left everything from his childhood behind.

Noah drove them back to the mostly empty campus for lack of a better place to go. Lainee wouldn't entertain the idea of going to her mother's and the thought of a cold, sterile hotel room somewhere nearby didn't feel right to either of them. So it was settled. They went back to what they knew, their shared, safe space that had become their sanctuary. There were no more cameras left, they'd made sure of that, and they wouldn't let his father take that sacred space away from them.

Noah didn't release Lainee's hand the deliberately slow, quiet two-hour drive back to campus and it was still tucked up securely into his own as they made their way to his room. He never thought he'd be able to let go, actually. He needed to make sure she was safe and secure at his side at all times.

They gratefully stepped inside the safety and privacy of their suite, though it was still in shambles from when they'd tossed it looking for cameras. Noah dropped their bags just inside the threshold and locked the door behind them.

Now he turned to her and just looked solemnly at her beloved, battered face, utterly exhausted in every way and unsure of what to do next. "Come here," Lainee said quietly after a moment, pulling Noah to the bathroom with their joined hands. She gently washed his bloody knuckles as he leaned against the counter. Then he gently cleaned her bruised cheek and bloody lip in return. Lainee decided a shower would help, too, and Noah understood that all too well, the compulsion to wash away his father's bruising fingerprints and the whole fucking trauma right along with it. If only it was that easy.

He left to find her some clothes and give her privacy. As he rummaged through his drawers, looking for something small enough to fit her, Noah listened to the shower with a twisted gut. He felt absolutely ill knowing Lainee was right now trying to erase his father's touch from *her* body and get clean from him, like Noah himself had so often done throughout his life. *I never should have taken her there,* he thought in residual horror for the millionth time. He was at a complete loss over how to deal with his overwhelming guilt and remorse.

Soon, he laid out his favorite grey hoodie and joggers for her on the bathroom counter, carefully keeping his eyes averted as she showered. It was the only thing he could think of to take care of her, to comfort her, as she recovered from the last few terrible hours.

But it helped. A feeling of relief, contentment and security settled into Lainee's bruised and battered body as she stepped out of Noah's bathroom, clean and fresh, in his oversize and comfy clothes that smelled just like him.

Noah was waiting for her in matching grey joggers and a white t-shirt. He was standing frozen in the middle of the suite, unsure of what to say or do next. Of course he'd turned on every lamp so the room was lit up from wall to wall. He watched her with shadowed, solemn eyes that spoke of remorse and tenderness both. Without a word, Lainee walked over to him, gently grabbing on to his bruised and swollen hand. Then she pulled him to his cozy bed where she'd sat many days and nights on top of his red plaid comforter studying with him, studying *him*, until she knew everything there was to know about the man.

That familiarity, that intimacy was as beautiful and immense as it was uncomplicated and intense. It was love in its simplest, purest form. No one and nothing, not even his father and his systematic abuse, could diminish it. She slid under the covers and pulled gently on Noah's hand, inviting him in, too, without a word.

Noah was drained to his core after pouring every ounce of emotion and strength into the beating he'd given his father, but still he hesitated. "Are you sure?" he asked quietly, standing by his own bed in hesitation, still holding her hand.

He understood if she didn't want him in the bed with her. There were plenty of reasons for that, starting with the horrid fact that he' led her straight into danger and ending with the simple truth that she was completely different from every other girl he'd ever had lying in his bed before, but there had been many. He could sleep in the chair if she preferred. Hell, he would sleep on the floor beside her so that he could still hold her hand. Whatever she needed to feel safe.

Then Lainee did the most miraculous thing. She smiled at him. Just a small one, but it was so sweet and shy, and Noah knew she was going to be just fine. Of course she was. She was the strongest, bravest person he knew. *My little warrior.*

"I'm sure," she answered him with no hesitation, gently tugging on his hand. "Please come into bed with me, Noah."

With his heart fluttering lightly after that smile, those words, he crawled into bed with her and tucked the sheets in tight all around her. He hesitated again, unsure how and if she wanted him to touch her. She seemed so damn fragile for the first time, her face tattered and bruised as she looked up at him with big, trusting eyes, and somehow he felt like an even bigger bastard.

She trusted him and he'd waltzed her right through his father's front door and practically told the sick fucker how much she meant to him. Of course that had incentivized the elder Riley into targeting her. Noah really should have fucking known better. So if she never wanted to see him again, let alone have him touch her after his father had, he would have more than understood.

But then she gave him another gift. She turned on her right side, pulled his arm over her left shoulder and snuggled back into him, inviting him not only to touch her but to cuddle her as well. Noah was spooning her then and he felt his whole mind and body relax for the first time in hours, days really. He hugged her to him tightly with an intense mixture of relief and joy.

His father had not succeeded in taking Lainee away from him despite his best, twisted efforts. Noah honestly didn't know what he would do without her now. Could he even function if she wasn't right there by his side? She seemed like the most important thing in his world and an integral part of who he was, like a necessary limb that kept him upright. He tucked her into him as close as possible.

Lainee was giving Noah as much comfort as he was giving her. They held on tight to one another, bodies touching from head to toe. And then they were quickly falling asleep, completely worn to the bone, able to rest at long last now that they lie comfortably in each other's arms, alone and safe in the sanctuary of each other.

They slept and cuddled for days, barely moving, only getting out of bed once in awhile to use the bathroom and shower. Noah was the only one to leave the apartment, getting them food, supplies and fruit snacks as needed but always rushing back as quickly as he could.

He carefully, methodically iced her split lip, her bruised cheek and cursed his father's name while apologizing to her repeatedly. There was now a bruise over her beloved scar and it pained him far more than it did her. He really couldn't say he was sorry enough. She always hushed him, took the ice pack and laid it on his bruised knuckles, assuring him that she was fine. She also pointed out that he'd rescued her. He was always quick to remind her he'd put her in harm's way in the first place.

Though it had finally galvanized him into action, it was his burden to bear, his father's hands on Lainee. She was so quick to forgive him and move on, being the survivor, the warrior with a heart of gold that she was, but it would take him much longer to forgive himself, if he ever could.

Lainee kept reassuring Noah and trying to ease his guilt as he worked through it. She knew better than to tell him of all the horrid things his father had said to her in that library before even laying hands on her. She had a feeling if she disclosed those additional details, he'd head straight back there and finish the job he'd started. She wanted to keep Noah out of jail, so she kept that all to herself, and tossed the cruel words aside rather easily.

There had been a time when Mr. Riley's words would have crushed her soul, haunted her for lengthy weeks on end, replayed endlessly in her over-active mind, but those days were in the past. Lainee was so much stronger now, and she actually felt very little insecurity about the scar itself anymore, all thanks to Noah. She'd even stopped feeling quite as guilty for being alive when her dad wasn't, though admittedly those thoughts and feelings were much harder to cast off.

That guilt and grief would undoubtedly be with her for the rest of her life, but Noah had saved her in more ways than one. If only she could convince him of that.

On the fourth day after they'd come back to campus, Lainee woke up, turned and looked at Noah's handsome face on the pillow next to hers with a fluttering heart. She greeted him with a soft smile. "Happy Thanksgiving, Noah."

And miraculously, it did seem like a happy one. Her smile and joy were contagious. "Happy Thanksgiving, Lainee," Noah responded gruffly with his own answering grin.

His mused hair, stubbled jaw and gorgeous, thousand-watt smile had her breath catching. She hadn't seen that smile all week and she was so very grateful for it now. And he thought her immune. As if that was even humanly possible.

"I would like to walk into town today," she told him sweetly, "maybe hit our favorite diner for breakfast, if it's open, then grab a latte at Crema Cafe. Then we can scrounge up a Thanksgiving feast for the evening."

Noah's heart leapt into his throat at the pure happiness her words caused him. She was ready to leave the suite and face the outside world. His little warrior was going to be just fine.

Noah managed to squeeze out through a suddenly tight throat even as he carefully ignored his morning boner, "That sounds like the perfect way to spend Thanksgiving day with the perfect girl." *His* girl. He was quite certain he didn't deserve her as he brushed her tousled, dark brown hair back from her face and over her shoulder, but damn did he need her.

His amber eyes glowed with intensity as the morning light streamed through the window and lit him up much like a spotlight. And despite her battered, disheveled appearance that contrasted starkly against his sheer perfection, Lainee felt absolutely beautiful beneath Noah's warm gaze.

How could she not when Noah was looking at her with such exquisite tenderness and awe?

CHAPTER 35

In the end, they could only find rotisserie chicken at the local grocery store this last minute. They made stuffing out of the box as well as green bean casserole, though Noah forewarned her that there was no way in hell he was eating that green gobbledygook. He was gagging at the mere sight of it which had her giggling uncontrollably. She knew she'd have fun with his sensitive gag reflex over the years.

They were drinking their dessert before dinner in the form of delicious pumpkin-pie-tinis that Noah had thrown together at his makeshift minibar. Next, they pulled his desk to the middle of the room, threw a red plaid bed sheet over it, lit a few candles and were ready for the most spectacular Thanksgiving of their lives.

Lainee had gotten a form-fitting black dress with spaghetti straps from her own dorm room that afternoon for the special occasion. She'd also packed a few more things, finally handing over Noah's large sweatshirt and jogging pants she'd been living in for the past few days. He quickly washed them for her downstairs in the house's laundry room and gave them right back to her. He loved seeing her in his clothes and, ridiculously, he looked upon her as if she was the most dazzling creature he'd ever laid eyes on in them, though they were about three sizes too big for her.

For tonight, though, she needed her little black dress and high heels. It was a special occasion after all. She even pulled her hair up as he liked and outlined her eyes. She may or may not have been trying to dazzle him just a little bit.

When she came out of the bathroom all dolled up, Noah thought his heart would burst. "Damn, Lainee," he whispered, slowly taking her in from top to bottom as if *she* was the feast. He'd never seen her in a dress before, her long, bare legs accented by heels. It did funny things to him. "You look gorgeous." She looked heaven sent. His guardian angel.

She blushed and encouraged him to put on a suit and tie to match her formal attire. He would have lit his hair on fire if she'd asked, so suddenly besotted and in need to please her he was. Thirty minutes later, a tie around his neck, Noah looked at Lainee across their unorthodox spread, the candlelight flickering between them and reflecting in her kind, blue eyes that he adored so much. They may have been his favorite feature, besides her scar.

Her bruises were fading and almost indiscernible to the eye beneath her makeup. Her split lip was also healing, made less noticeable by her red lipstick. Neither tried to think about her injuries now. Here and now was for celebrating the moment, and each other.

Noah was in awe of how utterly beautiful Lainee was, inside and out, as she smiled at him over their Thanksgiving spread. She was just so different from everyone that had come before her and, he had no doubt, everyone that would come after. She was sweet and strong, pure and good, so damn intuitive and intelligent. He'd tried to hide in shame from her for the longest time but she hadn't allowed it. She'd insisted on seeing him, all of him, and she'd stayed by his side anyway.

Noah had never been more damn grateful on Thanksgiving day. He was also quite hopeful that this was just the first of many they'd share together.

◆◆◆

There was magic in the air as they dined and drank that holiday night. They both knew that it wouldn't ever be better than this. It was the perfect moment in time, with a palpable promise of even more things to come. Simply, it was love at first bloom.

Suddenly his father and all the accompanying horrors were so far behind them in the rearview mirror that it barely warranted another thought. The celebration was pure magic. It was practically perfect because they let themselves feel it all without fear or hesitation for the very first time. They finally, at long last, let the love in.

They laughed and ate, talked and drank, happy to sit at that makeshift table for hours. Finally, around midnight, they blew out the candles and began to gather up the food, refrigerating what they could for leftovers the next day.

Afterward, Lainee didn't pull on Noah's oversized clothes to sleep in. Instead, she stripped down to her bra and underwear right before his bulging eyes, threw on one of his t-shirts and stood before him by the bed, both of their hearts pounding in their chests.

Noah was frozen in his spot, unsure of what she wanted from him. He couldn't seem to move and yet his heart was racing uncontrollably inside his chest as he looked down at her sweet, soft lips with a fair amount of yearning. That's when he saw the cut there that his father had caused, and remembered. And ached. He had the overwhelming desire to kiss her but, more than that, he had a sharp need to wipe away the remaining shadows of his father's savage touch. He couldn't do the latter so he wouldn't allow himself the former.

After a long moment, disappointed he didn't make a move,

Lainee took his hand and ran it lightly over her right thigh and down her upper leg where she had a long scar from her surgery, when they'd pieced her pelvis and femur back together after the car accident. She had to have him see it and touch it, all of her scars, all of her damage. She had to have him be okay with it so that she could be, too. Then she never had to think about it again.

Noah allowed himself to look down for the first time, taking in her creamy thighs and long, toned legs peeking out beneath his now favorite t-shirt. He looked closely at the prominent scar that trailed down the side of one thigh, running his fingertips gently down the full length of it, understanding she needed him to see her, all of her, and accept what she deemed her ugliest parts. None of them were ugly to Noah. Not a single scar, nor one inch of her amazing body. His building lust and rock-hard cock could attest to that.

"Beautiful," he finally breathed, looking up into her face. She saw it in his eyes, his obvious appreciation and adoration of her. It never waned and she *felt* beautiful under his gaze thanks to that naked, raw look reserved there just for her.

He'd stared at her just that way the very first time they'd met, she suddenly realized, when he'd reluctantly sat down across the table from her at the library. He'd locked eyes with her, just her, in such a way that had her slowly settling into her skin, her scars, with confidence and grace for the very first time. The way this man looked at her, whether she was in her argyle sweaters, his oversize grey jogging suit or her bra and underwear... *damn*. He looked upon her as if she was the eighth wonder of the world.

Face to face near the bed, something began to swell and build between then. Lainee was confused because *of course* she was attracted to Noah. He was literally the physical embodiment of the perfect male specimen. But he'd never been attracted to her in return... right? His appreciation of her seemed more like...

adoration, like she was something precious he'd put up on a pedestal to admire but never to touch.

She couldn't understand what his eyes were saying now, as they seemed to heat and burn at the centers. His hands were definitely touching her with something less earnest than reverence and more covetous like lust as he continued to skim the back of his knuckles along the side of her scarred thigh while lightly cupping the other hip in his second hand. It was the lightest of touches that had every one of her nerve endings on fire in sensual, suspenseful yearning.

They stood there breathing heavy in silence for long moments as he held on to her hips, and then finally she bravely asked, "Noah? Do you want to kiss me?" It was a question and an invitation both.

His breath caught and his throat tightened. He didn't think he could speak, so he simply nodded. *Of course* he wanted to kiss her. She was beautiful and sexy and everything in between. She was *Lainee.* A wave of happiness washed over her and a slow smile spread on her pretty face, making his heart flutter even faster.

Finally it was his turn to confirm with bated breath, "Y-you want me to kiss you?" He'd never been more nervous in his life, nor felt more unworthy. "Are you sure?" he whispered, wanting to give her time to reconsider. "Even after what my father did to you?" Even after his dad had done much worse to *him?*

As always the ugly images were all right there, ready to assault him, one after another, ending now with the newest one of Lainee pushed against the library bookshelves by his father, her beautiful face battered, her wet eyes large and round with terror. He closed his own eyes now and shook his head as if he could possibly stop playing the unpalatable horror movie on a loop in there. As long as he lived he'd never forget the sound of her calling out in fear and pain, or the devastated look on her face when he'd come running into the library and found her there with his father.

Lainee reached up and touched his face, bringing him back to the present and making him open his eyes and look at her again. "Noah, it wasn't your fault, and you saved me from him, don't you realize?" Why wouldn't he recognize either truth, she wondered helplessly.

He was shaking his head no, rejecting that description of the horrific events. "It was all my fault, Lainee. I brought you there and waved you in front of that sadistic bastard like a shiny new toy he had to have. I was so careless and stu-"

She put a finger over his lips to cut him off. She sighed then, but patiently. "You go to war, I go to war, remember? That was my call. You should be proud of *your* actions that day, Noah. You're so busy fixating on his behavior that you're overlooking your own. Don't you yet see what you accomplished in that moment? You stood up to him, Noah. You showed him you were strong and wouldn't take his abuse for another second more." She framed his handsome, beloved face in her hands. She needed him to really focus on her next words and take them in. "Noah, your father is never going to lay a hand on either of us again. *You* did that."

Noah was completely still beneath her touch, listening intently to every word and turning them over in his mind. He hadn't really given himself time or permission to appreciate the fact that yes, in fact, he'd stood up to his father at long last. *Fucking finally.* He'd put a stop to the abuse. It was really over.

Lainee was forcing Noah to stop focusing on her injuries and acknowledge his hard-won victory. And, now that he thought about it, he did feel different. At his core. Something had shifted within him immediately after knocking his father on his ass and pummeling the shit out of him. He felt... vindicated, powerful, and in control of his own world. Most importantly, he felt *unafraid* of his father for the very first time in his life.

He had taken his life back, Noah suddenly realized with immense relief. His father would never again terrorize either him or Lainee. He'd finally put a stop to his reign of terror. Ensuring the matter, Noah would soon file the legal paperwork to get control over his own finances, and then his father would be well and truly out of his life for good.

Noah felt a ground swell of relief and hope mixed with love and, yes, lust for this incredible girl standing in front of him now, making him the very best version of himself that he could possibly be. He was definitely a fixer-upper but he liked who he was becoming. He liked who he was when he was with her. For the first time in his life, Noah was unafraid of his father *and* he mostly liked who he was. It was no coincidence both things were happening simultaneously, and that Lainee had come first. She'd been the catalyst, the inspiration, the conviction he'd needed to get here.

Noah leaned in and kissed her tenderly then, as if she were made of precious, fragile glass. They kissed for long, tender moments and then they pulled apart and just stared at each other in amazement. It was the first time they both understood and acknowledged what had been changing between them.

They were falling in love. Slowly their friendship had turned into devout tenderness and now romantic love. It was all of that with more on the horizon.

They smiled gently at each other, enjoying the dear moment with all its sweet promise and potential. Finally, Lainee pulled Noah into bed, utterly content and fulfilled, not needing to push any further beyond that perfect moment. It was all she needed. She was peacefully asleep within minutes, him warmly spooning her from behind.

It was a long time before Noah could follow suit, though, as he tried to quiet his rioting hormones and traitorous hard cock. He shifted uncomfortably, trying not to poke her from behind and scare the living shit out of her. Eventually, his mind and body relaxed against her. Then he, too, was snoring softly, completely at peace with the world for the first time in his whole godforsaken life.

CHAPTER 36

The next morning after a fabulously deep sleep, Lainee woke up in the same position she'd fallen asleep in, on her right side, her back to Noah as he cradled her so perfectly with his longer frame from head to toe. She was getting used to his comforting warmth, that full-body hug, and she quickly pushed away the intrusive, sad thought that there was only one week of Thanksgiving break left now. She couldn't detach from this dream, or Noah, just yet. It was unfathomable.

So she snuggled back further into the warm depth of him with a happy little sigh. She couldn't seem to get close enough, deep enough, though she desperately tried. She pulled his arm tighter around her shoulder and tucked into him as far as she could go. Suddenly Lainee stilled her squirming body and her eyes flew open. Noah's rock-hard erection was pressing into her backside and she was frozen like a deer in headlights.

She heard him then, taking in a quiet, steadying breath. He was awake now, too, and trying like hell to control his traitorous body. He was attempting to deep breathe his way out of his painfully hard morning erection and it was most definitely not working.

Inexplicably she rubbed her bum against his cock then, making him inhale sharply and grab a bare hip underneath the covers, saying with a sleep-gruff voice through gritted teeth, "Lainee... please stop moving."

She went still again and her heavy, rapid breathing made Noah suddenly wonder if she was afraid to feel him hard like this up against her. She was so sweet and innocent. Untouched. A rush of guilt swamped over him, because he so was not.

Noah closed his eyes now and told her sincerely, "I'm sorry, Lainee." He took in a shaky breath, trying like hell to get control over his own body. "You're just so damn beautiful. I can't control my reaction to you. But don't worry, I won't do anything."

After a long, pregnant pause Lainee suddenly moved against him slowly, purposefully rubbing his hard cock with her ass once more, making Noah groan. "What are you *doing*?" he asked her rather helplessly.

She turned then to her other side, pushing off all their covers so that she could face him head on without any barriers. Her gorgeous face was serious and flushed as she watched him closely.

"I won't do anything," he promised her again, purposefully shifting his boner away from her while simultaneously trying to stave off the beating waves of lust and desire. "You know that right?"

She bit her bottom lip and nodded. "I know that, Noah. But... do you want to? Are you... attracted to me? In that way?"

He looked at her so utterly confused then, trying like hell to mentally keep up when he was fighting his body's rioting hormones within. They shook against the bars of his tenuous restraint because Lainee was mere inches away, in his bed in very little clothing with so much bare skin showing. He kept his eyes on her face, though it was quite a bit of effort not to look down at her naked bottom half. "Of course I'm attracted to you, Lainee. You're sexy as hell."

He said it like it was the simplest, easiest truth in the world and Lainee's heart leapt. She'd always been attracted to him but she'd assumed it wasn't mutual by his lack of actual effort in that department, combined with the sheer number of lovers he'd shamelessly bedded all the while.

Lainee couldn't help herself, she looked down at his penis then, and she swore it grew a few inches bigger in his tight, navy boxers right before her very eyes. She looked back up at his face in wonder. "Wow," she couldn't keep herself from saying. That was an impressive size. And it just kept getting bigger?

Noah huffed a laughed then and turned to lay on his back, flinging his arm over his eyes as he coached himself through more deep breathing, trying like hell to pretend Lainee wasn't laying there beside him with her black lace underwear peeking out from beneath his t-shirt while she eyeballed his penis like she'd never seen one before in her life.

And then he wondered if maybe she hadn't. He lifted his arm slightly to peek at her, asking gently, "Lainee, are you a virgin?"

She bit her bottom lip again and nodded, making his heart, and his penis, swell with emotion.

"Yes and I've never... messed around much," she admitted shyly. She had never let anyone physically close enough to her to even try before. After the accident, she hadn't felt attractive enough to even touch herself. "But I'm on birth control," she mentioned pointedly, blushing even as she said it, "to regulate my periods."

Noah groaned yet again, covering his eyes back up with his arm so that he couldn't leer at her suggestively for another second longer. Of course she was a virgin. On birth control. That was his girl. She had to make this as hard as possible on him, pun intended.

A thrill ran through him as he realized he could be her first, which was definitely not helping the cause of keeping his desire at bay. And then he registered that he wouldn't have to wear a condom with her, because he trusted her implicitly and she was on birth control. He'd be able to feel every inch of her without a barrier. He groaned rather miserably beneath his arm. *In through the nose to the count of three, Riley,* he reminded himself harshly, *out through the mouth. In through the nose -*

Lainee touched his rock-hard penis through his underwear and Noah went completely rigid. He didn't even breathe.

Slowly, hesitantly, she began to rub him on the outside of his boxer briefs. Noah lay frozen, not lifting his arm to look at her, his breathing shallow. He lay very, very still, not moving a muscle.

Finally she asked shyly, "Noah? Does that feel good?"

He groaned - again - much louder with mounting frustration, and flung his arms out wide, looking at her helplessly. "God, yes," he told her, panting as she stroked him up and down the length of penis through his boxers. He was staring into her eyes but gritting his teeth and unable to form an actual sentence.

"Tell me," she encouraged. "I don't have much experience as you know." And then she did the boldest thing she'd ever done in her life. She reached down into his underwear and took hold of his penis, making him jump an inch off the bed, freeing him from the fabric of his boxers. She gripped him firmly in her fist, some ancient and natural instinct taking over, a wave of pleasure washing over her at the same time it washed over him. She knew from the expression on his face, the labored breathing, his inability to speak, that she was doing something right.

Then she began moving her hand up and down his hard, smooth shaft and Noah was losing himself completely. She stilled after a moment but only to bend down and instinctively lick around the ridge of his crown, then over his tip, with a few flicks of her tongue, wanting to taste him. He jumped again. "Jesus," he panted as she took him fully in her mouth.

She slowly scraped her teeth up his smooth shaft and he inhaled sharply from the intoxicating mix of pleasure and pain. "No teeth," he managed through a jaw that was suddenly locked tight as she continued to suck on him experimentally. His girl was a quick learner.

Finally Noah stopped her head with both his hands and said quietly, tightly, "Lainee, I can't... I can't hold out much longer. You should stop."

She lifted her head, looking so supremely thrilled by him that he had to choke out a laugh. "You mean it's that easy?" she asked him, wide eyed and pleased.

He let out a long, shaky breath as he talked himself down from the ledge. Her hand was still wrapped around his penis which didn't help matters, but at least it had gone still for the moment. "With you it is definitely that easy," he answered her tightly, almost in warning.

Suddenly she felt shy but had to ask, "Noah? Will you be my first?"

Noah gawked at her, his mouth falling open. He may even have been drooling just a little bit. He simply forgot all of his usually suave and sophisticated moves that typically came so easily if robotically. He blinked, stuttered out, "Y-your first? Lainee... are you sure? You don't have to... to feel rushed or pressured. I can... I can wait." It was Noah's turn to feel shy even as Lainee held his dick in her hand.

With all the other girls that had come before it had been easy and effortless, because Noah hadn't been emotionally invested and, frankly, he had been putting on a show. He knew exactly the role that they all expected and wanted him to play: the smooth and flawless gentleman who was dashing, confident and generous. The expert lover who knew his way around a vagina and sometimes even spouted poetry and Shakespeare for bonus passion pints. He'd been playing that specific part for so long it had gotten rather stale and less fulfilling over time.

With Lainee, she never accepted anything less than his honest, authentic, complete self. Damage and all. She had so much integrity and intelligence herself that she would not, could not, be impressed by his performance, at least off the stage. He wasn't sure he could be good enough for her in the end, and he feared he would eventually disappoint her in every way. Especially in this.

But here he was, laying with her in his bed, his heart racing uncontrollably, his cock rock hard and throbbing in her hand while she offered him her virginity. As if he could say no to that.

Noah was scared shitless. Lainee was looking down at him so sweetly, blushing and smiling, hopeful and happy. And he couldn't deny her a damn thing, not his true, damaged self, his taut and ready body, nor certainly his pumping, bleeding, responding heart.

He reached up and gently cupped her still-bruised cheek with his hand. "Are you sure?" he asked her again, in awe of the gift she was offering to him as he attempted to settle his rioting nerves.

Her smile spread and she answered confidently, "Of me and you? Absolutely, Noah Bernard Riley."

His heart swelled to maximum capacity in his chest cavity and he sat up then and gently laid her back on the bed. "Lainee," he said achingly, at a loss for words. He struggled for any that might do this moment justice, and he came up with only two. "Thank you."

He ran a gentle hand over her silky hair. He was thanking her for her friendship and loyalty, her bravery and wisdom, her stunning, beautiful body, but most of all, he was thanking her for the rare, sacred gift of seeing and knowing her, all of her in her totality.

He leaned down and kissed her then, slowly, gently, cognizant that her lip was still probably tender. She was wearing his t-shirt which looked sexy as hell on her but he wanted it off as soon as possible suddenly. He tugged at it and asked tenderly, "May I?"

She nodded and bit her bottom lip with nerves and excitement. He easily pulled the shirt up over her head and unclasped her bra. Then he was running a gentle hand over her small breasts as he murmured, "Beautiful. Absolutely beautiful, Lainee." It felt exquisite to finally be touching like this for the very first time, skin on skin. Intimate. *Lainee.* In his bed. In his hands. His heart squeezed almost painfully.

Noah paused suddenly, pulling back to ask her, "Does that feel good?" He needed her permission and feedback every step of the way of this incredible journey, especially as it was her first time. He wanted to get it just right for her.

She grabbed his hands and put them back on her breasts rather desperately, impatiently answering, "Yes, yes. It feels incredible. Don't you dare stop, Noah."

CHAPTER 37

Noah was smiling as he brought his lips down to kiss Lainee, his tongue and hers lightly dancing, tasting each other even as he moved his hands gently over her nipples, his light fingers barely skimming back and forth over their taut, straining peaks. He kissed and teased her like this for long moments while a warm, liquid need unfurled at her core and swelled from her stomach outward to each and every limb.

She moaned, begged, really, as he continued kissing her, always kissing her, and he answered her plea by trailing his fingertips down her breasts, down, down the length of her flat stomach and then, ever so slowly, he slid the tips of his fingers underneath the ridge of her panties. Once again she groaned against his lips and lifted her hips instinctively, offering herself up to his seeking fingers.

Noah would not, could not deny Lainee the pleasure she was asking him for. Gently, he moved his fingers underneath the soft fabric of her underwear, sliding two fingers along her folds, making her gasp. It was his turn to moan when he felt how wet she was for him already. He sunk his fingers in and stroked her slowly, asking huskily against her mouth, "How does that feel, sweetheart?"

Calling her sweetheart felt like the most natural thing in the world just then as she was, indeed, so fucking sweet and had his whole bloody heart. She was also sexy as hell, writhing underneath him, now fully wet and almost completely naked. *Fuck*, she was delicious. He had the urge to take his mouth from hers and put it at her inviting center but he wasn't sure she was ready for that just yet. He reminded himself to go slowly with her, even as his body strained, pushed, prayed for immediate satisfaction and release.

Lainee took in shaky breaths and then flicked her tongue along his kissing lips while she moved her hips underneath his fingers. Then she bit his lip almost painfully, making him growl with a surge of surprise and lust.

"More, Noah," she begged, demanded of him, "I want more. Now." She was clawing at something unknown to her and though she couldn't see it through the blinding lust, she knew it was there, waiting to shine its warm, illuminating light on her. She just couldn't seem to find it fast enough.

He sucked on her nipples then while moving his fingers inside of her in a slow, steady pattern, and it was the most earth-shattering, pleasure-pain she'd ever felt. She called his name out, amazed, terrified almost, of what was happening to her body, and soon her hips were moving and pushing against his fingers desperately as she felt the something prowling ever closer in the blinding abyss, threatening to push her right over the edge. It was a swelling, building tsunami that began to tear at her mind, frustrating her beyond words.

"Noah, *please*," she choked out, writhing underneath him as he continued to lap at her nipples and rub her most sensitive spot. "Please, come inside me now," she asked, almost certain that would ease her need, pulling his head up from her breasts by his hair to look at his gorgeous face that she loved with all her heart. "I need you," she told him helplessly.

He nodded in complete agreement. It was time. They were both ready. Thank God. He peeled off his underwear and then hers and gently spread her legs with his hands, positioning himself between her thighs. His cock was hard and aching now as he patiently guided himself inside of her, ever so slowly, wanting to be as gentle as possible to minimize the inevitable pain of the first thrust. She inhaled sharply as he slowly pushed his way into her, trying to keep his traitorous body from immediately pounding in and pumping away as it so desperately wanted to.

"Are you okay?" he asked tightly, halting midway in when she gasped louder, looking at her with concern. "Do you want me to stop?" He thought he'd go absolutely mad if he had to pull out now but he left all the power in her hands. He would do whatever she wanted him to do, even if it killed him.

"Don't you dare," she said, boldly grabbing on to his bare ass with both hands and shoving him the rest of the way inside of her in one hard thrust. She inhaled sharply and they both stilled completely now that his dick was deep, deep inside her, as far as it could go. He waited patiently, panting, shaking slightly but otherwise completely still as her body adjusted to him being inside of her.

"Lainee?" he asked through gritted teeth after a silent, still moment, waiting for her to make the first move when she was ready.

Finally she rolled her hips underneath him and asked sweetly, with absolutely no embarrassment, "Like this?" For the first time in her life she felt like a brazen, sexy, confident woman, empowered and in control despite the slight discomfort she was currently experiencing. She hadn't known she could feel this all powerful. It was absolutely incredible and nothing short of life changing.

The Noah effect, Lainee thought tenderly then, reaching up to touch his beloved face in awe. She knew she would never, ever be the same and she gloried in the final stage of her physical and emotional metamorphosis. She rocked her hips again and Noah moaned, still holding himself completely rigid above her.

She rocked again, his penis sliding back and forth within her tight core. Then again. Noah was beginning to sweat with the effort it took to keep from fucking her hard and fast right then and there.

He licked his lips and nodded mutely to her question, so Lainee moved her hips again and again, testing, finding her rhythm, until Noah was losing his tight grip on his patience, his control, his sanity. Lainee focused on how glorious it felt to have his length stroking the deepest, most intimate parts of her, branding her and bringing her to life. Back and forth, back and forth his cock stroked her as she rocked against him.

"Jesus," Noah panted, beginning to pump away inside of her then, unable to hold off doing so for one more goddamn second despite his resolve to give her the power and the time to explore. After a minute of thrusting rather madly he made himself still again and it was an act of supreme will power he could only achieve by staring down into her dilated blue eyes. As always, she steadied him, righted him, brought him back to sanity. He needed to take his time with her, he reminded himself again.

Hovering over her, careful not to put too much of his weight on her, he gently pulled almost all the way out of her before gently pushing back in, all the way in, as deep inside of her as her body would allow him to go. Then he pulled all the way out again, the tip of his penis at her entrance, then all the way back in, slowly, gently, still fighting his natural instinct to pound away. *Take your time with her, asshole,* he coached and begged of himself on repeat. *This is Lainee in your arms, in your bed.* It was beyond his wildest dreams. *Take it slow.*

When he went even deeper inside her after a few more strokes, Lainee clawed at his back as he seemed to touch some nerve deep in the center of her being that she'd never even known existed. She moaned his name then and shamelessly begged for more.

He said her name in return against her lips, his voice rough and broken like gravel. He was kissing her while he thrust in and out of her slowly and gently until they were both shaking and sweating and consumed with lust and love and everything in between.

As he began to helplessly thrust away faster, his orgasm began to build and swell beyond his control. *No. Not yet,* Noah begged of his body. He couldn't leave her behind. He wouldn't. He reached a shaking hand down in between their pressed and hot, naked bodies to stroke her secret spot.

She gasped and ran her fingernails down the length of his back, clawing at him again, giving both pleasure and pain like he gave her as he pumped away inside her. Somehow Noah seemed to be touching all her most sensitive spots all at once and it was blowing her short-circuiting brain.

"*Lainee,*" Noah panted against her as they rocked and clung to each other's sweaty, naked bodies. "I'm close, baby. Are you?"

"Yes," she breathed, somehow knowing it, pounding her hips into his harder, faster, making him start to lose his last vestige of self-control and, right along with it, what was left of his rational mind. "Please, Noah. *Hurry.*"

Permission granted, he gratefully pounded hard with fierce desire as he'd wanted to do all along, his fingers stroking her while he French kissed her around their moans. Finally, at long last, she called out his name and her whole body shook and shuddered beneath him. Noah gratefully let go and climaxed right alongside her, pumping into her and calling out her name in return like a prayer, a promise, a confession and a curse.

Their bodies shook with their shared orgasm for long, glorious moments and Noah poured into Lainee everything he had, everything he was and yet could be. She wrung him dry and his body was the last to shudder into stillness. It took him many minutes more to catch his breath and still his pounding heart as he hovered over her. He stayed buried deep inside of her, never wanting to leave this sacred, heavenly place he'd miraculously found.

They stayed interlocked, foreheads touching while he braced his weight on his shaking forearms on each side of her. As they came down from the shocking high of their shared orgasm, the only sound they made was that of their ragged breathing as they both sucked in air after their rapid descent from the skies.

"Lainee," Noah whispered finally, at a complete loss for words. It had never felt like that before. It had been making love instead of having sex, an all-consuming pleasure wringing his body out head to toe even while his swelling heart felt like it might explode within his chest cavity. Every piece of him, every single cell had been engaged, lit up and present in the earth-shattering moment.

It was like a baptism, being submerged in her, and Noah felt brand fucking new. Lainee had given him all of her, mind, body and soul, and it was stunning in its gravitas. He was good enough to have earned her love? He was worthy of Lainee? Well then he was good enough and worthy period. He knew it for the first time in his life.

He was *good*, Noah suddenly realized as he stayed pressed to Lainee skin to skin. And he was loved, so well loved. It was true, everything Lainee had told him. He wasn't broken after all. In fact, still sheathed inside of her, Noah felt completely, utterly whole.

Lainee could feel Noah throbbing, pulsating inside of her for long moments more and it was the most exquisite feeling she'd ever known. "I can feel you throb," she whispered in wonder, her eyes wide with pleasure as she looked up at him as if he were the god of intercourse, orgasms and everything earthly delicious in between.

He huffed a laugh at her look of amazement and kissed her tenderly, taking his time with the precious moment. "Was that... was that okay?" he asked her huskily, suddenly hoping he hadn't rushed it or, God forbid, hadn't measured up to her expectations. Her first time was a lot of pressure at the exact same time that it made him feel like the luckiest, proudest man on earth.

"Are you kidding? That was amazing." She looked up at him in awe. "Is it always that good?" Now she fully understood the stream of girls in and out of his bedroom. "When can we do it again?" That was the more important question.

Noah chuckled and carefully, almost regretfully, pulled out of her and laid down beside her, exhausted from the all-powerful orgasm, pulling her close against his body so that they were still touching and connected. He never wanted her more than arms-length away ever again. "Soon," he promised, "but give me a minute. I'm only human after all."

"You can have two, but not a minute more," she teased as euphoria skirted along her nerve endings and her whole body rejoiced in what it had just experienced. Her first orgasm. *Wow.* It had been transcendent to be skin on skin with Noah, him literally inside of her body while they were touching *everywhere*. And then that crazy, startling burst of euphoria and pleasure at her core that extended from head to toe. Her nerve endings were even now singing at the stunning pleasure of it all.

She sat up just enough to prop her head on her hand and look greedily at his naked body fully on display for her for the first time. A thrill ran through her just from that new and naughty indulgence. She eyeballed him naked for a long time, head to toe, and the aching began all over again.

Damn, he was a beautiful man. He was lean but muscled with soft, golden skin. His abs were etched and a sexy V was carved out on his hips enticingly for her voyeuristic pleasure, pointing her way to his delicious cock which was front and center in the stunning masterpiece that was Noah Riley.

Lainee ogled said cock in wonder as it stayed semi-hard and an impressive length for many minutes more. She was completely in love with every inch of him, she decided then, inside and out. There wasn't a thing she would change about him. And, boy, the things that body could do to her body... She shivered in remembrance... and in anticipation of what was to come next.

Noah smiled up at her rather smugly then as she continued to stare with hungry, admiring eyes for long moments. His rogue, devilish grin only made her laugh. "You totally know how good looking you are, don't you?" she sighed, pushing at his shoulder. "Why are you so damn pretty?" she teased.

She laid down next to him then and asked seriously, "How do I compare to all your other girls?" To her surprise the question made Noah wince and tense, but it wasn't an inquiry born out of insecurity or jealousy, but rather intellectual curiosity. He was far more experienced than she, after all. And she did have a different kind of body with all her scars, though she knew he found her attractive despite them, maybe more so because of them somehow. Despite his perfection and experience, she hadn't felt self-conscious about one naked part of her body or one moment of their intimacy, not when his gaze and hands had been so gentle and loving.

Noah propped up then to look at *her* naked form, brushing his fingers gently over her scarred cheek in an automatic, loving gesture. "They don't compare to you, Lainee," he assured her quietly. "In bed or out of it. You are in a league all your own, sweetheart." She'd just given him the gift of her body, her virginity, and it was the best experience and orgasm of his life. Truthfully, he didn't have the words to adequately express how spiritual and transcendent it had been. All he could do was lean over and kiss her with exquisite tenderness.

He looked over the full length of her creamy, naked body then with equally appreciative eyes. She was so soft to his touch with hard, subtly defined muscle underneath. Damn, she was in good shape. He ran his hand down her hard, slightly outlined stomach and over her smooth, rounded thigh, admiring every inch.

Her scars did not detract from her beauty in any way, in fact, he found them endearing, alluring and uniquely sexy all at the same time. He stared at her vagina then, trimmed tidily and quite beautiful in and of itself. He was dying to taste it soon. *Mine,* he thought possessively as he cupped her between her legs now. He looked up the length of her beautiful body into her blue eyes with love and lust in equal measure.

Her lips turned up in a satisfied smile and she pointed out sweetly, "It's been two minutes, Noah."

CHAPTER 38

A half hour later as they rolled away from each other, panting and sweating, coming down from the high of another orgasm, Lainee began nuzzling Noah's neck, still hungry, somehow even more ravenous after her second orgasm. She licked, sucked and nibbled on him. She couldn't get enough of him and literally wanted to eat him up.

"Woman," he panted, swatting her away playfully, "let me rest, damn you. I'm not a battery-operated machine."

She giggled then and gave up, getting out of bed to fire up his fancy coffee maker. Unabashedly, she walked across the room naked, scarred and glorious. Noah put his hands behind his head and watched her all the while. He couldn't have been more impressed by her.

She finagled the fancy machine, whipped the milk and made them each a cappuccino with a dash of Italian sweet cream. She brought his into bed and served him like the Prince of Intercourse and Orgasms that he undoubtedly was.

"Mmm," he said thankfully, sitting up and sipping on the hot beverage. He looked at her over the rim of his cup with languid, loving eyes. "Thank you, lover," he said so shyly her heart squeezed.

"You're welcome... lover," she said back, trying it on for size. They grinned at each other.

They sipped another moment in silence and then she told him very earnestly, "I want to watch some porn."

Noah choked on his coffee.

"I want to know what's possible," Lainee explained very pragmatically. "I want to try *everything*."

Noah was still coughing and trying to digest this new bit of exciting information. He doubted she wanted to try *everything* but he was more than willing to explore with her.

"Show me," she challenged him. "I want to do it all with you, Noah. Today."

He laughed at that but loved her enthusiasm. "How about we start with massage oils, a vibrator... and some porn?"

She nodded enthusiastically. He was the teacher now and she the eager pupil. "Oh, yes, please."

◆◆◆

They spent the next week in bed, making love, having picnics on top of the tangled sheets, lounging and watching movies and then making love all over again. It was undoubtedly the best week in both their lives. It was one of those suspended moments in time, when everything in the world outside of their room just fell away. There was nothing and no one but each other and their love. They were mind, body and soul aligned, utterly content and fulfilled. They knew they would never be the same but there was absolutely no fear in that fact. They trusted the other with their heart implicitly.

Noah even began turning off all the lights at night, surprising them both. "No lights?" Lainee asked the first night he'd gone around the room turning them off before coming into bed and spooning her in the darkness.

He stilled for a second, holding her tight, letting the night settle in all around him. When he was satisfied no panic was forthcoming, he kissed her neck and asked huskily, "Who needs lights when I have Lainee?" They made love slowly and sweetly then under the mysterious shadows of the night which felt more like a light caress than a suffocating blanket with her in his arms.

Fear crept in later, though, for Lainee, when the other students started to arrive back on campus, interrupting their blissful corner of paradise with the startling, harsh reality of the outside world.

Two nights before classes were to start back up, Lainee tossed and turned and had a hard time falling asleep despite the multiple orgasms Noah had gifted her. He had no such problem as he lay snoring behind her, spooning her just as she liked. She was quite envious of him as she couldn't seem to turn off her brain to rest. She wasn't even worried about academics for once in her life. No, she was terrified this love bliss with Noah was all ending soon and she'd crash and burn. Abruptly. Painfully. Again.

She was certain *something* would change. They were all just atoms and molecules thrown together and reacting to one other in a random experiment, after all. How could she and Noah *not* respond when the other students came back into the mix, namely the hundreds of adoring, available women who threw themselves at him on a continual basis? Their chemistry would realistically be altered drastically. And now they would be apart all day for classes. She mourned the physical loss of him already. She was a love-drunk addict who would soon be without her designer drug. It was all so frightening and overwhelming.

She knew without a doubt her infamous killer focus had gone to hell but Lainee suddenly couldn't even care about that. What did it really matter if she was no longer top ten when she would still be summa cum laude, in advanced standing *and* she had Noah?

This paradigm shift had happened ever so slowly but decisively. Noah was definitely more important than her top ten status now. It was strange and... liberating. She wouldn't ever be sorry for it because she was more balanced and happy with him by her side. She had no doubt her dad would have been proud of that achievement over all her others.

But now Noah was *too* important, and everything was about to be turned upside down. Again. *Would this be almost as painful as the car accident?* Lainee couldn't help but wonder in horror as the hours slowly crept by. Would she lose Noah, too, and walk away even more scarred? Suddenly it was a real possibility.

Around 3am Lainee fell into an exhausted, uncomfortable slumber.

Noah stirred in the middle of the night as Lainee moved against him restlessly and whimpered. Her small little noises grew louder and her movement more distressed, making him come fully awake. He recognized instantly that she was having a nightmare and fought to pull her out. "Lainee," he said gently in her ear, kissing the side of her face from his position behind her. "Wake up, sweetheart. You're having a bad dream." Her whimpering only grew more frantic despite his efforts, and then she was crying, too.

Noah resorted to shaking her rather desperately, and Lainee startled awake, all but choking on her lingering fear and heartache. She turned in his arms then and curled up against him, burying her face in his chest. He soothed her with his hands and murmurs while she shook and cried.

Finally, as she started to get her emotions under control, he had to ask, his heart in his throat, "Were you... were you having a nightmare about my father?" Sometimes he had nightmares himself of his father putting hands on Lainee.

She shook her head against his chest and said quietly, "No, *my* father." And the flash of imploding glass and scraping metal had her gripping Noah for balance. She relived the horror of her accident and her father's death often in her dreams. Along with her scars, it was her penance.

"Oh, Lainee," Noah said gently, pulling her into him as tight as she would go. "I'm so sorry, baby. You're safe now. Don't be scared. I'm here. I've got you."

The tight ball in her chest slowly began to unravel as he kissed her, stroked her hair, and murmured soothingly. Eventually she was able to fall into a deeper, more peaceful sleep, right before the sun was about to peek in on them on their final day of break.

The next day Lainee forced herself to move back into her own dorm room, knowing she'd get them both in trouble if she was caught all but shacking up with Noah full time in his. When it came right down to it, though, it was really more of a test for herself, and preparation for the looming, daunting changes that lay ahead as classes started back up. It was the only way she could think to control the situation even a little bit.

She had to be stronger, smarter, better... She had to be in control at all times... It was the first time she'd replayed that mantra in her head in quite awhile, she realized. Her worry was spiking her stress and triggering her old coping mechanisms, alarming them both.

Noah watched her pack up her things with a heavy heart, quite sick with worry. He couldn't understand her reasoning and he felt panic rising with each article of clothing she threw in her bag.

"Don't go," he told her repeatedly, swallowing around a lump in his throat. *Why was she going?* "You really don't have to go." *Ever.* Noah was seriously ready to throw all pride out the window and beg her to stay. He felt her pulling emotionally away as well as physically and his heart *hurt.* He absently rubbed his chest and watched her finish packing in horror, as usual so out of his league with this girl and uncertain what to do or say next.

Lainee shook her head sadly, unable or unwilling to share the full depth of her concerns and why this painful separation seemed the best preparation for tomorrow's changes.

She assured him she would spend the night on the weekend but that did little to stem his panic and heartbreak. Noah had to let her go, and that night he slept with every lamp on in the place, when he slept at all.

Lainee felt downright bereft across campus in her own bed for the first time in weeks, alone and quite cold and uncomfortable. Her heart was inexplicably broken to be so far away from Noah after living with him in his room for days on end. Even before that, she'd been in his room way more than her own on a daily basis. Now this place felt foreign to her.

She barely slept again, tossing and turning only to find light sleep for a few hours just to be awakened by her ongoing nightmare of the car crash. This time there was no Noah to soothe her and Lainee recognized for the first time as she stared up at the ceiling in the middle of the cold, unsettling night that she was in trouble. *Serious* trouble.

What have I done, she wondered in a panic. She'd lost *all* control. She'd given herself completely over to Noah. He now felt like a necessity, like she *needed* him right along with air to live, and she'd never felt more vulnerable or fragile.

He had all the control now it seemed and she had none. He could totally and systematically annihilate her with a simple change of heart, she realized. It infused the night with more terror.

Lainee gave up trying to sleep around 5am. She got up, showered and dressed for the difficult day ahead.

Noah must have been feeling much the same way because he was at her door at sunrise with a bagel and coffee, surprising her. He looked a bit disheveled with shadows under his eyes as if he hadn't slept well either. It did her heart so good to unexpectedly see him there at her threshold. She threw herself at him as if he'd just returned from raging war after a lengthy stint apart.

"That was the longest night of my life," Noah admitted sheepishly, "and the dumbest idea you've ever had." He leaned in for a kiss after passing her a coffee. "I don't think I can survive another night like that, honestly." He was only half joking, and beyond relieved when she vehemently agreed.

"What are we going to do?" Lainee asked forlornly, as if it was the worst diagnosis they could have gotten from the best doctor.

"I'll tell you what we're going to do," Noah said with absolute conviction, leaving no room for argument. "You're packing that bag again and coming right back." He pulled her close with one arm until she was flush against his body, where she belonged. "I'm pretty sure I need you to sleep now. And I'll get you another vibrator and more porn, woman, whatever it takes." He wiggled his eyebrows suggestively, making her giggle.

Seriously, how could she pass up that offer for even one more night? Perhaps the better question was, why *would* she? None of the reasons from the day prior seemed viable now that she was back in his warm, soothing arms. "We both completely failed this test, you know," she pointed out with a sigh.

"I better get myself a tutor, then," Noah quipped with a relaxed smile, all worry evaporating into thin air now that she was in his arms clinging to him. "Know of a good one?" He French kissed her long and hard then, reminding her that he had his own master class to teach *her*.

Lainee's roommate suddenly came up behind them, barging in on their intimate moment, stating the obvious in wide-eyed wonder, "You're Noah Riley." She blinked at him as if he was a thirst-inducing mirage that would disappear soon in the dry desert heat. When he still remained standing before her after a few more hard blinks, she asked incredulous, conveniently overlooking the previously locked lips and his arm still around Lainee's waist, "What are you doing here?"

Noah didn't frequently come to Lainee's room due to said roommate and lack of privacy, so now he introduced himself, looking over at Lainee lovingly, explaining with quite a bit of joy and giddiness, "I'm Lainee's boyfriend."

Her roommate about fainted from shock.

A flood of emotion washed over Lainee at his loving words and his adoring look. It was a balm to her worried, sleep-deprived soul. She was reminded then that they would figure this out, together, and she needn't worry, at least not on her own anyway. She could trust Noah with her entire heart and soul. How could she have forgotten even for one night? This was Noah, for God's sake, the best man on planet earth, her prince among men.

Lainee grabbed her backpack and they walked hand in hand to class, sipping their coffees and purposefully ignoring all the stares and dropped jaws along the way. They truly could have cared less about any other person on campus as they happily held on to one another.

CHAPTER 39

Noah rushed to the gym at lunch time to meet Lainee. Damn, he missed that girl despite having seen her just three hours prior after holding her in his arms all night. It was a little embarrassing, he wasn't going to lie. Overeager like a little boy with his first school crush, he rushed into the MAC, looking towards the elliptical machines where he knew he'd find her. He came up short inside the entrance when he saw she was talking close with someone by the machines, a dude in a tank top with broad shoulders and lots of arm tattoos whose face he couldn't see from behind.

The burly bloke turned slightly and that's when Noah recognized Ryker Wallace, who'd grown an impressive, thick, full-on brown beard since the last time he'd seen him. Somehow it looked rugged and manly on the good-looking motherfucker instead of unruly and unkempt. Noah's protective instincts had him pushing forward again. If that abrasive asshole said one derogatory thing toward Lainee, he swore to God they'd come to blows.

Then Lainee threw her head back and laughed at something Ryker was saying to her, making Noah slow his march forward once again. Wait, was Ryker *hitting* on her? Oh, yeah, they were for sure coming to blows. Noah picked up his pace, not able to reach them fast enough now. Suddenly Lainee began unzipping her hoodie, pulling it down over her shoulders, revealing a sports bra and her rock hard abdomen underneath, making

Noah's eyes round in shock. *Since when did his sweet and shy girlfriend start showing so much skin in public?!*

Noah was scowling when he finally reached them. He threw a protective arm around Lainee's shoulders and squared off with Ryker through narrowed eyes, recalling uncomfortably that the guy had called his girl "Scar Face" not too long ago at the Pats' viewing party. Ryker was both an asshole and a ladies' man, and Noah didn't want him this close to Lainee for any of those reasons.

"There you are," Lainee said with a sweet smile, obviously pleased to see him, completely oblivious to the murderous thoughts currently running through his head. She kissed his cheek lovingly, which made his ire lessen considerably, still he stared down Ryker just daring him to be disrespectful.

Ryker lifted an eyebrow and tried to push back a knowing smile behind his new manly beard. "33," he said quite courteously, calling Noah by his lacrosse number, but he was smirking at him.

Always smirking, this one. Noah was tense from head to toe, wanting to wipe that smug look off Ryker's face as he waited on edge for him to say something inappropriate and rude to Lainee. The guy really was an arrogant, muscled, tattooed asshole. Now that Noah thought about it, he wasn't sure he ever really liked Ryker that much. He wasn't sure anyone did. He muttered, growled really, Ryker's number in return, "17."

Ryker's smile spread from ear to ear, enjoying himself immensely as he easily recognized Noah's jealous alpha rage bubbling just underneath the surface. Ryker was always up for a fight, be it verbal or otherwise, especially with Golden Boy Riley here. "Ready to start lacrosse practice soon so that I can kick your lily ass, Riley? You clearly have one coming to you."

Before Noah could retaliate, Lainee spoke up, still oblivious to the very real testosterone-filled tension between the two teammates, saying, "I'm going to go fill up on water." She turned to Ryker and added with a polite smile, "Nice to meet you, Ryker." Then she headed over to the drinking fountain across the room with her water bottle, giving the teammates some time to catch up. And square off.

Noah commenced with his scowling until Ryker outright laughed at him. "Dude, why don't you just pee on her to mark your territory and get it over with?"

Noah didn't back down. "Ryker, dude, I'm warning you. Don't be a dick to her..." *and don't fucking hit on her either.*

Ryker threw up his hands in defense. "Whoa. Chill out. Jesus. I was just introducing myself as one of your buddies - or at least I thought we were buddies - and inviting you two to a party off-campus this weekend." Ryker scoffed at him, glanced over his shoulder at Lainee across the room and added, because he just couldn't help himself, "I'd ask what's gotten into you but *dayuuum.* Now I get it. She is hot as fuck." Just as Noah saw red, Ryker punched him in the shoulder playfully. "Seriously, I'm a little bit jealous, man. Good for you. Now stand the fuck down and quit being the angry asshole here. That's *my* job, on and off the field. And, frankly, you're not very good at it."

Noah huffed a laugh and scrubbed a hand over his face just as Lainee came back to his side. She kissed him again on the cheek, looking up at him as if he were the sun, the moon and all of the stars combined, punctuated by a bunch of electrifying orgasms. His heart flip flopped and he kissed her hard on the lips.

"Alright, lovebirds," Ryker all but snickered at them. "Have fun and hopefully I'll see you at the party. Go Crimson!" he shouted, walking backwards and throwing them a peace sign, flexing his big bicep with a Japanese serpent tattoo wrapped around it. He was out the door thirty seconds later and Noah watched the door close behind him in relief.

"You okay?" Lainee asked then, gently tugging on Noah so he'd turn to look at her. "You seem a little tense."

She had no idea. Noah looked at her bare midriff. She was by far the sexiest girl here, probably the sexiest girl everywhere. "Do you have to show so much skin?" he growled at her, fully realizing he was being obnoxious and insecure but not able to help himself.

"Wait." She eyeballed him in shock. "Are you jealous?"

She outright laughed in his face then. Noah leveled her a grumpy and slightly pouty look. It was decidedly *not* funny.

"Oh, this is rich," Lainee said with a quick peck to his lips. She climbed up on an elliptical and looked over her shoulder at him. "Now you know how I feel every time we step foot outside your dorm room."

This had Noah pausing long enough to recognize that, indeed, Lainee had to deal with girls hitting on him multiple times a day. Everywhere they went. In her face. God, that sucked.

He climbed on the elliptical beside her with a chagrined look. She really was the bravest, strongest person he knew. How could she deal with *that* shit multiple times a day? One round of protective jealousy had him wanting to annihilate a teammate, throw her over his shoulder and take her back to his room to hide her away forever.

"I can make all the bad guys good for a weekend," Lainee teased, putting in her ear buds and hitting play on Taylor whom she frequently quoted now. She blew him a kiss and then got to work.

Noah still couldn't take his eyes off her as she worked out, her lean body glistening with sweat and her cheeks turning pink, reminding him of how she looked right after she'd just been tumbled... by him. He loved looking upon her flushed face as she lie in his bed, coming down from the high of a shared orgasm.

The sensual memories were still so new and fresh. He couldn't stop thinking about it as he kept pace with her on the elliptical. His hard-on was making it a bit difficult to concentrate on the workout and move comfortably. Finally he paused his machine and then hers, saying with a pointed look when she tried to protest, "I know of an even better workout, baby girl... in my shower."

Her eyes lit up instantly and then they were rushing to his suite, hand in hand. As they stumbled through the doorway they were already grabbing on to each other and kissing. They dropped their bags at the threshold and made their way to the shower, kissing, tripping, breaking apart only to help each other rip off another article of clothing.

Then finally they were standing in the warm spray of the shower, rubbing each other's bodies down with soap and kissing all the wet, exposed skin everywhere. When they were both completely clean, Noah again took the Johnson & Johnson's baby shampoo and poured some in to his hand. He then gently reached down between their hard, wet bodies and slid his hand between her legs, along her center, his amber eyes burning with lust as they held fast to hers.

Her breath caught as he rubbed her ever so gently down there, cleaning her with the most gentle and reverential touch possible. Then he turned her so her front was getting the full blast of the shower spray, her back against his chest, and he opened her wide, making her gasp as water hit her erogenous zone that he'd just awakened and stroked to heightened awareness. As all of the soap washed away, Lainee pressed back in to his hard, wet chest and Noah began stroking her again. He moved his other hand up around her throat as he bit and suckled the column of her neck.

Lainee rested her head back on his shoulder, moaning and

writing against him, repeating his name like a litany, a prayer. "*Noah*." After a moment he moved his hand from around her throat to her breasts. He ran light fingertips over both wet nipples. Almost immediately, her body spasmed against his and she called out in pleasure and triumph.

Noah stroked her gently as she came down slowly from the high of her orgasm. He whispered in her ear, "So beautiful, Lainee, all of you. Every single inch." He was kissing her gently down the column of her neck again as she melted against him and sighed, completely satiated and fulfilled in that moment.

She took a minute to revel, then Lainee turned in Noah's arms and faced him so that the shower spray was hitting her back. She gave him a wicked, wolfish grin he'd never seen before, making him chuckle. "Was that good, sweetheart?" he asked lovingly, pushing her wet hair back from her glowing face. There was that post-orgasmic flush he loved to see. He felt pride, tenderness and quite a bit of awe that he was the one to put it there.

"So, so good, Noah," she assured him, licking his bottom lip with a flick of her tongue. "Now it's your turn, lover." She held his eyes as she slowly sunk to her knees before him in the shower. His hard cock swelled in anticipation as she grabbed on.

CHAPTER 40

Suddenly, inexplicably, Lainee was popular for something other than her scar. Girls who'd never glanced her way came up to her and struck up random conversations, only to inevitably ask, "Are you, like, dating Noah Riley?"

Noah was asked more blatantly rude questions throughout the following days by the guys. "Dude! The girl with the scar? Does she put out?" Noah had actually rounded on a few of the assholes that had dared asked, showing a temper for the first time in his life and ready to throw a punch. They'd backed off immediately.

Soon everyone understood they were together, really together. Most people accepted it, except for a few diehard fans who'd been waiting impatiently in line to get a bite out of one Noah Riley.

Caroline Lucas was one such fan. She could have cared less about Lainee Reed. She dismissed the disfigured girl immediately as no threat to her. One look at Caroline and Noah would prefer *her* to *that*, she had no doubt.

She'd been stalking Noah before Thanksgiving break, following him around covertly, discovering his routine and, most importantly, the location of his bedroom. She decided she'd waited in the wings long enough a couple days after returning from break. She skipped her class after lunch and hung around inconspicuously in the hallway until she saw Noah sauntering towards his door, looking absolutely delicious in his workout gear, all flushed and sweaty from his lunch-time workout at the MAC. She'd discovered long ago from afar that he worked out religiously at this time. This habitual habit made him an easy target.

Noah didn't even glance her way as he removed his ear buds, unlocked his door and stepped through. Caroline caught the door a half an inch before it closed shut, waiting a full minute before following Noah inside. She looked around the suite a moment, hearing the shower through the open bathroom door. She smiled to herself and sauntered around in exploration. It satisfied her beyond measure that he had no pictures, not even of his supposed new "girlfriend." This validated her assumption that Miss-Scarred-Vanilla-in-an-Argyle-Sweater was a passing phase, a pity project probably, not to be taken too seriously by the likes of her. She blatantly ignored the open bag containing women clothing sitting beside a leather chair.

Caroline quietly opened Noah's dresser drawers, one by one, running her long, manicured fingernails over his underwear, his t-shirts. Then she lifted a plain white t-shirt up and put it to her face to take in his smell. She decided she'd keep this shirt for herself, for later. She set it aside and slid the drawer shut when she heard the shower turn off.

Without hesitation, she quickly took off all her clothes and came to lay on his large bed. She was so ready, practically purring, as Noah came out of the shower, wet, shiny and gloriously naked himself.

Noah was toweling his hair off as he came out of the bathroom. He stopped dead in his tracks when he saw her there, some complete stranger he'd never seen before, spread out on his bed in the buff. His heart flipped, but not in a good way. He quickly covered himself with the towel he'd been using to dry his hair and growled gruffly, "Who the hell are you?"

The girl looked utterly satisfied with herself as she all but purred, "I'm Caroline, darling, your next and best lover." She opened her legs wide in invitation and he couldn't help but look.

Noah caught himself and quickly glanced away. "Caroline, you need to leave. *Now.*" He would normally have at least thanked her for the compliment if not jumped at the opportunity conveniently laid out before him in his bed. But he was a different man now. He was a *better* man, thanks to Lainee. "I have a girlfriend now and you can't just break into people's rooms-"

"Oh, you want to play hard to get, do you?" Caroline returned with a sly smile, sliding off the bed and waltzing over to him slowly and leisurely in all her naked glory as if she owned the room. She was stalking him, really, like she was the predator and he the prey. Even as Noah backed away, Caroline advanced with cold purpose. She came within an inch of his naked body and brazenly ran a hand down his hard, wet chest even as he had a horrific flashback of his father and flinched away. "I'll chase you and hold you down if that's what you want, big guy. I'll tie you up, whip you hard and make you beg for it, too."

Noah took another step backward in stunned silence as he tried to process what was transpiring. He'd never had a girl break into his room and pounce on him like this before. He was momentarily taken aback by her overbearing and arrogant actions that left him uncomfortable and wrestling with painful memories from the past. He felt flustered and on edge over the blatant violation of his privacy that he'd fought so damn hard for. "Caroline," he warned, taking another step back from her. "I said no and I meant it. Please get out of my room."

She was relentless, though, leaping at him and grabbing up his hand. She placed it over one exposed, ample breast and rubbed her nipple against his palm. Noah jerked his hand away in disgust at the forced gesture and warned angrily, "Caroline, I'm not playing this game with you. You need to get the hell out of my room. *Now.*"

Though there was very little space separating their bodies to begin with, she stepped even closer. She was eyeballing him as if he was a delicious snack, not listening to a word he said. Suddenly, her hand darted forward again and she ripped the towel away from him, catching him off guard and throwing it clear across the room.

They stood there then, face to face, both of them now completely naked, and damn his body if it didn't respond to her despite himself. She was a physically attractive woman after all, though he kept his eyes on her face at all times.

Caroline smiled victoriously as she watched Noah's cock growing hard despite his feeble protests. She pushed him against the wall that was suddenly at his back. "I see you like my games, darling, and I promise you that we will both have a really fun time." She grabbed his dick then, making it harden fully in her hand, and Noah felt instantly disgusted at them both. She pushed her body into him then so that her hand holding his cock was trapped between their two pressed, naked bodies.

"What the fuck, Caroline," Noah growled angrily in growing repulsion, grabbing her hips to push her away. "Get off-"

It was right then that Lainee walked into the room and everybody froze.

CHAPTER 41

Lainee took in the scene before her, Noah naked against the wall, his hands on an equally naked woman's hips, his penis in her hands. Her heart plummeted into freefall and she stumbled backward towards the doorway as if the earth's plates had suddenly shifted beneath her.

"Right," she whispered after a shocked, silent moment, nodding even as a numb, trance-like wave of self-preservation washed over her. This was Noah Riley, ladies' man and lover extraordinaire. Beautiful women threw themselves at him every day and he ate it up. He'd slept with dozens of them before her, all throughout the duration of their friendship. So why would things be different now? Why would he settle just for her, when she was average at best, scarred at worst? Their little moment in time was just that, a short scene in the overall full-length feature of his life starring hundreds of beautiful leading ladies. It was now over, whatever they'd had. Clearly.

Here was that moment that Lainee had feared, the one when Noah had a simple change of heart and totally and systematically annihilated her.

The aching lyrics of Exile suddenly floated through her stunned brain as it stopped and started again. *I think I've seen this film before, so I'm leaving out the side door. You're not my homeland anymore, so what I am defending now? You were my town, now I'm in exile seeing you out...*

Without another word, Lainee turned and ran.

"Lainee!" Noah called after her, pushing Caroline away without a second thought. He ran after Lainee only to remember one step outside into the hallway that he was buck naked. He cupped himself, darted back inside, pulled on some shorts as quickly as humanly possible and ran back out. Caroline was instantly forgotten.

Noah caught up to Lainee halfway across campus, between his dorm house and hers. "Lainee, stop!" he begged, running full steam and catching up quickly.

She went from a brisk walk to an almost full run herself as he neared. He was lunging for her arm, begging her to stop, when suddenly she tripped and fell. He didn't have time to catch her and she went down hard on the cold, unforgiving ground face first.

Fuck. "Lainee, are you okay?" Noah asked in alarm and concern, reaching down to help her up.

She turned and scooted back on her butt, looking up at him and his outstretched hand in horror, as if... his heart stopped dead in his chest... as if she was scared of him. Her panicked, pained look had Noah stopping cold in his tracks, his hand outstretched and frozen between the small space that now separated them.

"Don't touch me," she whispered hoarsely, still scooting backward along the ground and looking up him with large, tear-filled eyes.

Noah had seen that look before on Lainee's face. She had looked at his father in the library just that way, after the bastard had struck her and pinned her against the bookshelf. Lainee was looking up at him now in much the same way as if... as if... *Oh, God.*

She's afraid of me, Noah realized with a start, and he felt bile rise in the back of his throat. *Jesus.* Lainee was actually looking up at him in fear. *What the fuck have I done?* The bruises his father had given her had only just faded and now he'd knocked her to the ground with his own hands.

"Don't ever touch me again," Lainee choked out louder then.

Her words were like a physical blow to his core and Noah flinched, dropping his hand to his side in stunned silence. He stared down in horror at the scene unfolding before him. Lainee on the ground looking up at him in fear and loathing, backing away from him and telling him not to touch her.

In that moment, Noah was his father.

As Lainee scrambled up to her feet and ran from him, Noah let her go in stunned silence.

Noah stood there long moments, ignoring the stares of everyone around who had witnessed the dramatic scene unfolding, feeling utterly shocked and sickened to his soul. He didn't even acknowledge the cold December air hitting his naked chest or the patches of snow crunching beneath his bare feet. He couldn't feel anything besides the rising tide of panic and nausea.

Oh, God. He was going to be sick. He leaned over and put his hands on his knees, trying to breathe and keep from heaving.

He'd pushed Lainee down. He'd hurt her. He'd *scared* her. His body shook as he tried to process this horrible turn of events over the last few unrecognizable minutes of his now distorted reality. *What the fuck had just happened to his life?* His whole world had just imploded in a matter of minutes and he couldn't even grasp at the magnitude of it. *What have I done? Is Lainee alright?* There was a stabbing in his chest that kept him bent over in pain, trying to process and somehow persevere.

Noah gagged as he thought of Lainee's shocked, terrified face looking up at him as if he were a monster. As if he were his father. His worst fear had just been realized. Oh, God. *Lainee.* His sweet, beautiful Lainee. His best friend. His lover. *Was she okay?*

He wanted to go after her and comfort her, and it was a need he could not deny even now. Especially now. She was the only thing that could ever pull him up out of his head and his swirl of self-destruction. She started pulling at him now, and Noah absolutely had to make sure she was alright. He knew she didn't want to see him but he had to check on her this one last time. He had to make sure she was okay and then he would never, ever bother her again.

It would all but kill him to walk away from her now, but he would do it. For her. It was the least he could do, really, spare her another brutal moment like this one, with his narcissist bullshit and the latent abuse that seemed embedded into his very DNA.

Noah all but stumbled the rest of the way to her dorm room then, still sickened, dazed, unaware of the biting cold against his half-naked body as well as the gaping, puzzled stares. *He had to get to Lainee.* He had to make sure she was alright. It was his north star in the chaos of his shredding mind.

CHAPTER 42

Noah knocked on Lainee's door, biting back the nausea. Of course she didn't answer. Why would she answer? It took all of his courage to knock again. Then he splayed a hand on the door as if he could feel her right through it.

"Lainee," he called out when there was still no answer. "God, I'm so sorry. I swear I never meant to hurt you. Are you okay? I just need to know you're okay."

Tears were stinging his eyes as he was greeted with nothing but heavy, telling silence. *"Fuck,"* he spat, more angry at himself than he'd ever been in his life. *How could he have let this happen?* "Tell me I'm a heartless bastard, Lainee, a piece of shit that doesn't deserve you, the biggest fucking moron at Harvard. Don't take it easy on me, just let me know you're okay and then I'll leave you alone, I swear. I just need to know you're alright." And then quieter, the door holding him up as he began to crumble in on himself, "I'm so fucking sorry I scared you. "

Suddenly the door began shifting underneath him and he managed to stand upright as Lainee swung it open and looked up at him between narrowed, flashing eyes. "I'm not scared of you, Noah," she seethed, righteous fury making her eyes blaze as she all but pinned him to the wall behind him with her angst. "I'm heartbroken." And then her eyes filled with tears and she said much quieter, "You broke my heart."

The door slammed in his face then.

Noah was left reeling, processing. She wasn't scared of him? But she was heartbroken? Even more uncertainly he knocked on the door again. "Lainee, I-I'm sorry I pushed you down. I didn't mean to. I don't even know how it happened. I'd never hurt you on purpose... you know that, don't you?"

But there was no answer. He wanted to tell her again and again that he was sorry. He was a piece of shit. He wanted to promise he'd never hurt her again. He wasn't his father.... right? He didn't want to hurt the one that he loved. And then something shifted in his mind, a slight, imperceptible cloud lifted from his thoughts... That's right. He loved Lainee but he'd never actually told her. *Seriously, what the fuck was wrong with him?* He rested his forehead on the door, defeated.

"Lainee," he said quietly then, "I'll go now and leave you alone if that's what you want. I'll do whatever you tell me to do. Just know that I'm not my father. I would never hurt you on purpose. Lainee... I love you."

Silence.

But Noah had no pride left, and it felt absurdly good to say it out loud, so he said it again, louder, "I love you, Lainee. I fucking love you."

He stood there in the silence for what seemed like hours but was probably more like minutes, and then slowly the door opened to him again, making his heart leap. "Lainee," Noah said in relief as he took in her beautiful, beloved and dirty face. She had opened her door to him again. It was more than he deserved.

"I know you're nothing like your father," she said gently, slowly, her blue eyes shimmering with more tears. "You didn't push me down, Noah. I tripped and fell." She paused a second, making sure the words were sinking in. "I was never and will never be scared of you."

Noah's over-taxed mind almost audibly whirred with her words, but he still couldn't understand. "Then why did you run from me?"

She sighed at him then, one of her irritated, you're-so-slow sighs that he'd gotten many times over the course of the last few months and it did his heart so good to hear it now. "Because, Noah... you were in your room with another girl. Naked."

Noah blinked a couple of times, still processing, and then a look of surprise and fresh horror crossed over his face, "Lainee, I didn't do anything with that girl. I'd never seen her before in my life. I came out of the shower and she was there in my bed, naked, throwing herself at me. You should have stayed and let me explain. I mean, why would you just assume anything was happening?"

He seemed genuinely hurt by the mere suggestion but, for once, Lainee wasn't about to let him off the hook quite that easily. "Because, Noah," she said dryly, pointedly, "you were both standing in your bedroom... naked... She was literally holding your penis in her hand."

Noah had the decency to blush then and admit, "That *would* look a tad suspicious. But I swear absolutely nothing happened. I didn't even kiss the nut job! She was all grabby and aggressive and I only put my hands on her a brief second to get her off me."

Lainee blinked up at him then, the fire leaving her instantly as she accepted his words at face value. Her heart was still sore, though, and she said quietly, "But you're Noah Riley and women throw themselves at you all day long and you like it. You've slept with scores of them."

"That's not fair," he pointed out with a grimace but no heat. He cupped her face with both of his hands then as his world became upright on its axis once more. *She wasn't afraid of him.* "That was before you and me." His amber eyes burned bright at the centers with the truth of his words now. "I love you, Lainee. This body is yours. This heart - this *mess* - it's all yours... if you still want it." Truthfully, she'd ruined all other women for him a long time ago.

Lainee searched Noah's face as she let his words sink in. "You love me?" she whispered breathlessly. "Are you sure?"

He smiled rather shyly at her then and repeated her words back from the day they'd made love for the very first time. "Of you and me? Absolutely Elaine Rose Reed." He'd been untethered, unseen, unknown until her. He wouldn't love her perfectly, but he would love her completely and like no other.

Lainee took in a big, deep breath then, letting go of the self-imposed nightmare and all of the misconceptions of the last half hour. She easily let go all the self-inflicted hurt and heartbreak. Because Noah loved her. *Wow...*

"I love you, too, Noah," she told him gently then, giving him the greatest gift of his life mere moments after he'd thought it was completely over.

He pulled her to him then so fast it knocked the breath out of her. "Oh, thank God. Thank you, Lainee, thank you for not giving up on me, for giving me another chance... for loving me." He said the last part very reverentially. A beautiful, special soul like Lainee loved him?

As she reached up to pull him down for a kiss, he knew with absolute certainty and great relief then that he was nothing like his father. If Lainee loved him, he couldn't be.

CHAPTER 43

She trusted him implicitly then, though it wouldn't be the last time Lainee found another woman in Noah's bedroom. She shook her head as another overzealous fan forced her way in, this time while she was there naked in bed with him.

"I'm so sorry, Lainee," he said chagrined, angry beyond words. It was one thing for an aggressive admirer to intrude on his privacy and see him butt naked but he was damn sure not going to put up with anyone barging in on Lainee and seeing her at her most vulnerable. These private moments, her naked body in his bed, that was for him and his eyes alone.

"We really need to start locking that door more often," she said dryly, pulling the sheet up around her chest. "Maybe get a deadbolt while we're at it."

The next day Noah had a deadbolt installed and Lainee smiled in satisfaction as they fell into bed once more.

They couldn't bear to be apart another night after her failed experiment, so Lainee pretty much moved in little by little. She was defying school rules which went directly against the grain of her being. Noah, on the other hand, was utterly unconcerned about the letter of the law. He was downright cavalier about it as they undressed each other after a full day of classes. "They aren't going to kick either of us out," he promised her knowingly, smugly, patiently unbuttoning her white dress shirt like he had dozens of times before. It never got old. "The administration wouldn't dare."

Lainee rolled her eyes at him as her bra and underwear came off next. "I know, I know. You're Noah freakin' Riley. Harvard theater gem who can shamelessly exploit his popularity and power thusly."

"More importantly," Noah said, cupping her naked butt in his hands and lifting her right up off her feet entirely, making her squeal in surprise and delight as she wrapped her legs around his waist, "I'm Lainee Reed's boyfriend and lover," he carried her right back to his bed, where she belonged, "more than prepared to shamelessly exploit my popularity and power over this body," he laid her gently down, pulling her legs apart with loving hands, kissing her inner thigh, "thusly."

She looked down at him between her legs with adoring and hungry eyes. She asked quietly then, in awe of him and all that he was able to give to her, "Do you think there's ever been two people more in love than me and you, Noah?"

His heart swelled to max capacity and Noah crawled up her body to hover over her so that he could look down into her beautiful, beloved face. He cupped her scarred cheek in his large, gentle hand, answering honestly, gruffly, choking a little bit on his overwhelming emotion, "No, Lainee, I don't believe there has been."

Romeo and Juliet had *nothing* on them, save perhaps the tragic ending... hopefully.

"I love you, Lainee," he said gently, reverentially, leaning down to brush his lips over hers. He'd never get tired of saying it and she'd never get tired of hearing it, so he gladly repeated it again and again. "I love you." Then he moved back down her body and placed his mouth right at her core.

◆◆◆

As they slept later that night, a familiar whimpering sound woke Noah up. He immediately recognized the nightly pattern. Lainee was having another nightmare about the accident. He knew what to do now. He shook her slightly on her shoulder and whispered soothingly in her ear from behind, "Wake up, baby. It's just a dream." He continued to gently shake her until she slowly came out of the nightmare. Then she turned and cried in his arms.

His heart broke for as she struggled through reliving her worst moment once again. He just held her tightly to him and murmured, "You're safe, sweetheart. I'm right here. Everything is okay." He wished he could do more.

Noah had studied up on survivor's guilt and knew he had to accept and allow all her feelings. He had to give her ample time to process each one every time she had this nightmare, but it was damn difficult week after week when all he wanted to do was fix it and make the pain go away immediately. But it would never really go away. Not completely. So he would patient, and work through it with her. Over and over.

Tonight after her tears ran out, Lainee pulled away from Noah to lay on her back. He felt adrift as she stared up at the ceiling with raw, red eyes. She choked out achingly after a moment, "It should have been me. I should have been the one to die that day."

The panic mixed with anger was an instant rush that had Noah sitting up in bed. He knew he was supposed to allow for all her feelings, but not that one, not the suicidal one. He couldn't stomach it. "Don't you ever say that to me again, Lainee, don't you dare." He was angry with her for the very first time and she looked up at him in surprise. "Don't even *think* it, do you hear me? For your father's sake, for my sake." He looked at her achingly then and added, a hitch in his voice, "For the sake of our future family."

Lainee blinked at him then, coming out of her dark thoughts as realization slowly dawned on her. *She had a full and bright future with this amazing man.* It occurred to her for the first time. She gazed up at Noah in wonder and really took it in.

There was an achingly beautiful life ahead for her, full of love and joy, a fulfilling career, friendship and family. It was suddenly all so clear and exquisite. *This* was the beautiful gift that her father had given her. This right here.

How dare she take it for granted and disregard her dad's last, loving wishes, his most sacred hopes and dreams, his willing sacrifice? And how dare she take Noah's undying love for granted, too?

She owed it to them both to take hold of this gift of life and love with two firm hands and give it everything she had to give. Lainee was suddenly more grateful than guilty for having walked away from that car accident, because she had an amazing, beautiful future ahead. With Noah. *Wow.*

Lainee reached up a hand then and touched Noah's cheek as he hovered over her, concern etched into the shadows of his handsome face. She promised them both then that she would never take her life for granted again. "For my father," she vowed, "for you, Noah... for our future family."

Relief and an immense love that his body couldn't properly contain within the confines of its structure overtook Noah. He bent down and took her lips, her love, her whole body with urgency.

Lainee's worst thought, her ongoing nightmare, held less weight and frequency from that moment on.

A few weeks later as fall exams and Christmas break loomed nigh, they were sitting in the Dunster House library and Noah was eyeballing her weirdly from across the table, like she'd grown a second head or a third eye. She could see him relentlessly staring her down in her periphery as she attempted to write her final paper for engineering thermodynamics. It reminded her of the early days in the gym, before they knew each other, when he'd stare her down just this way from across the room. Even then they'd been painfully aware of each other.

After a moment she gave up trying to ignore him and looked up, locking eyes with him. "You're staring," she pointed out with an attractive flush. "Why are you staring instead of studying?"

Caught in the act, Noah cleared his throat. "Um, well, I was wondering... do you..." She'd always had the ability to turn him into an awkward, stumbling idiot. He supposed she always would. "Do you think we should... you know... maybe get a ring when we're in New York over Christmas?"

Lainee tilted her head at that, taking a second to turn this over in her mind. Finally she asked incredulously, "Noah Bernard Riley, are you asking me to marry you? *Now*? Like *that*?" She shook her head even as her heart fluttered in glee. "That is the worst proposal in the history of mankind. You should ask me again, with a ring of your choosing, on your knee and in a much more romantic fashion... though in a library would be nice." She gave him one of those ear-to-ear, brilliant smiles that had his heart doing a somersault, even as she added pointedly and pragmatically, "In a few years."

She could tell he didn't like the sound of *that*, the waiting plural years part. She reached across the table and grabbed his hand then. "We are in no hurry," she reminded him, still smiling. "We both have to establish our careers before marriage and kids." But it all seemed like a blissful foregone conclusion now.

They'd already spoken excitedly about setting up home base together in New York City once they graduated from Harvard, where both of their careers could thrive. They were even taking a flight to NYC over Christmas break to get to know the city a bit better. It was all terribly exciting, so Lainee couldn't blame Noah for getting caught up in the moment and thinking of getting a ring while they were there on holiday. It was quite sweet and romantic, actually.

Lainee sat back then and studied Noah in return, as only she could, her blue eyes looking straight through him and into his soul. Her laser focus had Noah squirming in his seat a little. "I kind of botched that, didn't I?" he asked, wincing with chagrin.

"A little," she said gently, "but just then I was thinking of what a phenomenal husband and father you're going to be one day."

Noah was floored and flattered, asking uncertainly but with great hope, "You think so?" It's not like he exactly had a stellar role model in either department.

"I know so," Lainee answered him with a tender smile and it felt like the highest of compliments. "My prince among men."

Noah flushed with pleasure at her words and it hit him square in the eyes. Lainee Reed-Someday-Riley was going to marry him and have his children. It was an unwavering belief, as solid of a concept as an aged weeping willow tree digging in and standing strong for decades upon decades, its roots firmly planting deep down inside the earth.

"Sign me up, my little warrior," Noah said gruffly as emotion tightened his throat, his heart squeezing almost painfully with exquisite tenderness. She thought he was good enough? She thought him a prince among men? Because Lainee said it, Noah believed it.

It was downright Shakespearean, and Taylor Swift could have written one helluva song about it.

Noah and Lainee.

A prince and a warrior.

Superimposable.

Scarred but strong and symmetrical, spending forever side by side.

The End...

And just the beginning.

EPILOGUE

Five years later...

They were watching Grey's Anatomy and eating dinner in their tiny New York City apartment when suddenly the blood and guts on the operating table up there on the television screen looked suspiciously similar to the Bolognese spaghetti Noah was eating.

He involuntarily gagged and asked, "Could we please watch something else while we're eating?"

Lainee looked over at him in amusement, asking with sudden certainty, "You're going to gag in the delivery room when I'm having your children, aren't you?"

"Undoubtedly," he answered matter of fact, turning his head so he wouldn't have to see the messy medical procedure being acted out on the large TV screen.

She sighed knowingly. "And you're going to gag when you have to change a diaper, too, I suppose?"

"Most likely," Noah answered, grabbing the clicker out of her hand. He quickly turned the channel to a much more palatable Hallmark movie, breathing in a sigh of relief.

Lainee leveled a look at him. "You're still going to have to be in the delivery room *and* change diapers, Noah Bernard Riley."

Noah gave her a big, besotted grin then and promised with great tenderness, "Absolutely, Elaine Rose Reed-Riley. Sign me up, my warrior wife."

ABOUT THE AUTHOR

A. WHITCOMA

"This fast-paced Ivy League romance satisfies with memorable characters and a dash of spice... as an expert in fast-moving romance, Whitcoma hits all the right spots for fans who prefer hot and spicy reads that still deliver the perfect amount of complexity." - BookLife by Publishers Weekly

A. Whitcoma is an author, dreamer and mother, as well as an advertising professional in Metro Detroit. To find image boards and Spotify playlists inspired by the Crimson Crew universe, please visit www.whitcoma.com.

A special thanks to Rowan Arts Graphic Design (rowanartsdesign.com) for the amazing cover, and to you for reading!

THE CRIMSON CREW SERIES

Meet the Harvard men's lacrosse team as they compete and come into their own with the help of some very smart and talented women.

2021/2022 Men's Roster:

Noah Riley #33
Ryker Wallace #17
Laith Brinley #5
Mack McLaren #23
Quinn Carr #47
August Warwick #64

The Higher Education of Noah Riley (Crimson Crew Book 1)

Both in their third year at Harvard, it would seem that theater gem, lacrosse superstar and pretty boy Noah Riley is the polar opposite of top-ten-ranked Lainee Reed with her facial scar and hard-won stoicism. But when the tutor forced upon Noah in biochemistry is none other than Lainee, they are suddenly face to face and wondering if appearances aren't always what they seem.

The Recoding of Ryker Wallace (Crimson Crew Book 2)

Ryker Wallace, #17 of the Harvard men's lacrosse team, is always up for a fight, be it on the field or off. The muscled, tattooed attackman has more penalty minutes per game than any other player in the whole Ivy League. He also scores more than anyone, in the game or otherwise, save perhaps his teammate and buddy Noah Riley, #33.

Even as Ryker helps the Crimson Crew establish an illustrious winning streak, his brutal anger disguised as insatiable hunger begins to tear him apart at the seams from the inside out. Manifesting itself in insidious ways, he becomes a borderline alcoholic with barely passing grades and a detachment disorder with a dash of God complex. What no one knows is that Ryker comes by these attributes justly, and painfully so. It's his very birthright.

Programmed by harsh hands, he's been hardcoded with a particular algorithm born of fire and brimstone that burns within his veins. Its code is that of discipline and despair added to severity and scarcity. Can Ryker learn to evolve and adapt, to recode the initial instructions laid into his very foundation before he implodes? Or is his ultimate output inevitably that of self-destruction?

The Liberation of Laith Brinley (Crimson Crew Book 3)

Laith Brinley, #5 of the Harvard men's lacrosse team, is a swift and stealthy player, quiet and unassuming on and off the field. One would never know behind his silent stoicism that he is Boston royalty, coming from old money and generations of influential politicians, including a father in Congress and older siblings groomed to follow suit. One would also never glean he harbors a shocking secret that must never leave the walls of the Brinley compound.

Laith seemingly has it all as he carefully downplays his heritage and shiploads of family money and influence, trying to blend into the background behind a wall of quiet fortitude as he's been carefully trained to do all his aristocratic life. He never seems to notice or care about the attention he unwillingly garners. He never, ever wants to be in the spotlight. He just always steps up for his family and teammates on the Crimson Crew, quiet and steadfast, like a rock.

But even the hardest and most polished of stone can crack under too much pressure. As Laith bears the weight and utter lie of perfection in silence, he must eventually choose once and for all: legacy or liberation?

BOOKS BY THIS AUTHOR

There is a Place

Samantha, Erin and Madison are roommates in the modest metropolis of Detroit on a modern-day quest to find love in all its forms, including the most elusive of all, self-love.

****

There is a place I run to when I'm scared or lonely. I wonder if you know that place is you." - Flavia

****

Samantha, Erin and Madison are best friends and roommates in the modest metropolis of Detroit, each struggling to find their place in the world. As they each search for purpose and strive for fulfilling careers and relationships, they rise and fall, side by side, as sisters-in-arms on the precipice of something truly great but unnamed and frustratingly evasive.

Their interwoven journeys take them on a modern-day quest for love in all its nuanced and layered expressions: the intricate and essential kind between friends, the more conspicuous and lauded romantic manifestation and, the hardest and most elusive of all, self-love.

Printed in Great Britain
by Amazon

19786020R00169